BENEDICTION

BENEDICTION

Kent Haruf

ALFRED A. KNOPF

New York

2013

THIS IS A BORZOI BOOK
PUBLISHED BY ALFRED A. KNOPF

www.aaknopf.com

Knopf, Borzoi Books, and the colophon are registered
trademarks of Random House, Inc.

Library of Congress Cataloging-in-Publication Data
Haruf, Kent.
Benediction / Kent Haruf.—1st ed.
p.   cm.
"This is a Borzoi book."
ISBN 978-0-307-95988-1
1. Families—Colorado—Fiction.   I. Title.
PS3558.A716B46 2013   813'.54—dc23   2012028744

*This is a work of fiction. Names, characters, places, and incidents either
are the product of the author's imagination or are used fictitiously.
Any resemblance to actual persons, living or dead, events, or locales
is entirely coincidental.*

Jacket photograph by Lorry Eason/Millennium Images, UK
Jacket design by Carol Devine Carson

Manufactured in the United States of America
First Edition

For Cathy

Benediction—the utterance of a blessing, an invocation of blessedness.

BENEDICTION

I

WHEN THE TEST came back the nurse called them into the examination room and when the doctor entered the room he just looked at them and asked them to sit down. They could tell by the look on his face where matters stood.

Go on ahead, Dad Lewis said, say it.

I'm afraid I don't have very good news for you, the doctor said.

When they went back downstairs to the parking lot it was late in the afternoon.

You drive, Dad said. I don't want to.

Are you feeling so bad, honey?

No. I don't feel that much worse. I just want to look out at this country. I won't be coming out here again.

I don't mind driving for you, she said. And we can come this way again anytime if you want to.

They drove out from Denver away from the mountains, back onto the high plains: sagebrush and soapweed and blue grama and buffalo grass in the pastures, wheat and corn in the planted fields. On both sides of the highway were the gravel county roads going out away under the pure blue sky, all the roads straight as the lines ruled in a book, with only a few small isolated towns spread across the flat open country.

It was sundown when they got home. By then the air was starting to cool off. She parked the car in front of their house at the west edge of Holt on the gravel street and Dad got out and stood looking for a while. The old white house built in 1904, the first on the street which wasn't even much of a street then, and still only three or four houses there yet when he bought it in 1948, the year he and Mary were married. He was twenty-two, working at the hardware store on Main Street, then the old lame man who owned it made up his mind to move away to live with his daughter and he offered Dad the option of purchasing it, and he was a known man in town by then, the bankers knew him, and gave him the loan without question. So he was the proprietor of the local hardware store.

It was a frame house sided with clapboard, two-story with a red shingled roof, with an old-fashioned black wrought iron fence around it and an iron gate with spears and hard loops at the top. Out back was an old red barn and a pole corral grown over with tall weeds, and beyond that there was nothing but the open country.

He went inside to the downstairs bedroom to put on old pants and a sweater and came back out and sat down in one of the porch chairs.

She came out to find him. Do you want supper now? I could make you a sandwich.

No. I don't want anything. Maybe if you could bring me a beer.

You don't want anything to eat?

You go on ahead without me.

Do you want a glass?

No.

She went inside and returned with the cold bottle.

Thank you, he said.

She went back in. He drank from the bottle and sat looking out at the quiet empty street in the summer evening. The neighbor Berta May's yellow house next door and the other houses beyond it, running up to the highway, and the vacant lot directly across the street, and the railroad tracks three blocks in the other direction, all of that part of town still empty and undeveloped between his property and the tracks. In the trees in front of the house the leaves were blowing a little.

She brought a tray of crackers and cheese and an apple cut up in quarters and a glass of iced tea. Would you like any of this? She held out the tray to him. He took a piece of apple and she sat down beside him in the other porch chair.

Well. That's it, he said. That's the deal now. Isn't it.

He might be wrong. They're wrong sometimes, she said. They can't be so sure.

I don't want to let myself think that way. I can feel it in me that they're right. I don't have much time left.

Oh I don't want to believe that.

Yeah. But I'm pretty sure that's how it's going to be.

I don't want you to go yet, she said. She reached across and took his hand. I don't. There were tears in her eyes. I'm not ready.

I know. . . . We better call Lorraine pretty soon, he said.

I'll call her.

Tell her she doesn't have to come home yet. Give her some time.

He looked at the beer bottle and held it in front of him and took a small drink.

I might get me some kind of better grade of beer before I go. A guy I was talking to said something about Belgian beer. Maybe I'll try some of that. If I can get it around here.

He sat and drank the beer and held his wife's hand sitting out on the front porch. So the truth was he was dying. That's what they were saying. He would be dead before the end of summer. By the beginning of September the dirt would be piled over what was left of him out at the cemetery three miles east of town. Someone would cut his name into the face of a tombstone and it would be as if he never was.

2

NINE O'CLOCK in the morning, he was sitting in his chair beside the window in the living room looking out at the side yard at the dark shade under the tree and at the wrought iron fence beyond the tree. He'd eaten his breakfast. He hadn't been hungry but he'd eaten it and he was thinking he wasn't going to eat anything anymore he didn't want to eat, and he was thinking how he wasn't going to paint the iron fence again in this life, and then Mary came in the room.

She was carrying a watering can. She had washed and dried the breakfast dishes and put them away in the cupboard and had gone out back to set the sprinkler going on the lawn, and now she had come inside to water the houseplants. It was a clear hot day. Not a cloud anywhere. But crossing the room she all of a sudden went down on the floor like a little loose pile of collapsed clothes. She threw the water can away from her as she fell. The water splashed up on the rose wallpaper and there was a stain growing on the wall.

Darlin, Dad said. You all right? What's going on?

She didn't move, didn't answer.

Mary. Goddamn it. What's going on here?

He stood and bent over her. Her eyes were shut and her face was sweating and very red. But she was breathing.

Mary. Sweetheart.

He got down on his knees beside her and felt her head. She felt hot. He pulled her toward him and slid his arms under her, propping her up against the couch. Can you hear me? I got to call somebody. I'll be right back. She made no sign. Is that all right with you if I leave a minute? I'm coming right back. He hurried out to the kitchen and called the emergency number at the hospital. Then he returned and got down on the floor again and held her and talked to her softly and kissed her cheek and brushed back her damp white hair and patted her arm and waited. After a little while he heard the siren outside and then it stopped and people came up on the front porch and knocked.

Come in here, Dad called. Christ Almighty. What are you knocking for? Come on in here.

They entered the house, two men in white shirts and black pants, and looked at Dad and his wife on the floor and knelt down and began to attend to her. What happened?

She fainted out. She was walking across the room. Then she just went down on the floor.

The younger of the men stood up and went out to the ambulance and brought back a gurney.

Can you move back, please? he said.

What's that? Dad said. What are you saying?

Sir, you'll need to move back so we can take care of her. Are you all right yourself? You don't look too good.

Yeah, I'm all right. Do what you got to do, and hurry.

They lifted the old white-haired woman onto the wheeled cart and buckled the straps across her chest and legs. Dad got up from the floor and stood watching. He put his hand on her.

You won't let nothing happen to her, he said.

No sir. We'll do our best.

That's not what I'm saying. Your best might not be good enough. This is my wife here. This lady means everything to me in the world.

I hear you. But—

No. I won't have no objections on this. You do what I say. Now go on. He bent over close to her face and patted her cheek and kissed her.

The two men wheeled her out to the ambulance. Almost immediately he heard the siren start up again in front of the house, then the diminishing sound of it retreating up the street.

3

SHE STAYED in the Holt County Memorial Hospital at the south
end of Main Street for most of three days. They could find nothing
wrong with her except that she was old and she was working too
hard and she had exhausted herself by taking care of her husband by
herself.

By nightfall of that first day she was a little better. But at the hospital they said she still needed her bed rest. The nurse said, Don't you
have somebody that would come in and help you?

I don't know, she said. Maybe. But I'm worried about my husband.
He's all alone.

Your husband told them he was all right there in the house.

Told who?

The men who brought you in the ambulance. They asked him and
apparently he said he was all right.

Well he isn't all right. He wouldn't let on how he really is. Not ever
to strangers.

They said he seemed like he could be a little bit hard to get along
with.

No, he isn't. He just gets set in his ways about things. He doesn't
mean anything bad by it. But he's not well at all. He's alone in that
house without me.

Isn't there a neighbor or somebody?

Maybe there is. She looked across the room. Would you bring me
that phone?

You want to call a neighbor? It's kind of late, Mrs. Lewis.

I want to talk to Dad. I want to speak to my husband.

But you shouldn't be talking to anyone on any phone right now. You're not supposed to be upsetting yourself.

Would you bring it to me, she said. I want to make a private call, please.

The nurse looked at her and then brought the telephone and set it on the bedside stand and went out. It took a long time for him to answer.

Yeah. This is Dad Lewis. His voice sounded rough and old.

Honey, are you doing okay?

Is that you?

Yes. It's me. Are you doing okay?

You're supposed to be asleep. I thought you'd be resting.

I wanted to see how you are.

Did they say I called this morning and another time this afternoon?

No. They didn't tell me that.

Yeah. Well. I did.

What did they tell you about me? she said.

They said you need to rest. You need to take it easy and get your strength up.

I'm all tired out, honey, she said. When I got here and woke up I was all wet with sweat.

You were wet when they come for you. You don't remember that.

No.

But will you be all right, do they say?

I don't have any pep. That's all.

Outside the room people were talking in the hallway, and the nurse had come back in to check on her.

She's telling me I got to get off the phone now. Did you get some supper, honey?

Yeah. I had something.

What did you have?

I heated up some soup. But you need to take care of yourself, Dad said. Will you do that?

Good night, honey, she said.

———

They still always slept together as they had since the first night so long ago, in the old soft double bed in the downstairs bedroom, even though he was sick and dying now and moved restlessly in the bed in the night. She insisted on being there close beside him, she wouldn't have it otherwise. Now in the night it was unfamiliar and lonely, and he was desolate without her. At three o'clock he woke and went to the bathroom and came back to bed and lay awake thinking for a long time, until the room began to get a little gray and he could make out the brass handles on the dresser drawers and the mirror on the door to the closet.

In the middle of the morning the old neighbor woman came over and knocked on the front door and then cracked it open without waiting. Hello? Dad, are you here?

Who is it?

It's Berta May from next door.

Yeah. All right.

Can I come in?

Come ahead.

She came in with a young girl behind her and they stood in the living room looking at him. He was in sweatpants and an old flannel shirt.

Mary called, Berta May said. She said you was alone here by yourself.

Well I don't know what she did that for.

Well she was worried about you.

Yeah, but I'm okay.

Maybe you are. Maybe you aren't.

Dad looked at her and looked at the girl. You going to sit down? I'm not going to stand up.

No. I come over to see if I could help. To see if you needed something.

I don't.

You're sure of that.

I'm doing all right. Who's this here you got with you? he said.

This is Alice, my granddaughter. Haven't you met her before?

I see her out in the yard over there across the fence.

She's living with me now. Say hello to Dad Lewis, honey.

The girl was eight years old, a thin brown-haired girl in blue denim shorts and a white T-shirt.

Hello, she said.

Hello back to you, Dad told her.

Berta May said, You don't mind me looking out in the kitchen to see if anything needs to be done, do you.

It's okay out there. It's just not tidy.

Well, I'll just take a look. She went out. The girl remained, looking around the room and then at Dad Lewis in his chair.

Why do they call you that? she said.

What?

Dad.

Because I got a daughter like you. People started calling me that when she was born. A long time ago.

I don't have a dad. I don't even know where he is. I don't ever see him.

I'm sorry to hear that.

Are you sick or something? she said.

You could say so. I got this cancer eating me up.

She studied him for a moment. Is it in your breast? That's where my mother had hers.

I got it all over me.

Are you going to die?

Yeah. That's what they tell me.

She looked out the window. You can see Grandma's house from here. You can see the backyard.

That's where I saw you. I noticed you yesterday back there, Dad said.

What was I doing?

I don't know. I couldn't tell what you were doing.

Was I down on the grass?

Yes. I believe you were.

Then I was working.

What kind of work?

Digging dandelions. Grandma pays me for every one. She's got a lot of them.

Why don't you come over here and dig some.

How much would you pay?

The same as your grandmother.

I don't know, she said. I better go see if she needs any help.

The neighbor woman Berta May washed up the dishes and swept the kitchen and afterward she and her granddaughter went back home and at noon she sent the girl over with a tray covered with a white dish towel. Alice came in and said, Where do you want me to put this?

What have you got?

Grandma made you some lunch. The girl set the tray on a chair and removed the dish towel. There were potato chips and a ham sandwich and a little hill of cottage cheese on a paper plate and a piece of cake wrapped in wax paper. Grandma said you could drink water or make your own coffee.

You want some of it? I'm not hungry.

Grandma's waiting for me to eat with her.

Tell her I appreciate this. Will you do that?

The girl went out, and through the window he could see her going along the fence and on into the yellow house.

Late in the afternoon of the third day, without any warning Mary came through the gate out front and up on the porch and into the house. In the living room Dad was sitting in his chair by the window reading the *Holt Mercury* newspaper. He looked up and she was just standing there.

Well, what in the hell. What are you doing here?

They let me out, she said.

I didn't hear any car out front. How'd you get here?

I walked.

What do you mean you walked?

I walked home.

You walked home from the hospital.

They couldn't bring me right away. They were out on some other call, I guess. And I didn't think we had to have the expense of that anyhow. It's going to cost too much as it is. They told me I had to wait but I didn't want to. I wanted to get home.

Well, Jesus Christ, Dad said. You were in there because you got too worn out and now you walk home in the hot afternoon clear across town.

It's not so hot out right now, she said.

What's wrong with those people, letting you go like this.

They didn't want to let me go. I just left. I wanted to make you some good supper.

He was staring at her. Well, by God, he said. If you keep this up, I'm going to die right now and not put it off any longer, just to keep you from doing this again.

She came across the room and stood in front of him, small and straight and old, and spoke slowly, directly. Don't you say that to me. Don't you say such a evil thing. Don't you ever say it again. You don't have any right. Are you hearing me, Dad?

He looked away from her.

I mean it. I won't have it. You're going to break my heart yet, you damned old man. I believe you will. But you can't say something like that. Now what would you like for supper? I don't remember what we even have in this house for sure.

I don't know. It doesn't matter to me.

I want to fix you something nice.

She bent forward and kissed him on the head and wrapped her arm around his shoulders and raised up his old age-spotted hand affectionately and held it to her cheek for a long time.

I'm going out to the kitchen, she said. It seems like I was gone for three weeks instead of three days.

———

After supper, after she had washed the dishes and had put Dad to bed, she called Lorraine in Denver. I think it's time to come home now, dear. If you can.

Is Daddy worse?

Yes. I wasn't going to tell you yet.

Tell me what?

The doctor said he only has about a month more.

Mom, when did you find this out?

Last Friday.

Why didn't you call me?

Oh honey, I'm trying to get used to it myself. I can't talk about it yet. She started to cry.

Mom.

I was in the hospital too, she said. You might as well know that too.

What's this now?

They took me to the hospital a few days ago.

Why? What was wrong?

I was just too worn down, they said. I fainted on the floor, right here in the living room.

Jesus, Mom, are you okay?

Yes, I am. But I'd appreciate it if you could arrange to help out here a little. I had Berta May come over, but that's not right. You're our daughter.

I'll be there as soon as I can. I'll have to tell them at the office. But I'll be there.

That'll be good. Now I didn't ask you—are you all right yourself, dear?

Yes.

And Richard?

He's all right. Richard doesn't change.

Well.

I know. It doesn't matter. I'll be there as soon as I can.

———

The next day Lorraine drove into Holt on Highway 34 after the sun had already gone down and the blue street lamps had come on at the corners. It was all familiar to her. She turned north off the highway and drove along past the quiet night-lighted houses set back behind the front yards, some of the yards bare of trees or bushes next to vacant lots filled with weeds—tall sunflowers and redroot and pigweed—and then there was Berta May's house which had been there when she was a child, and then their own white house. She got out and went up to the porch, a pretty woman in her mid-fifties with dark hair. The air was cool and smelled fresh of the country in the evening out on the high plains.

In the house Dad was already in bed and she went with her mother back to the bedroom.

Is he asleep already? It's only eight thirty.

I don't know if he's actually sleeping. He goes to bed early. He always did. You know how he does.

They stood in the doorway. He was lying in the bed with the window open and the sheet drawn over him. He opened his eyes. Is that my daughter? he said.

It's me, Daddy.

Come over here so I can see you.

She crossed the room and sat down on the bed and kissed him. Mary went out so he could have Lorraine to himself. Dad stared up at her for a long time. Lorraine's eyes were wet and she took one of his Kleenexes and wiped at her eyes and cheeks.

Oh, Daddy.

Yeah. Ain't it the goddamn hell.

She took his hand and held it. Are you in a lot of pain?

No. Not now.

You don't have any pain?

I'm taking things for it. Otherwise I would. I was before. Well, you look good, he said.

Thank you.

How was your drive?

Okay. A lot of traffic but it was all going the other way, to the mountains.

How's work?

It's okay.

They let you off to come here.

They'd better, she said.

Yeah. He smiled. That's right.

Can you sleep now, Daddy?

I can still sleep, that's one thing. As long as Mom's here. I didn't sleep much when she was gone. They had her to the hospital. Did she tell you?

She told me.

She walked home. Did she tell you that too?

No.

She did. It was hotter than billy hell out there. I'm glad you've come. She's all tired out. I'm afraid she might get down too far. I never wanted her to have to take care of me like this.

I know, Daddy.

Well. All right, then. You're here now.

You go to sleep. I'll see you in the morning.

She kissed him again and went out to the kitchen. He looks so bad, Mom.

I know it, honey.

He's gotten so thin. His color's so bad.

He won't eat. He isn't hungry he says. He just fusses with it.

Sunday morning at the Community Church on Birch Street on the back page of the bulletin there was an announcement about Mary Lewis. It said she had been admitted to the Holt Memorial Hospital and had been released, and it said Dad Lewis was no better. The congregation was asked to continue their prayers for him. There was another brief notice that said Lorraine had come back home.

On Monday, Reverend Lyle and the two Johnson women came to the house to call on the Lewises in the afternoon, all of them within the same hour. Rob Lyle was a man in his late forties, new to town, a tall thin man with black hair and dark eyes. The Johnson women were longtime residents of Holt County. Willa Johnson was a widow with long white hair worn in a knot at the back of her head in that old way and she had thick glasses; and Alene, her unmarried daughter, was over sixty and had taken early retirement after teaching children for almost forty years in a little town on the Front Range, and was back home for the summer now and maybe longer. They lived east of Holt, a mile south off the highway on a county road in the sandhills.

Lyle was in the living room when they came to the house, sitting on the couch talking to Dad Lewis and Mary, and Lorraine had brought him a cup of black coffee and some cookies on a little china plate. Then the Johnsons came to the door and Lorraine got up and showed them in and Lyle stood up. They shook hands. Lorraine carried in a chair for herself and one for Alene from the dining room.

Well, Dad, how are you doing today? said Willa. Are you doing any better?

If I am I can't tell it. I'm better to have my daughter home, I can say that.

Yes, it said in the church bulletin she was here. Willa turned to Lorraine. You couldn't stay away now, could you.

Not after Mom was in the hospital.

It announced that too, how she was admitted to the hospital. It was the first we heard of it. You might have called us, Mary.

I didn't want to bother you, Mary said. You wouldn't of either, if it was you.

Well, Dad could have.

I'm glad he didn't.

Lorraine's here now, Dad said. That's enough.

All right, I'm going to be quiet, then. I can tell when to keep my mouth shut.

You don't have to be quiet. It's not that, said Mary.

That would be the first time if she did, Alene said.

Oh now my daughter's attacking me too.

They all laughed a little.

On the couch Lyle watched them talk. After a time he said, I think I'll have to go now. Before I do I wonder if we might pray together. And he bowed his head, they looked at him, at his dark head, and they all bowed their heads too and he prayed, O God, Our Father, we ask you to take particular care of this family and this man here. We ask in your infinite mercy that you bring him the comfort and peace that passeth all human understanding and the assurance of thy son's own death and resurrection. While he prayed Lorraine looked at him sitting on the couch across the room with his head lowered and his hands folded together and she looked at her father and he was watching the preacher too. Then Lyle finished and said, May you hear our prayer, oh Lord. Amen. He stood and shook hands all around and touched Dad Lewis on the shoulder and Lorraine went with him out the front door onto the porch.

Thank you for coming, she said.

I don't want to bother your father, but I'll come again if that's all right.

Yes. I think it would be.

I don't know that he's very religious.

No. Not in any orthodox way.

I understand that. In his own way perhaps.

Perhaps.

Well. I'll be going. He held out his hand to shake hers and instead she surprised him and hugged him. He was a good deal taller than she was.

Thank you for coming, she said again.

He went down the walk to his car parked at the street and she stood and watched him drive away. Then she sat down on the porch swing in the shade of the house and took out her cigarettes and smoked. The air was hot and dry and clear, but it was better in the shade. Then Alice, the girl next door, came up in front of the wrought iron fence. She turned and looked out at the empty street and then turned and looked at Lorraine.

Hello, Alice.

How do you know my name?

My mother told me. Why don't you come up here and talk to me.

I don't know who you are.

I used to live in this house. When I was a girl like you are.

I don't know if I should, Alice said.

You can ask your grandmother, if you want to. Your mother and I used to play together.

The girl stood looking at her, then she looked out at the street again and finally she opened the gate and came up on the porch.

You can sit down if you want. Here, beside me.

The girl slid onto the swing and they began to move it slowly. Lorraine took out her cigarettes again.

Do you always smoke?

Once in a while.

My mother's boyfriend smoked all the time.

Lorraine blew smoke out to the side and they rocked the swing in the hot air so that it felt a little cooler as if there were a breeze.

What did you play with my mother?

Well. She was younger than me. She was closer to my brother Frank's age. We played at night under the streetlight at the corner up there and we played out back in the barn.

What was she like, my mother?

She was very nice. She was fun to be with.

Oh.

That's right, she was, and I'm so sorry she died like she did, so young, Lorraine said. I'm very sorry. She was a good person. I miss her.

Grandma says I'm lucky to have someone to take me in.

Yes, I guess so. I guess you are. And you can come over here and see us if you want anytime.

He's dying too, isn't he.

My father?

He's dying, isn't he.

But you don't have to be afraid of him. He's just an old man who's sick. He wouldn't hurt you. You can come over and see me. We can do something together.

Like what?

I don't know. We'll have to think of it.

Are you done smoking now?

I'm done with this one.

Alice got up and brought the ashtray from the porch rail and held it for her.

Thank you, Lorraine said and stubbed out the cigarette.

You're welcome.

She put the ashtray back and sat down again and they swung in the hot afternoon.

In the house the women were still talking.

Is he Mexican, did anyone ever say? Willa asked. He's so dark.

No, Mary said. I don't think so.

On his mother's side, I mean.

No.

Or Italian maybe.

Not if he's in the Community Church. A Mexican wouldn't be a preacher in a Protestant church. He'd be a Catholic.

He's kind of good-looking, Alene said.

Her mother turned toward her, her eyes seeming overlarge behind the thick lenses.

He is, Alene said.

He's married. He has a wife and a teenage son.

He can still be good-looking.

They sent him here from a church in Denver, Willa said. He was an associate minister there.

We heard he was, Mary said.

I doubt if he's accustomed to small towns.

He better start getting accustomed to them, Dad said.

The women turned and looked at him. They'd thought he was asleep. His head was turned toward the window and he wasn't looking at them when he talked.

Nothing goes on without people noticing, he said.

They waited. But he said no more.

After a while Willa started talking again. He had some kind of trouble in Denver, I heard. I believe that's why he was sent here.

What kind of trouble? said Mary.

I heard he was disciplined by the church for supporting some other preacher who came out homosexual in Denver. I believe it was something of that nature.

Wherever did you hear that, Mother?

A woman friend. Somebody from out of town told me about it.

Well, they're people, Alene said.

Well, of course. I know they're people. I'm not saying that. I'm only saying as an example of the kind of man he is. What we might expect.

The room was quiet then. They could hear Lorraine and the young girl on the front porch, the soft talking and the regular small complaint and recover of the porch swing. The hot sunlight streamed in through the window beyond Dad.

I think I'll go outside, Alene said. Excuse me, please.

There's more coffee, Mary said.

No thank you. It's good to see you, Dad. He looked over at her and nodded.

She rose and straightened the skirt of her dress and went out to the porch. Willa and Mary watched her leave.

I don't know what I'm supposed to do, Willa whispered. You see how she is. She's been this way ever since she came home.

She's not happy, Mary said.

Nobody's happy. But she doesn't have to be unpleasant in somebody else's house.

We're glad to see her, Mary said, and stood and went back through the dining room to the kitchen. She looked out the window to the west. The backyard was in shade from the trees, and beyond, the corral and barn were in hot bright sunlight. She brought the pot of coffee and poured some into Willa's cup.

Just half, Willa said. I need to go pretty soon.

Mary looked at Dad. He was asleep now, his old bald head fallen onto his chest, his big hands folded in his lap.

Out on the porch they made room for Alene on the swing and the three of them, the two women and the young girl, moved slowly in the heat. Lorraine introduced the girl to Alene.

I've been waiting to meet you, Alene said.

Do you know my grandmother?

I've known her a long time. She and my mother have been friends for years.

Grandma has a lot of friends.

Yes. She does.

But she doesn't do anything with them.

You don't when you get older. But maybe you and I could do something together.

That's what she said. The girl looked at Lorraine.

We'll all do something, Lorraine said.

What grade are you in, honey?

I'll be in the third grade this year.

That's the grade I taught.

I don't know my teacher here. I don't know who she'll be.

Do you want to find out?

I guess so.

I'll take you up to school if you like. Maybe we can meet her. Or at least find out who she is.

Do you teach here?

No. I taught in another town close to the mountains. I've stopped teaching now.

We used to live close to the mountains. When my mother was alive.

Willa came out on the porch and they introduced her to Alice, and then the two Johnson women went out to their car and drove home to the sandhills and Alice went back to her grandmother's house.

4

FORTY YEARS AGO, when it was over, Dad Lewis was only surprised that it had taken so long to find him out. He hadn't been all that clever about it.

After he'd made the discoveries, Dad wouldn't put it off and on Saturday after they'd closed for the day and the last meager purchase had been made and the change tendered across the scarred wood counter and the last customer had gone out the front door onto the cold darkening sidewalk on Main Street, Dad said, Are we locked up?

Clayton was standing before the front door looking out at the empty winter street. It looks like it wants to snow, he said.

Does it, Dad said. Has everybody gone?

Yeah, they're all out. I'm ready to go too. I'm wore out today. We were busy.

Come back here to the office first, Dad said.

Something more to do?

No. Just come back to the office.

He turned and walked past the long narrow ranks of plumbing supplies and the assortment of plastic elbows and metal clamps, past the spools of chains and nylon ropes and thin cording hanging at the end of the aisle and went into the office at the rear of the building back at the alley and sat down behind the desk.

Clayton, the young clerk, followed him and stood at the door, leaning against the doorframe, rolling down his blue shirt cuffs as he did every day after they closed.

Sit down, Dad said.

Something going on?

Come in and take a seat.

I hope this won't take too long. Tanya's waiting on me. We was talking of getting a sitter and going out for dinner somewhere. Having a night out.

Were you. Have a seat first, Dad said.

Clayton stepped into the room and sat down. What is it? he said.

Dad looked at him and looked past him out through the open office door for a moment. A car went by in the alley, the top of it visible through the square window in the outside door. He turned in the swivel chair and took down the wide blue-backed cash receipts ledger from the shelf behind him and turned forward again, coming around slowly in the chair, and opened the book on the desk, finding the pages he wanted, and turned the book a half turn so it was right side up to Clayton. You want to say something about this? Dad said.

Clayton looked at him and then down at the ledger pages. He studied the figures and then looked up quickly. I don't get what you mean.

I think you do.

No, I don't neither. Are you accusing me of something?

Are you going to make this harder than it needs to be? Dad said. You sure you want to do that?

He pointed his finger at the total for the month just finished and turned back a page and indicated the total for the previous month.

Have you got those numbers in your head?

I don't get what this is about, said Clayton.

I'm showing you. Keep watching.

He turned back the pages in the ledger to the same months four years earlier. You see these? he said. He pointed to the total for the earlier year.

The store's making an average of three hundred dollars a month less than it did four years ago, Dad said. How would that be? What would be the cause of something like that, do you think?

I don't have no idea. People started going someplace else maybe.

Where would they go? This is the only hardware in town.

Maybe we're just not as busy.

No. We're still as busy. Inventory tells us that.

Then I don't have no answer for you.

You could be missing something.

Like what do you mean?

Like something you lost. Something that might of fell out of your jacket pocket when you hung it up on the back hook this morning and never noticed.

Dad leaned sideways and stretched his leg out straight so he could reach into his pants pocket, he withdrew a small key and bent forward and unlocked the bottom drawer of the desk. He sat up again and laid out on the desktop a small receipt book that had half of the pages missing. The perforated ends inside the binding were still there but the carbons that should have been in the book were torn away.

I found this laying on the floor below your coat back in the hall, he said. Kind of leaning up against the wallboard. So then I could see how you were managing it. A customer comes in and buys something and you give him a receipt out of this private little extra book here of yours and then after he goes out the door and the door is shut good you pocket the money and nothing shows. It couldn't be nothing too big. Because I would notice that. And you had to be sure I was at the back of the store or back in the office here or maybe gone home to lunch, and I don't guess you could of done it too often or even somebody as trusting as I used to be would get suspicious. Then too I suppose you had to worry about somebody returning some shovel or garden hoe and presenting this false receipt to me and not you, to get reimbursed. You had to worry about that a lot, I guess. But somehow that never happened, did it. But I figure after a while you got too greedy, didn't you. If you was only taking three or four hundred dollars a year I'd never of noticed anything. Or maybe even a thousand dollars a year. But that would have to be only if you hadn't of lost this little ticket book out of your coat pocket, isn't that right.

Dad stopped and stared at him. Clayton didn't say anything.

Well, I'll tell you, Dad said. It makes me sick. That's what it does. It makes me wonder about the whole goddamn human race. And I don't want to think that way. What's wrong with you anyway?

Across from him Clayton's round face had begun to sweat. Later Dad would remember that, how Clayton appeared to burst out in a sudden sweat, and it was wintertime, February, cold outside, and it was not even warm in the little windowless office there at the rear of the hardware store.

How much time will you give me? Clayton said.

Time for what?

To pay you back.

You can't pay me back.

Not right away. But I could if you gave me enough time.

No you couldn't. I'm not going to have you around here anymore. You don't work here. I don't want to see you again.

But I got a wife and two kids to think of.

Yes, Dad said. I know you do. You should of been thinking about them, what you brought them to by this.

Clayton stared at him. He wiped his hand across his forehead and dried it on his pants leg.

Are you going to the sheriff? he said.

No. I decided not to. On account of your kids. But I'm going to have you sign this.

Sign what?

This paper here.

What is it?

Dad removed a sheet of paper from the drawer in front of him and pushed it across the desk. Clayton read it. The paper was typed out neatly, telling how he'd stolen from the store and admitted as much and it said how many thousands of dollars the sum was and it said he admitted that too and then there was a place at the bottom of the page for him to sign his name and to provide the date.

What will you do with this if I sign it?

Oh, you're going to sign it. There's no question about that.

All right. Say I do. Then what?

Then I'll keep it locked up in the safety box at the bank. In case you ever think of moving back to Holt.

But I'm not leaving Holt.

Yeah, you are.

You mean you want me to leave town too?

I'd have to run into you sometime, Dad said. I'd have to see you again on Main Street someplace.

But I grew up here.

I know. I knew your father and mother. Son, this is a sorry goddamn mess all around.

But what am I supposed to do?

You'll have to figure that out. That's not for me to say. Maybe you will learn something. I don't know about that.

What about—Clayton looked desperately around the little office—what am I going to tell my wife? How can I explain this to Tanya?

That's one more thing I don't have no idea about. It's not going to be a lot of fun, I know that. It wouldn't be for me.

Clayton studied Dad's face, but there didn't appear to be anything forgiving or tractable there. All right then, goddamn you, he said. He took up a pen from the desk and signed the paper quickly and shoved it away from him back across the desk.

Dad reached forward and took up the paper and looked at it, examined the signature and the date, and folded the paper twice and put it in his shirt pocket.

Now I think you better go.

This isn't treating me fair, this way.

No? I thought to myself I was being more than fair.

I deserve better. I've been working for you for going on five years.

That's why I'm saying you better go now. Otherwise I might forget that.

———

The next day, Sunday, Clayton phoned Dad at home early in the afternoon. I need to talk to you, he said. .

We did all our talking last night.

I know. But I need to have one last talk with you.

About what?

Can you meet me at the store?

What are you going to do, shoot me or something? Dad said.

No. Christ. It's nothing like that. I just need to try to make this right.

You can't make it right.

I'm asking you. I'm saying please will you. Just talk to me.

Dad thought about it for a moment. All right then, he said. I'll go in by the back door and let you in the office. In one hour. Two o'clock sharp. Don't make me wait. This is not going to make no difference though.

Thank you.

Just before two, without telling Mary what he was doing, Dad went out to his car and drove across town to the hardware store and went in by the alley and left the door unlocked and turned the lights on. He entered the little office and switched the light on there and checked to see that the gun was in the drawer of the desk and then put it back, then he heard the car and Clayton was coming in at the alley door. He sat and waited, only it wasn't Clayton who appeared. It was his wife, Tanya, the young blond woman.

Where's your husband? Dad said.

He isn't coming. I'm here.

What are you doing here?

She stepped into the little close windowless office. She was wearing a long coat, a man's raincoat, a kind of slicker. She came around the end of the desk and stood three feet away from Dad. Then she opened the coat. She was naked under it. A young woman who had had two children in rapid succession and she showed it. Her belly was round and slack and had white stretch marks. She had wide hips. Her large breasts sagged a little. But she wasn't bad-looking.

You can have all this, she said. You can have all this as often and regular as you want it for an entire year. I know some special things too that might interest you.

If what, Dad said.

If you tear up that paper he signed last night and we all forget anything ever happened.

He looked at her face. Her face was quite pretty. She was watching him closely, her eyes fierce and hard and scared, daring him. Waiting.

No, he said. No, I'm not interested. You're going to take this wrong but I'm not going to do anything like that. Your husband's wrong as hell to get you into this.

I don't care about that, she said.

You will.

She opened the front of the raincoat wider, as if she hadn't offered herself sufficiently. She changed her stance, pushing herself forward, displaying her body. She put a hand on one hip, moving the skirt of the coat out of the way. She turned slightly to show herself in profile.

Do you see? she said. Are you looking?

Yes, he said. And I'm married and my wife is all I want and all I'll ever want.

You're not looking good enough, she said.

Yeah I am. I think you better go on now.

You're going to regret this. You're going to wish you could change your mind.

No. That's not going to happen, Dad said. Now I want you to get out of here.

She pulled the coat together and looked at Dad sitting in the swivel chair at the desk. Then the coat came open once more and her breasts swung and bobbled with the violent motion and she slapped him as hard as she could across the face. It left a bright red mark. Then she turned and went out of the office.

It snowed that night as Clayton had predicted the day before that it would. A wet snow more like one in March or April than one in

February, and the next day Clayton and Tanya took the two children and some few quick belongings in suitcases and cardboard boxes
and drove a hundred miles south and moved into a house with her
parents.

In the spring a couple of months later on a slow day Dad received
a call. He was in the little office again, in the middle of the morning.
The voice on the other end, a female voice, was already screaming
when he picked up the phone.

You son of a bitch! He killed himself! You son of a bitch.

Who is this?

You know who it is. He went to Denver and started drinking and
took a gun and blew half his head off. He never even left a note.
Because of you. You did this. You're the one that made him. Oh I
hope you rot in hell! Oh goddamn you! I hope you burn in hellfire
forever.

5

MIDMORNING she was out on the front porch in the still fresh bright heat of the day with the old wooden-handled broom she kept for the porch and sidewalk, sweeping across the gray-painted wood boards, some of them warped and coming apart at the joints. At the front window she looked inside and Dad was sitting in his chair staring out into the side yard. She wondered what he was thinking about. If he was thinking about how his death would come for him, in what manner it would take him away. He never talked of it. She swept up the dead tree leaves and the dirt that had blown in. There was always dirt on the front porch, even in winter. She was glad of that, in a way. She was sweeping it off onto the bare ground next to the cement foundation of the old house when Lorraine came out and said she had a phone call.

I didn't hear the phone.

It's some woman asking for you.

Did she say who it was?

No. But I wish you'd let me do this, Mom. You don't need to be sweeping out here.

Yes I do. I have to get outside. This gives me an excuse to be out here. She leaned the broom against the house wall and Lorraine handed her the phone and went back inside.

Yes. This is Mary. She stood facing out across the street.

This is Doris Thomas calling. I saw Frank.

What did you say?

I saw Frank.

What do you mean?

At the airport in Denver. He was in the lines at security where they make you walk back and forth between those straps and we kept passing each other and I knew right away it was him. He was wearing a cap so I couldn't see the top of his head but it looked exactly like him. Like your husband used to look when he was that age.

What did you say to him?

I didn't say anything to him. I didn't want to embarrass either one of us.

He was flying someplace?

Yes. I just thought you'd want to know.

When was this?

Two weeks ago. I was on my way to Seattle to be with my daughter. She had her baby.

Did he look okay?

Frank? Yes, I think he looked okay.

I mean, did my son look happy?

Oh. I wouldn't be able to say about that.

She stood facing out across the fence and gate and the street to the empty lot on the other side. Inside the fence the shade under the silver poplar trees was shifting and moving on the grass. There were tears in her eyes now and she stayed for a long time crying quietly and thinking. Then she wiped her face and went back into the house. Lorraine was upstairs in her bedroom. At the foot of the stairs she called up to her. Will you come down now?

Is something wrong?

I want to tell you and Dad at the same time.

What is it?

She turned and went into the living room. Dad was sleeping and she went over and put her hand on his arm and held it there until he opened his eyes and looked up at her. Are you awake, honey? she said.

I am now.

I want you to hear something.

Lorraine came into the room.

I want to tell you both something, Mary said. About a phone call I just got from Doris Thomas. You remember her.

No. I don't, Dad said.

Yes, you do. She had the daughter that moved out to Washington State. She and her husband lived over on Detroit Street until he died.

Don Thomas.

That's right.

He always talked a lot, said Dad.

Well, I don't know about that.

They had a boy my age, Lorraine said. I never heard what became of him.

What about this phone call? Dad said.

Mary looked from her husband to her daughter. Doris said she saw Frank. At the airport in Denver.

How could she see Frank?

That's what she said. She said she saw him at the airport.

When?

Two weeks ago.

Why is she just calling now?

Because she was in Seattle seeing her daughter. Her daughter had her baby. She just got back.

What did he look like? Dad said.

She said he looked like you when you were his age.

I doubt that.

That's what she said.

I doubt it.

Dad, she said she saw him.

I don't believe any of this for a minute. It isn't possible.

But, honey, what if she did.

No. Frank's gone off someplace far away. He's not coming back here or anywhere near here.

I don't think she saw him either, Mom.

Oh why do you say that?

I don't think she could have. I don't think Frank would be flying anywhere.

Mary looked from one to the other, her eyes filling again with tears. Shame on you both, she said. Shame on you.

She left the room and went out through the front hall to the porch and carried her broom to the swing and sat down.

In the house Dad said, Go see about her, will you? She won't talk to me now.

Lorraine went out to the porch. Can I sit with you, Mom?

No, I don't want any company. I don't want to speak to you or anybody else right now.

6

THE NURSE from hospice was a small active woman with beautiful teeth and shiny hair. She came into the living room on a sunny
morning in her pink shirt and vest and blue jeans and came over to
Dad, walking slowly so as not to surprise him, and he turned from the
window to look at her. Lorraine brought her a chair and she sat down
in front of Dad and took his hands and examined them, inspecting
his fingernails, and smiled and he looked at her soberly, not smiling
but not frowning as he sometimes did. She said, Mr. Lewis, how are
you this morning?

About the same.

You're out of bed and in your chair. You still feel well enough to
sit up.

Yeah.

What did you have for breakfast? Did you eat breakfast?

I ate something.

What did you have?

He looked at Mary who was standing behind the nurse with
Lorraine.

You had your oatmeal, she said.

I had some oatmeal, Dad said.

He didn't eat very much of it. He didn't want his toast.

I'm tired.

Yes, the nurse said. You eat whatever you want to.

She thinks I need to eat.

Of course. Because she cares about you.

I'm not hungry anymore.

I know. That's what happens. We get like that. Did you have a shower today?

No, he said. Later maybe.

All right.

We'll see. I don't know if I will.

Do you mind if I check your breathing and pulse?

If that's what you want to do.

I do.

She took his temperature and his pulse and put the clothespin-like oximeter on his finger to gauge the oxygen level.

What is it today? Mary said.

It's ninety-two. Still satisfactory.

Can I listen to your heart and your breathing now, Mr. Lewis?

She took the stethoscope out of her bag and he unbuttoned his shirt and pulled up the undershirt. His chest was white and bony and almost hairless, the ribs jutted out. She bent forward and listened to his heart and his chest and his stomach.

You sound all right for today. Do you feel okay?

Well. I know I don't have long. If that's what you mean. But I don't feel too bad.

Are you in any pain today?

Some.

A lot of pain?

There's some pain. Yeah.

Honey, you don't tell us that, Mary said. I wish you would say something.

He looked at his wife and then turned and stared out the window.

He can take the Roxanol too, the nurse said. Along with the MS Contin.

How often can he take it? Lorraine said.

Whenever he wants, the nurse said. It won't hurt him. Every fifteen minutes if he needs it. Mr. Lewis, will you listen to me? she said.

Slowly he turned back around. His eyes were flinty now.

When you're in pain you need to tell your wife or your daughter. They can give you something that will help right away.

I don't plan on getting addicted, he said.

You won't.

It's morphine, isn't it?

Yes. It's a form of morphine. But it won't matter.

He studied her face. Because I won't last that long. That's what you're talking about. Not long enough to get addicted.

That's right. But it'll give you immediate relief. I've told them about it and they can help you take it.

He looked at her and then he began to rebutton the front of his shirt, fumbling with the buttons. The nurse took his hands again.

What are you going to do today?

Today?

Yes.

Not much.

What are you thinking about? Will you tell me?

I was thinking I'd like some peace, he said. He withdrew his hands and turned and peered out the window once more.

Well, you seem to be doing pretty well here. I'll come again next week. Is that okay?

He was looking at the side yard and at the tree and the shade on the grass. There was less shade now, the sun had moved higher in the sky. That'll be fine, he said. Thank you for coming.

The nurse took her bag and equipment and rose from the chair. Do you need any more of any of the pills?

No, Mary said. Do we, Lorraine?

I don't think so.

The women went out to the sidewalk in front of the house and stood talking quietly. Does he seem worse to you? Mary said.

He's still getting out of bed and he's sitting up. He's still fairly responsive to questions when you ask him something.

When he wants to be, Mary said.

He's sleeping more now, Lorraine said.

He'll probably begin to sleep even more. You understand he can have Roxanol throughout the day.

And it won't hurt him.

No. You have the journal I've left, with my phone numbers on it, and you know what to do when things change. And you have that little blue book I gave you to read. You can call me anytime, night or day.

Thank you.

You're doing a wonderful job taking care of him. I want you to know that. He's lucky to have you.

I don't want my husband to suffer.

Lorraine put her arm around her mother. The nurse said good-bye and they watched her go on to the car.

7

WHEN LYLE heard something and looked up they were standing in the doorway watching him. He was seated at his desk in his office at the rear of the church with the shelves of books behind him and the framed print of Sallman's *Head of Christ* hung on the wall together with the picture of Christ knocking at the door wearing the crown of thorns, lifting aloft a lantern. They were a young couple, the boy maybe twenty-one or twenty-two; the woman looked to be older. He was a big strong tall boy wearing new jeans and brown boots and a suede vest over his white shirt and holding a good Stetson hat in his hand, and the girl, the young woman, was dressed in a short white sleeveless dress with a silver belt and she had on white high-heeled shoes. Can I help you? said Lyle.

Are you the preacher here? he said.

That's right.

We were looking to get married.

Would you care to come in?

They stepped into the office. They did not appear to be nervous or uncertain. The boy looked around.

Would you care to sit down? Lyle said.

He removed some books from the couch next to the wall and wheeled up his office chair from behind his desk and sat near them. The woman was not tall and the short skirt of her white dress rose up on her thighs when she sat down. She took the boy's hand on her lap.

This is Laurie Wheeler and I'm Ronald Dean Walker, he said.

It's good to meet you.

You too.

When were you thinking of having the wedding? Lyle said.

Today, the boy said. He looked at the woman. Now. If that's possible.

Yes. That's possible. May I know something about you first?

What do you want to know?

Well, I wonder where you come from. How you met each other.

He comes from over by Phillips, the woman said. He grew up there. Didn't you, Ronnie.

I was born there. I've been other places but I come back.

He works in a feedlot over there, riding pens. But he can do a lot of things.

I've done a fair number of things so far, he said.

He can fix anything you want fixed.

And yourself, Lyle said. What about you?

I came from South Dakota. But I've been in Colorado for about seven years.

I see. And what do you do?

I run a café in Phillips. That's how we met. He came in for supper one night and didn't have his billfold.

I forgot it out at the trailer. And I didn't have no money on me to pay with. No checkbook neither. She thought I might be pulling something.

I didn't really think that, she said. But you don't know. You get all kinds in a public café. So we got to talking and then the next day he brought me back the money. And then he said, When do you close up shop, ma'am, if I may be so bold.

I was trying to kid her a little.

He's got a good sense of humor.

And that was the beginning, Lyle said.

That was the beginning, the boy said. That's how we got started. He looked at the woman and then at Lyle seated in the chair beside them. Can you marry us this morning like you said?

Yes. But you're aware you need a license.

The boy reached inside his vest and unsnapped the pocket of his white shirt and took out a marriage license that had been duly prepared and stamped and handed it to Lyle. It had been folded and unfolded and was frayed at the creases. Lyle inspected it. Yes. This looks fine, he said. It looks legal and official.

They said we could get married if we was over eighteen and we are. Both of us.

I'm older than he is, the woman said. You probably noticed.

That don't matter to me, the boy said. It's only five years. She knows a whole lot more than I do.

Isn't he nice, she said.

He seems like it, Lyle said.

He is.

But you know in Colorado you could marry yourselves, Lyle said. You don't need me or someone like me or a judge even. Just the license and saying to each other we're married and then afterward you return the license to the county clerk.

We know, she said. They told us that. But we wanted a preacher in a church. And in some other town than Phillips.

It'll be a pleasure, Lyle said. You do seem to love each other.

We do.

Could you tell me why you love each other?

You want us to tell you why we come to love one another.

If you don't mind. I'd like to hear it.

You go on first, the boy said.

All right, the woman said. She spoke very seriously. I love him because he's such a nice man as I said before. He treats me gentle and careful. Not all men are like that you know.

No.

He's reliable and he's a hard worker. He's not afraid of work.

I've held down a job ever since I was ten years old, the boy said.

He pays attention to things, she said. He pays attention to me. She looked at Lyle. All those reasons are why I love him.

I can see that. And why do you love Laurie?

The boy turned to look at her. They looked solemnly at each other.

They were still holding hands on her lap and he was holding the hat on his knee with his other hand.

My life is altogether different ever since I met her. My life is every way changed. The way I look at things. He stopped, then went on. I want to say this girl has altered just about everything in the world for me. To the good, I mean. He stopped again. This girl here is the best person I know on earth. I don't ever hope to meet no one any better.

She smiled and there were tears in her eyes now and she leaned toward him and kissed him on the mouth.

She's awful good-looking too, the boy said and grinned.

They turned forward on the sofa and looked at Lyle.

I think that'll do, he said. That'll do just fine. You know about love, I can see that. But let me just add my own thoughts. Love is the most important part of life, isn't it. If you have love you can live in this world in a true way and if you love each other you can see past everything and accept what you don't understand and forgive what you don't know or don't like. Love is all. Love is patient and boundless and right-hearted and long-suffering. I hope you may love each other all your days of life together. And I hope you may have a great many years of those days.

They sat looking at him talk. Yes sir, we will, the boy said. He glanced at the woman. Can you perform the service now?

We'd like it in the church if you could, the woman said.

Of course. It requires a big room, doesn't it. Something more than a small ordinary place like this. Come in here.

He rose and they followed him into the sanctuary.

Afterward, after Lyle had said the words out of the old book, holding it open in his hand, and after the boy and woman had repeated what he'd said and they had kissed each other for a good long time and were still standing in front of the altar with the sun streaming through the stained-glass windows, the boy took out his wallet from the rear pocket of his jeans and presented a fifty-dollar bill to Lyle.

I never forgot my wallet this time, he said. Will that be enough?

It's more than enough, Lyle said. It's too much.

No sir. It's worth every dime to me to have this wedding here. To have Laurie and myself be connected together.

Then thank you, Lyle said. I'll find something good to do with it.

The boy shook his hand briskly and turned and picked up his hat from the pew behind them and he and the woman twined their arms together and walked up the aisle, and outside the boy set his hat firmly on his head and they stepped down the shining concrete steps to the freshly washed pickup parked at the curb and drove off.

That evening, over the dinner table, Lyle told his wife and his son about the wedding and about the way the boy and the woman talked and conducted themselves. That was love, he said.

His wife and son didn't say anything.

That was an example of love for anyone to see.

He took out from his shirt pocket the fifty-dollar bill and set it on the table.

I'm going to put this money in the World Mission Fund. I think it's important to use this particular bill and not some other or some check but this one specifically. I won't use his name. Let it be anonymous. It represents a half, better than half a day's work for that boy. Maybe even a whole day. Something good should come of it. Nobody but the three of us will ever know. An anonymous gift. To somebody somewhere else in the world who needs it without the giver even knowing he's made the gift.

Later in the evening while Lyle was out of the house making calls at the hospital, John Wesley went into his parents' bedroom at the top of the stairs. His mother, a pretty dark-eyed woman, lay in bed reading, the bedside lamp shone onto her face and shoulders. She had on a summer nightgown and her shoulders were bare. She pulled the sheet up and put down her book. The boy stood at the foot of the bed.

Why does he have to talk like that? It makes me sick.

Don't talk about him that way.

He's not preaching here. At the table to us. But he still sounds like he's preaching or pointing up some moral.

He means well, you know that. He was trying to tell us about something that was important to him.

He's full of shit, Mom.

Don't talk like that. It's not true.

It is. I can't stand it when he sounds like that.

Be patient, you'll be gone to college before long.

Two years from now. I want to go back to Denver.

We're living here now.

These kids are all going to be hicks. You know they are.

You'll find someone to like. You didn't like everybody in Denver either, don't forget.

I liked some of them. I still have friends there. I'm never going to have any friends here.

Yes you will. Somebody'll come along.

You don't have anybody here yourself.

We just got here. I have your father and you.

The boy looked at her and looked at himself in the bureau mirror. You don't have him very much.

Don't say that.

I haven't forgotten what happened in Denver.

I know and I wish it had never happened. Go to bed. You'll feel different tomorrow.

8

It was her way, Willa's manner and her character to keep the house clean and in good repair out in the country east of Holt though few people drove by to see it and almost no one ever visited and entered it. A white house, with blue shutters and a blue shingled roof. The outbuildings were all painted a deep barn red with white trim and they were in good condition too though they had not been used for thirty years, since her husband had died.

She still drove a car. Her eyes were failing but not so much nor so fast that she was ready to give up driving. She had the thick prescriptive glasses. She leased the land to the neighbor and he had black cattle in the pastures and did the haying and what he paid her was enough to live on if she were careful. She liked seeing the cattle standing at the stock tank at the corral beyond the barn. She liked the sound of the windmill working and cranking, the sight of the spouting water. She still kept a garden and she canned the vegetables and fruit and gave most of it away, and went into church on Sundays and attended various church meetings and served on the boards and did her grocery shopping on Wednesdays and ate in the Wagon Wheel restaurant on the highway east of town. Now her daughter had come home again.

On a hot day in June she and Alene went into town and ate and then shopped for groceries at the Highway 34 Grocery Store, then they drove past the Lewis house on the west side of town and drove slowly past the yellow house next door where Alice lived with Berta May and they both envied the other old woman. They didn't see the girl out in the yard as they had hoped so that they might talk to her. They drove back home to the country once more and put the groceries away in the kitchen and then went upstairs and got out of their town clothes and put on thin cotton housedresses and lay down and napped in their separate rooms with the windows open letting in the hot summer air and woke in the afternoon and rinsed their faces at the bathroom sink and dabbed water on the thin napes of their necks and returned downstairs and later they ate their quiet supper and sat out in the yard in lawn chairs and watched the sky color up and darken on the flat wide low horizon.

What are you thinking, dear? Willa said.

About what?

I mean what are you going to do now? Have you decided?

No. I don't know.

You know you can stay here with me. You're very welcome. You don't have to go anywhere. You don't have to leave at all if you don't want.

Alene looked out toward the fading sky. There was only a little light remaining. It would turn nighttime now and soon they would return to the house. It would be too cool to sit outside. It would get dark out. I'm so lonely, she said. I had my chance and I lost it.

What do you mean?

My chance at love and a life.

That wasn't much of a chance, I don't think.

It was.

You did well to get out of it. You were wise to end it.

No. It gave my life some direction. It was my chance, Mother, and I lost it. It was probably my only chance. Oh what's wrong with me? Why have I ended up like this? I'm not even old yet.

Of course not, dear.

But why am I this way? How did you live after Father died?

I just went on. I was lonely too.

Aren't you still lonely?

I don't think about it anymore. I've learned not to think about it. You have to.

I haven't yet.

You will, dear.

But I don't want to. I don't want to be one of those sad old lonely women and not even old but just one who has lost her life and her nerve. I don't give off any intimation of sex or even the possibility of it anymore.

Sex.

Yes. I don't put anything out anymore for anyone to sense.

What are you talking about?

I mean that quality, that condition of being alive and interested and vital and active and passionate in my life. Oh I hate this. I'm going to die and not even have lived yet. It's so ridiculous. It's absurd. It's all so pointless.

You'll get better, dear.

How will I get better?

It gets better. Everything gets better.

How?

You forget after a while. You start paying attention to your aches and pains. You think about a hip replacement. Your eyes fail you. You start thinking about death. You live more narrowly. You stop thinking about next month. You hope you don't have to linger.

9

LORRAINE SAT SMOKING in the evening. Rocking in the porch swing, scarcely moving. There was a little summer night's breeze. In front of the house the wide street was quiet and empty, at the corner the street lamp shone blue. Then Dad was coming out and she got up to help him through the door, he stepped out carefully and came past the swing to one of the porch chairs and lowered himself and set his cane on the floor.

You doing okay, Daddy?

Yeah.

Will you be warm enough out here?

This air feels good. It was too hot today. It doesn't need to be that hot.

Lorraine watched him and sat down on the swing.

But it always cools off, he said. You can count on that much. He looked out at the street. Nothing happening. Quiet, he said.

Yes. It's nice.

They sat for a while, not talking. She took out her cigarettes again.

Let me have one of those things.

You want to smoke?

I like the smell of it. I can still smell it.

She stood and shook out a cigarette from the pack and he took it in his thick fingers and she bent and lit it for him, his face illuminated now for a moment, pale and thin, his cheeks drawn in, his eyes sunken. He puffed at the cigarette and blew out and looked at the end of it. Lorraine sat back down. Mary came out on the porch and stopped, looking at Dad.

What are you doing?

Nothing.

Oh don't give him one of those things. He doesn't need something more to make him worse.

What can it hurt, Mom? Come sit down.

I'm just holding it, Dad said.

You're both foolish, Mary said. She seated herself and after a while she and her daughter began to move the swing.

Do you remember when you caught us smoking in the barn? Lorraine said.

Corrupting your brother, Dad said.

It was my job. I was the big sister.

By three years.

Big enough.

I made you smoke the whole pack afterward.

It was only a couple more cigarettes.

Was it.

But you stood there and made us.

It didn't do any good. Did it.

No.

How old were you?

I was eleven, Frank was eight. About Alice's age.

Who's Alice?

The little girl next door with Berta May.

All right.

Her mother died of breast cancer.

I remember now, Dad said. I know.

Later, when the three of them were still talking, Dad said: You could come back and run the store. You're already here. You wouldn't even have to leave. You could stay here and run it.

I don't know if I want to do that, Daddy.

It's all in the will, he said. It goes to Mom and then to you after she's gone. You could learn how. You're quick and you know how to manage people. You manage people already.

Just four people in the office.

That's enough. You wouldn't have to take care of that many here. There's Rudy and Bob and the bookkeeper. They've been with me so long they don't need much managing.

They're used to you, Lorraine said. They wouldn't want somebody new coming in and telling them what to do.

They'd get used to it.

I doubt it.

They'd get used to it. Or else, you'd let them go. You can think about it. Will you do that?

I don't know, Daddy. We'll see. What do you think, Mom?

I think it'd be nice to have you here. You could live with me in the house.

We'd make each other unhappy. You know we would.

Well, I don't either know that, Mary said. You wouldn't make me unhappy. But you mean what I'd do to you.

I didn't mean anything, Mom. I've just been away for so long.

They looked at Dad. He was staring out into the street past the trees and the fence. Does it hurt you, Daddy, for us to be talking about what will happen after you're gone?

I don't want to know all of that. What I want to know about is the store. I want that figured out.

But if I took over, what about Frank?

What do you mean? Frank won't be coming back.

But what about him? How is he mentioned in the will?

He's not mentioned.

Why isn't he?

Because he left.

So did I.

But not like he did. We don't know where he is or what he's doing. We don't know nothing about him no more. We haven't had contact in years.

I used to hear from him, Lorraine said. He'd call me on the phone at work.

When was this?

When he was still in Denver. Then I didn't hear from him anymore. I tried to find him but I couldn't. We used to meet and go out to a bar and talk.

Honey, we know you did that, Mary said. We thought you were talking about something different.

He always wanted to meet at a particular bar downtown. He'd come in as he always did, like he was sick, or hungry. Maybe he was, both. He'd sit down and look around. I'm paying, I'd tell him. Then I'll have something good, he'd say. We'd smoke and when the drinks came he'd take a long swallow and say, Goddamn. Here's to happier days, and then he'd start talking.

About what? Dad said.

Oh anything. His work. His friends. What guy he was living with.

We don't need to hear about that.

I know, Daddy. He was just so sad sometimes and so blue.

He was always sad, Mary said. As he grew older, I mean. Not when he was little.

He'd be drunk by the time we finished for the night. Sometimes he'd get funny too.

What do you mean?

Oh, he could be funny. He had style. He could be really witty. Did you know that?

We never heard much of that here, Dad said.

No. He wouldn't here. But he could be very funny.

Like how? said Mary.

Oh, just clever. Not telling jokes, I don't mean that. But talking in a funny entertaining way about different people. About his life. About his friends and the people he worked for.

I suppose he said something about us, Dad said.

He talked about you. About both of you.

What about us?

What his life was like here, Daddy. When he and I were growing up here in Holt.

It was all bad, I suppose.

Not all of it. He had some good things to say too.

Well, I don't know.

I hope he did, Mary said. She got up and went into the house and brought back a blanket and spread it over Dad. He sat in the chair looking out at the street, the blanket drawn up to his chest.

The millers were swirling under the porch light and bumping it and dropping to the floorboards and fluttering upward again. Mary went back and switched off the light and returned and sat down. The millers still singed themselves against the hot bulb and fell or fluttered away. From beyond Berta May's house the corner street lamp cast long shadows through the trees that moved a little in the night air.

10

YEARS AGO Alene walked along a wide Denver sidewalk with her arm in a man's arm. That was in wintertime. A snowy evening. The snow was falling thickly and it was pleasant under the lights along the street, walking slowly past the city stores, looking in the windows, delaying going back to the hotel for the pleasure of being out in the cold air together. She was a young woman then, just thirty-three, nice-looking and slim and tall and brown haired and blue eyed. He was a little older, closer to forty, a tall man with the gray starting to show at the sides of his head. A principal in a school in the same district as the school she taught in. Which was how and why they met, at a district-wide school meeting. She had felt something at once. And then she had found a way of saying something to him. She couldn't remember what it had been but it'd made him laugh and then they'd met again at another gathering and he had wanted to know if she would join him for dinner sometime in Denver. They both understood what he was saying. She said yes, she'd like that. And that was when it began.

The snow had started to collect on the sidewalk. The cars were beginning to pack it down out in the street. Going quietly by, quieted by the snow.

At the end of the block they stood waiting for a city bus to pass, the interior illuminated in the evening, the people in the bus moving past them as in a kind of movie. An old woman alone in her seat on the bus. An old man wearing a hat. A young girl at the back looking out the window as the bus passed and went on up the street. They crossed the street, she held on to his arm so as not to misstep.

Are you ready to go up? he said.

Yes. Are you?

Yes.

They turned in at the lobby of the hotel. It was a block east of the train depot, an old hotel, one of the oldest in the city, a tall square redbrick building with an ornate front. She stood near the elevator while he got the key from the desk clerk and they rode up to the third floor, another man with them, and she felt his now familiar hand pressing the side of her hip through her coat and that was something she would remember afterward, the feeling of that and the secret of it, while he and the other man made conversation about the weather. What about this snow? It might go up to a foot. Is that right? That's what they were saying on the news, if you can believe them, and then the elevator stopped and they got out and walked down the long narrow hall, following the runner tacked to the floor, she in front, he following, and came to the room and she stepped aside so he could open the door with the key.

The flowers he had brought her that afternoon were still there on the mirrored buffet. Their fragrance was in the room. She waited as he locked the door and then he turned to her and she kissed him, she was full of joy and happiness. Then he undressed her. The bed was cold and they clung to each other until they were warm and the sheets were warm.

The room had been rich once, beautiful, with wallpaper that had dark red roses aligned up and down, and with an elaborate brass light fixture in the ceiling and a tall mirror on the wall and a narrow door letting into the bathroom, you took a step up to enter, and inside were the claw-footed bathtub and the free-standing sink with the two porcelain faucet handles, and an oval mirror with tiny silver cracks around the edges.

She rose above him in the bed and kissed him and looked down into his face. He had a good face. And brown eyes, looking at her. Oh God, she said.

I know. Don't think about it.

I'm not thinking. I just was going to say—

I know.

She reached under the sheet and found him and made the adjustment, shifting a little.

Afterward lying in the bed in the old beautiful room, feeling warm and happy, she said, Don't go yet.

I have to. You know I do. I still have to drive home. It'll be late as it is. And I can't tell what the roads will be.

Stay here. Stay overnight. Please.

How can I?

Call her. Say you're snowed in, you can't leave. You got delayed at the meeting and didn't get started when you thought you would.

The meeting was over this afternoon.

Make something up.

I can't.

Of course you can. You do already. We both do.

I can't tonight.

When will you? When is it going to be any different? Will it ever be?

Yes.

When?

I don't know. I can't say that.

Go on then. Leave if you're going to. She turned away from him.

Don't be like this.

You don't know what it's like, she said. You have no idea.

She lay in the bed and turned toward him again and watched him dressing in the dim room, in the winter light from the street coming in at the window, his long legs, his bare chest and back and arms before he covered them, dressing, and watched how he stood while he tucked in his shirt, and then he came across the room and sat on the bed and bent and kissed her and reached under the cover and touched her breast again.

Are you going to say anything?

No, she said.

He kissed her cheek and went out of the room and she got up quickly and wrapped herself in the bedcover and stood at the window and saw him far below picking his way across the street in the darkening car-packed snow and then she watched him walk down the block in the snow that was still falling and go around the corner out of sight to his car, to drive home on the icy roads to his wife and children in the town where he was principal in the high school.

She imagined his arrival at home, his wife's worry and complaint, and his consoling her, joking a little, making his excuses and explanations, and she could see them then in the familiar pretty picture walking arm in arm, looking in at the sleeping children, and entering their own bedroom, lying in bed with her head resting on his shoulder and her hair spread out like a fan, and then she saw him kissing her and doing what he had just done with her, and she realized she was crying again and after a while she got up and went into the old tiled bathroom to rinse her face.

II

AFTER IT WAS announced at Annual Conference where they would be sent, Lyle drove his family the two and a half hours from Denver out onto the high plains to look at the town. Main Street with one traffic light blinking on and off at the corner of Second Street, the business section of three blocks, the old brick buildings with high false fronts, the post office with its faded flag, the houses on either side of Main Street, the streets on the west side named for trees, those to the east named for American cities, and Highway 34 intersecting Main and running out both directions to the flat country, the wheat fields and the corn and the native pastures, and beyond the highway the high school where John Wesley would be going, and far away the blue sandhills in the hazy distance.

After they had moved to Holt, John Wesley spent the first week up in his room at his computer writing long letters to his friends in Denver. Then on Sunday he was forced to attend the morning service since it was the entire family who made up the preacher's presence in town and the church expected them all to attend. On the third Sunday he got a surprise.

There was a girl who attended church who was tall and thin and strange, dressed in black with bright red lipstick, and with very pale skin. She always sat in the back pew. She caught up to him after the Sunday service when he was walking away from the church.

Wait, she said. Are you trying to escape from me?

He stopped and turned toward her.

They told me about you. You're going to be a sophomore in high school. It's too bad you're not still a freshman, I could initiate you. Well I can anyway.

She had her own car and they went out at night driving all over the town and out into the country on the gravel roads as far south as Highway 36 and as far north as Interstate 76, John Wesley in the seat beside her, the windows open, the cassette player playing her music, the two of them talking, and then they would pull off the road onto a farm track or an unused side road and she would move him into the backseat and unbutton him and teach him what she knew, and afterward sweaty and red-faced they would get back in the front to drive some more. The air would be coming in cool and fresh and the dust boiling up behind them on the county roads, with rabbits and coyotes and red foxes and raccoons all out at night on the road, and once suddenly the great white shape of a Charolais cow broadside in the headlights together with its pale calf, and occasionally they'd stop again for another time in the backseat. She was on birth-control pills. Are you stupid? she said. I thought you city boys knew something. I'm not going to get pregnant and fuck everything up. Don't worry about it. Come on, preacher's boy. Don't you want to go again.

Then he'd return home. She'd drop him off in front of the parsonage and drive away and he'd walk up onto the porch and enter the dark quiet house. His father and his mother would be asleep in their bedroom upstairs, and he'd go back to the kitchen and make something to eat, and take the food up to his room, and enter the bathroom and lower his trousers and inspect himself and soothe his soreness with hand salve and return to his bedroom and turn on the computer and eat the food he'd brought upstairs and read his messages.

It went on for most of a month this way. He and this older girl, Genevieve Larsen, out in the country in the dark in Holt County driving and stopping and climbing into the backseat. And then starting the car again and turning back out onto the gravel roads and always the dust swirling and rising up behind them.

You should have known me in Denver, he said. It was different in Denver. I had friends there. I was known there.

What'd you do? Sit around and play with your computer?

No. We had fun. It was interesting.

Doing what?

It was different. There's so much to do. We went out at night and talked and saw people. Ate in the cafés. We laughed and laughed. We hung out at the malls.

We're out at night. We're talking. Don't you like this?

Yes. Of course.

You didn't have somebody like me there, did you?

No.

Well.

I don't know, it was just different there. That's all I'm saying. You'd have liked it.

You're going to mess this up, do you know that? You don't even see what's in front of you. You're like everybody else.

No, I'm not.

You're dreaming backward.

One night his mother was waiting in the living room, reading, when he came in. It was late. He stood in the doorway. She was watching him over the top of her book.

Come here, she said. I want to look at you.

Why?

I want to see what you look like when you come in so late after being out with her all night.

It's not all night.

Don't be literal. You know what I mean.

He went over and stood before her. She studied him, a tall skinny thin-faced boy, his hair a mess.

You smell like her, she said. Don't you.

No.

Yes, you smell like her. You have her odor. I hope you're not being foolish about this. I hope you're not going to get this girl pregnant.

She's on the pill.

Is she. Did she tell you that?

Yes.

Do you believe her?

Yes.

Well, we can hope she's not a little liar. Do you love her?

It's none of your business.

Do you or not?

Yes, I do.

That's good. I wouldn't want it all to be for nothing. Just sex.

Mother. What are you doing?

You'll get tired of her. Or she you. It doesn't last. Love doesn't last. You look like you're losing weight. Are you?

No.

Well go to bed. You must be exhausted.

12

At the window sitting in his chair Dad Lewis was awake in the late morning when the Johnson women drove up and stopped in front of Berta May's house and got out of the car in their summer dresses. They went up the walk onto the porch and knocked and stood waiting.

Dad turned his head and called toward the kitchen.

Yes? Mary said. Do you want something?

Would you come out here?

She came out through the dining room. Is something the matter?

They're over at Berta May's.

Who is?

Willa and Alene.

Mary looked out the window. The Johnson women were still standing on the porch.

What are they doing over there? Dad said. I thought they'd be coming here again.

Maybe they're just paying a call.

Berta May came and drew back the lace curtain at the front window and peered out and opened the door.

I didn't hear you knock. Will you come in?

Is this a bad time to come? Willa said.

No. I don't guess it is. Is there something I can help you with? Come in, please.

They stepped inside. Alene looked at her mother and said, We just wondered if we might take Alice out for lunch today.

Take her out for lunch.

Yes. If you wouldn't mind.

Well, I don't know. You only want her. Is that what you're saying?

Oh no, we'd like you to come too if you want to.

She looked at them. No. I see now. I'm afraid I'm getting slow. You thought you might take her for a treat. Is that it?

If you wouldn't mind.

I don't mind. But we'll have to ask her.

Is she here?

Out in the backyard. I'll call her.

She went out and stood at the kitchen door and called the girl in and they came back together to the living room. The girl was tanned and freckled, in shorts and T-shirt.

Her grandmother stood with her arm around her. They want to ask you something. Go ahead and ask her, if you'd care to.

Willa smiled at Alice. Do you remember meeting us next door when we were visiting Dad and Mary Lewis?

Yes.

We wanted to know if we could take you out for lunch today.

The girl looked up at her grandmother's big red face.

If you want to, Berta May said. It's up to you.

For a little excursion, Alene said. Just the three of us.

Isn't Grandma coming?

No, I'm staying here. I got too much to do right here.

We'd bring you back home as soon as you would want.

Where to?

Where would we go to eat?

Yes.

We thought the Wagon Wheel Café out on the highway. Have you been there?

I don't think so.

You haven't, Berta May said. We go to Shattuck's if we eat out.

I guess I can go, Alice said.

Then you better go change your clothes. You can't go out in public to eat with these ladies looking like that.

What should I put on?

You decide.

The girl looked at them again and went back into the hall to her bedroom. The women stood and talked, waiting for her.

Then she came back in a yellow shirt and green shorts.

Well, those are some bright clothes, her grandmother said. You won't get run over at least.

They're my new clothes.

I know. They're clean anyway.

Would you like to go now? Willa said.

They went out to the car in the dazzling sun of midday and Alene drove and Willa sat beside her in the front seat and the girl rode in the back and watched out the window and looked at the back of the heads of the two women. They went up to the highway and turned east past the Gas and Go and on beyond the Highway 34 Grocery Store into the country past the implement dealership.

They parked and went inside the café and waited at the counter until a woman in a white blouse and a black skirt came and led them past the bar and the salad buffet into the second room to a table where the woman put down menus at three places and took away the fourth place setting. Luann will be your waitress today, she said. She'll be with you in a moment.

Where would you like to sit? Willa said.

Alice looked at the table and then around the room.

Do you want to face the doorway so you can see who's coming in or look out the window toward the fields?

The doorway, the girl said.

She pulled her chair out and took her seat and the two women sat on either side of her. They took up the menus.

What do you feel like eating? Alene said.

I don't know what there is.

Alene pointed in the menu. There are salads and sandwiches listed on this side and main dishes on this page.

Do they have hamburgers?

Yes. But you can have anything you want.

The waitress came and they ordered drinks. She had blond hair, teased out around her face, and was nice-looking.

Who's this now? she said.

This is Alice. Berta May's granddaughter.

Oh my, aren't you a pretty girl. I like your outfit.

Thank you.

I could take you home with me, you're so pretty. Do you want to come and be my little girl? I just got boys.

I don't know.

Maybe some other day.

The girl shrugged.

The waitress left and came back with glasses of tea for the Johnson women and a Coke for Alice. Willa ordered soup and a salad and Alene a club sandwich and Alice said she still wanted a hamburger.

How do you want it cooked, honey? the waitress said.

The girl looked at Alene.

Do you like it pink inside or all brown?

All brown.

With fries? the waitress said.

The girl looked at Alene again.

I think you'll want some fries, don't you?

Yes.

The waitress went off to the kitchen.

Rose Tyler's here, Alene said to her mother. By herself.

They looked at the old woman sitting alone by the window.

She's never going to get over him, Willa said.

Why would she? People don't.

The girl watched them talk and looked out through the doorway to the other room where people were coming and going.

After the waitress brought their food Alice started to pour ketchup on her hamburger but it spurted out, covering it all and she set the bottle down and stared at her plate and put her hands in her lap. She looked as if she would cry.

We're not going to worry about that, Alene said. We can just scrape it off. Do you want me to?

I can do it, the girl said. She scraped and spooned the ketchup off onto the side of her plate.

There, Willa said. That's better. Isn't it.

The girl nodded and began to eat her French fries, picking them up one at a time and dipping the end in the ketchup and biting off the end and dipping it in again and eating the rest by small bites. The Johnsons watched her.

I've only used squirt bottles, Alice said. I used to help my mother fill the ketchup and mustard bottles and the salt and pepper shakers.

Your mother worked in a restaurant?

Yes. She always had me help her.

Do you have any pictures of her?

I do at Grandma's. The girl looked around the room. She looked back at her plate. That old man's dying like my mother did.

You mean Mr. Lewis, the man next door to you.

He's got it all over him. My mother had it in her breast.

We heard about that. We're very sorry.

Alice looked out the doorway and said, She didn't have blond hair like that waitress.

Didn't she?

She had brown hair like me.

Then she must have been a very pretty woman. I wish we had known her.

How does she get her hair that way? So puffy like that.

Well. She must blow-dry it and tease it and then pick it.

As they drove back to town in the car after lunch, Alice was looking out the side window at the trees and the houses going by. My mother said teasing your hair could damage it, she said.

13

ON THE PHONE Dad Lewis told Rudy and Bob to bring him the sales numbers in the morning this time since in the afternoons he wasn't much good anymore, then he hung up and turned to Lorraine. Don't you want to sit in with us so you can see for yourself what these store accounts look like?

Daddy, they don't want me there.

How do you know that? It doesn't matter what they want. If I tell them you're sitting in, that's what will happen.

I'm still trying to decide if I want to at all.

You have to make up your mind pretty soon. This isn't going to go on forever, you know that. You can't put it off much longer. If you don't want to, I've got to do something else.

I know, Daddy.

So at midmorning the clerks came up on the porch and Rudy knocked quietly on the door. They removed their caps and Mary ushered them into the living room and served them coffee, and again they sat side by side on the couch as they had each time, as if they were attending a funeral service, and Dad was in his chair as always with a blanket over his knees and with his wood cane laid on the floor beside him.

Rudy was a little quick voluble middle-aged man, with a balding head, and Bob was tall and skinny and slow, with thick graying hair combed straight back. Rudy held the store accounts in a file on his lap.

You boys doing any good today? Dad said.

We're doing pretty good, Rudy said. How about you, Dad? It seems like you're looking a lot better.

Dad looked at him. Now that is bullshit and you know it.

Well, you don't look too much on the worse side, Bob said.

Yeah. All right. He looked out the window and looked back. You want something to go with that coffee, you boys?

No thanks, Rudy said.

You, Bob?

No thank you, I don't think so. It's still pretty early in the morning.

All right then. Let's see what you got there.

Rudy stood up and set the file in Dad's lap and sat back down. Dad took out the reading glasses from his shirt pocket and fit the thin bows over his ears and studied the pages. The two men bent forward and sipped their coffee, watching him.

After a while Dad looked up. Any problem with any of this? he said.

No. Not to speak of.

Anything we do need to speak of, then?

No. Don't believe so, Dad.

How many lawn mowers we sold this summer by now?

Ten, Rudy said. He looked at Bob. Wasn't it?

That sounds about right.

Last summer we sold fifteen, Dad said.

Things have been slower this year, Rudy said.

Why's that now?

They're not building no new houses in town. That's mainly it. That's how I account for it.

What do you say, Bob?

It's like what he said. And it's this new mower we ordered in. It costs more.

It's a better machine, Dad said.

Yeah. But it costs more.

Well yeah, it costs more, Bob. Goddamn it, it's got to cost more.

Bob inspected his hands. People don't like to spend too much money on a lawn mower.

All right, Bob. I take your point. Dad opened the file again. He found the line he was looking for. What about this accounts receivable? How come that's still so high?

That's old Miss Sprague, Rudy said.

What about her?

She bought that freezer.

I remember she bought it. She bought it before I got sick.

Well. She stopped paying anything on it.

Did you call her?

Yes sir. I called her. Called her two times.

Then did you go to see her?

I went.

Well. Why don't you just go ahead and tell me, Rudy. This ain't some kind of mystery, is it?

No, but it's a bad mess, Dad. He stared across the room for a moment. I figure I can go over to her house and get it back if that's what you want.

You mean repossess it.

Yes sir. Repossess it.

How come?

You ever been in her house?

About thirty years ago.

Well, I doubt she's thrown anything away since then. Dad, it's just an all-out bad situation. She sits in her rocking chair or walks up and down in that mess and confusion all day long. She's left herself little narrow trails to walk in. And she's put that freezer out on the back porch loaded up with things. It ain't even food that she's got inside. She's put her old leftover bank papers and family letters and old yellowed newspapers in it. And she's got it plugged in and turned on, keeping it running, keeping the papers cold. She showed me. She insisted on it. I didn't want to look at it. I didn't know what I'd see. Why hell. It just kind of made me feel sick to myself to see all those papers iced up like that. You want me to take her freezer back?

You think she's lost her mind now? Is that it? Gone over the hill?

I guess that's what it is. Or just pure old age.

You don't think she's going to pay.

I don't think she can pay. It don't look likely to me, Dad.

Well. We don't want it back. We don't ever want to have to take anything back.

She's just all alone over there, is mostly what it is.

Nobody to take care of her? Nobody to talk to?

No sir. Not that I know of.

Well. We can't take back her freezer. It's like she had some idea but whatever it was she forgot it. Let her go. It'll be laid onto bad debts, that's all.

Yes. That's the best way.

What else? Anything happening around town or out in the country?

You heard they started cutting wheat, Bob said.

They should. It's almost the start of July.

You heard about that custom combiner from Texas.

I don't know. I guess. You mean that fellow that claims when you cross into Oklahoma it makes you want to steal?

You heard his story about old Floyd.

I don't guess I heard that.

Well, as he says, last year they come into this little town down in Oklahoma just before the Fourth of July and the hands, they all wanted a day off. He said he didn't trust them but they'd been working pretty hard and deserved some vacation. All of them was pretty much a bunch of alkies, he said. Anyway so they was down there in this little place and he let them go for the one day like they asked. Then the next day when they come back one of the men isn't with them. What happened to Floyd? he says.

Well, one of them says, he's sort of scratching his foot in the dirt, I guess we lost old Floyd.

What do you mean you lost old Floyd?

Well. We went out fishing in a boat on this lake and I guess we had a little bit to drink and then old Floyd, he falls in. He never rises back up.

Goddamn. Didn't you look for him?

Yeah. We looked for him. But we couldn't find him.

So finally this Texas guy telling the story he says he had to call Floyd's mama to tell her they'd lost old Floyd. His mama tells him, Well, just give his things to the hands.

Dad shook his head, grinning. Hell of a deal. I guess it's funny, in a sort of way. He stared for a moment at the two men sitting on the couch. They say drowning is the way to go, isn't that right? But how anybody would know that I don't know.

That's right, Bob said. How would they know?

But you boys now, you could take me over to Bonny Dam and tip me in, couldn't you.

Hell now, Dad, Rudy said. That ain't no way to talk.

It ain't no way to talk maybe, but it would settle things. It wouldn't be a lot of trouble for you.

They looked down at their coffee cups. It ain't that it would be any trouble, Rudy said. That ain't at all the point, Dad.

All right then. I suppose not. He studied them for a while longer. I guess we're done here. You boys want some more coffee before you go?

We wouldn't care to bother you.

You don't bother me. I just appreciate you coming. It's good to see you.

It's good to see you too, Dad.

You know I'm going to have Lorraine sit in with us next time.

Oh? How's that now?

In case she takes over for me.

They stared at him, not speaking.

Afterward, he said. When I'm gone.

I don't know as we get what you're talking about here, Dad.

You will. Nothing's definite yet.

14

THE ONLY REASON Dad Lewis was home midweek on a winter's day thirty-seven years ago was that he had contracted some form of intestinal flu. And the only reason he saw Frank and the Seegers kid out in the corral with the horse in the afternoon was that he'd had to get up from bed to go into the bathroom when he thought he was going to be sick again as he had once in the night and twice already that morning, and it was then, when he looked out through the bedroom window toward the barn out across the backyard, that he saw the two boys. They were wearing winter coats and stocking caps, Frank a good head taller than the Seegers kid. The wind was blowing hard and they looked cold.

Dad was alone in the house. Mary was gone, working at the bazaar, selling chokecherry jam and homemade quilts and crocheted dishcloths in the basement of the Community Church for an African fund-raiser. And Lorraine hadn't come home from school yet.

He went to the bathroom and was sick for a while and afterward returned to bed, looking again out the window, but didn't see the boys this time and didn't think anything of it, but when he got up from bed an hour later and looked once more and didn't see them in the corral this time either, he wondered what was wrong. He thought they might have gotten hurt. Or were having trouble with the mare. He stood looking out the bedroom window for some time.

Finally he went out across the kitchen to the back porch and watched out the window. He pushed open the door and stepped out into the howling raw day and cupped his hands and hollered toward the barn. The wind tore his voice away. He could barely hear it himself. He hollered again. He looked left and right and saw nothing but Berta May's yellow house to the south and the empty windblown weed-grown undeveloped lots to the north and the raised bed of the railroad tracks. He stepped back into the house and shut the door. Weak and sick, he stood shivering on the back porch in his pajamas, shaking steadily, looking out the window.

He put on his winter coat and boots and work cap and scarf and gloves and crossed the bare winter lawn in the backyard and went on into the corral. The wispy dirt was swept up by the wind into little drifts across the bare ground. The wind cried and whistled in the leafless trees. He came around the south end of the barn out of the weather and opened the door and peered in at the dim and shadowy center bay. Shafts of sunlight from the cracks in the high plank barn walls fell across the dirt floor. Dust motes and chaff drifted in the air. There was the rich smell of hay and the good smell of horse. He stood for a moment to allow his eyes to adjust. Then he could see Frank and the Seegers kid.

They were mounted on the mare, riding her around in a circle in the closed area of the dirt-floored barn, Frank behind the other boy, their heads close together, and each of them was dressed in one of Lorraine's frilly summer dresses, trotting in and out of the shafts of sunlight. Riding the horse bareback, bouncing, their thin bare legs clutching the mare's shaggy winter-coated barrel. Frank held the reins in one hand and his other hand was wrapped around the Seegers kid.

Then Frank saw Dad standing in the barn doorway. He reined the mare in sharply. Dad stepped inside and moved over to them. The Seegers boy was a redheaded twelve-year-old kid, skinny, his neck scrawny above the square-cut yoke of the pink dress. He looked cold and scared. He and Frank both had lipstick on their mouths.

Get down from that horse, Dad said.

Dad, Frank said. It's all right.

Get down from there.

Frank slid down, then the other boy slipped off. They stood waiting, watching Dad.

What in the goddamn hell do you think you're doing? he said.

We weren't hurting anything, Frank said.

You weren't.

No.

Let me have the goddamn horse. And get the hell out of those goddamn dresses.

Dad took the reins and led the mare across to the big sliding door and shoved it open and jerked the bridle free and slapped the mare hard on the rear, and she trotted out across the empty lot, then he came back. The boys had removed the dresses and were working at getting the brassieres off. They looked like thin hairless animals, frightened and cold. They turned their backs to him and took down Lorraine's silky underpants and stepped shivering over to the manger to their own clothes draped on spikes and got into their pants and shirts and coats.

Are you going to tell my mom? the Seegers kid said.

What? No. But if I see you in here again, by God, I'm going to whip you.

The boy looked at Frank once, quick, and stumbled across to the door and hurried outside. They could hear him running across the corral.

You want to tell me what this is about? Dad said.

There's nothing to tell, Frank said.

Those were your sister's dresses.

Yes.

Does she know you took them?

No. But we weren't doing anything to them.

You think she'd see it that way?

Frank looked at him and looked out the open door where the boy had gone. She wouldn't care, he said.

Why wouldn't she care?

She just wouldn't.

How do you know that?

I don't know it for sure.

Have you talked to her about this, what you've been doing?

No.

She doesn't know anything about it? How you two were wearing her dresses?

No.

Jesus Christ. He looked at Frank, watching his face. What am I supposed to do about this?

Leave me alone.

Leave you alone.

Please.

Dad stared at him. Christ, he said. What are you anyway?

I'm just your boy. That's all I am.

Dad grabbed him and shook him, hauling him around in the cold air, they staggered in and out of the bars of light fallen across the floor, and then Dad stopped shaking him and grabbed the bridle reins and whipped at him. Frank pulled away, and in his wildness Dad whipped him once across the face and then he suddenly threw the reins away and grabbed the boy, holding him in his arms, hugging him and sobbing. Oh my God, oh my God, oh my God.

Frank held himself rigid in his father's arms and finally Dad let him go, then Dad hurried out of the barn, stumbling across to the house into the bathroom and was sick and then went back to the bedroom, his head aching and throbbing now. When he was lying in bed he turned his head and looked out the window. The sun was going down. His eyes welled up and he straightened his head on the pillow and folded his arm over his face in the darkening room.

After a while he heard Frank enter the house and climb the stairs to the second floor. He could hear him in his sister's room where he must have been hanging up the two dresses in the closet, and putting away her underwear, then he heard him cross the hall to his own bedroom and he thought he could hear the bed as he lay down, and he thought he must be touching at his cheek now, fingering where the welt was.

———

At suppertime Mary stood beside the bed in the dark downstairs bedroom. Are you awake, dear?

I'm awake.

Can you get up for supper?

I don't want anything.

You don't sound good. Are you all right?

He nodded slightly.

Okay then. But you seem sicker than you did this morning. Call me if you need something.

In the kitchen she sat down with Lorraine and Frank and she noticed his face immediately.

Honey, what happened to you?

I ran into a post in the barn.

It must hurt. You need something on it. Let me look at it.

He pulled away. Leave it alone, Mom. Never mind.

15

DAD CAME OUT from the bedroom through the hall in the hot still summer afternoon using his wood cane, with Mary following behind, her hands held out in case he needed help, and they came on into the living room where the preacher and Lorraine were sitting together on the couch. Lyle had said not to disturb Mr. Lewis if he was sleeping but Mary told him she'd go back to see if he was awake yet. Now Dad moved across to his chair and sat down and put his cane in place on the floor, looking up at Lyle, who rose and stood next to him and touched him on the shoulder and reached down to take his hand. It's good to see you, he said. How are you doing today?

Getting slower. Going downhill more.

Are you in pain?

No. They got that taken care of.

I won't trouble you for long. I just came to see how you were feeling.

You don't trouble me. Sit down a while if you care to.

Lyle turned and sat again beside Lorraine. Mary seated herself in the rocker as Dad glanced out the window at the sprinkler that was throwing rings of water onto the grass between their house and Berta May's.

What's the weather doing out there today? he said. Too hot again?

They say it's going to rain, Lyle said.

It might. It's turning off dark right now.

The farmers won't like that, will they, Daddy? Lorraine said.

Not if they're trying to cut wheat. The guys with corn won't mind it.

Sounds like a mixed blessing, Lyle said.

Dad looked at him. Yes sir. Lots of things turn out to be blessings that got mixed up.

You've seen some in your lifetime here.

I was raised out on the west plains in Kansas.

You've seen some changes.

One or two. He looked out the window again. The sprinkler had moved on its cleated wheels. He looked back. This was the only house on this street when we bought it. Isn't that right, Mary?

It was nothing but prairie and wind and dirt, she said.

The wind still blows, he said. That doesn't change. You got to have some wind.

It doesn't have to blow on my account, she said. I'm tired of it.

They never paved our road over. I don't guess I'll see that. If they ever do.

What about people you've known? Lyle said. Do you think people have changed?

People?

Are we any different now?

I don't know. He stared at the preacher. We got more comfortable. We're not as active or physical. We don't even go out as far as the front porch as much as we used to. We sit around and watch TV. TV is what's become of people.

My folks always used to sit out in the evenings in the summer, Mary said. I remember that so well.

We did when I was a kid too, Lorraine said. When Frank and I were still little, before junior high. Do you remember?

Frank's your brother, I understand, Lyle said. May I ask about him? I hear his name mentioned.

No one said anything. After a while Dad said, You can ask about him but it won't make no difference. He left here a long time ago. Two days after he finished high school, he took off.

That's pretty young to leave home, Lyle said.

He only come back twice, Dad said.

But he'll come back now, won't he.

Back here?

Yes.

Why would he?

To see you. He'll want to say good-bye.

He won't come back for that, Dad said.

Honey, he might yet, Mary said. Oh I want to think he will.

He doesn't know I'm dying. He won't be coming back.

Haven't you told him? Lyle said.

We don't know where he is.

But would you like to see him?

I'm not waiting on Frank so I can die. If that's what you're get-ting at.

Most people want to see all their family before they go.

I got my family right here.

No, this is not all of us, Mary said. Don't say we're all here.

As far as I'm concerned we're all here, he said.

No, we're not, Daddy, said Lorraine.

He looked hard around the room, at each face, then pushed him-self up from the chair and bent over and picked up his cane and stood still to get his balance. Lorraine came across the room and put her arm around him, holding him, and kissed him on the cheek.

Don't leave, Daddy. Stay and talk to us. It's all right. Don't go, please.

He looked at her face so close to his and looked away and closed his eyes and stood for a long time and finally sat down. She took the cane and set it on the floor, bending over him, kissing him again, putting her cheek against his old age-spotted gray face, and sat down once more beside Lyle. There was silence for a while.

Daddy, why don't you tell Reverend Lyle about some of the preach-ers we've had, Lorraine said. Like that one you always talk about.

Which one is that?

The one that the woman saw Jesus standing on his head.

He looked at her, then at Lyle. All right, you asked about changes, have people changed, you said. They have in church. Church used to be a long serious affair. None of this bell ringing and people's dogs getting blessed down at the altar and kids dancing around during the service.

Sounds like a good time for a nap, Lyle said.

I had me some good ones on Sunday mornings. That's a fact. Anyway, on one of those long hot Sunday mornings there was this woman that was visiting town. Who was it she was seeing, Mary?

The Thompsons, Mary said.

That's right. . . . But you tell it. I won't remember it right.

Yes, you will.

No. Go ahead. Why don't you.

She was visiting the Thompsons, Mary said, and while the preacher was giving his sermon this woman, she was only a little thing, didn't weigh as much as a cat, all of a sudden she jumps up from the pew and starts wailing and crying. The preacher, it was Reverend Cooper then, wasn't it, interrupts his sermon and this tiny little woman cries, Glory! It's the Lord Jesus! Praise God Almighty!

Reverend Cooper says, Yes, ma'am. Can I help you?

He's right there over your head! Dressed all in white and walking in the air!

She shoves her way out of the pew and comes running down to the front of the sanctuary and starts shouting how she's changed this very hour. On account of what she's witnessed. Oh heavenly days! Hallelujah! Then it's like she faints out or has a spell, she kind of sinks down in front of the altar and Marla Thompson rushes down and lifts her up and hauls the poor thing back to her pew.

What did the preacher do all this time? Lyle said.

Oh, he's watching her like the rest of us and then he just goes on with his sermon from where he left off. And afterward we sing the last hymn and he gives out the benediction.

It woke us up at least, Dad said. I couldn't sleep through that. But there was another one too. You remember, Mary. Reverend John Dupree.

You're not going to tell about him.

What was that about? Lyle said.

He was a preacher here too. About twenty years back.

What happened?

Well, him and his wife, she was a lot younger, they had a boy about eight. They were having some kind of trouble and got separated from one another. She went off somewhere and left him.

She just went back to Denver, Mary said.

She went back to Denver and that put Reverend Dupree here alone with the boy. It was a god-awful mess. Dupree, he wasn't any good at church anymore, wasn't much good at anything at all, couldn't concentrate on practical matters, and the boy was moping around town getting himself into trouble. Then the Sunday comes, and during the time for announcements he says, I got an announcement myself. My bride is coming home! She's coming back to me this week. People in the church just applauded. The women, mostly.

There were men clapping too, Mary said.

Clapping at the news. I never heard such a thing in church before in my life.

Did she come back as he said she would?

Yes sir, she come back. All in good time. And shows up in church sitting with the boy and singing hymns. She seemed more or less all right, didn't she, Mary.

Not really.

No?

No.

Well, she seemed all right to me, a man, but Mary's correct, she must not of been completely all right because two Sundays later the preacher's boy is sitting in the pew by himself again and we find out the woman has left Dupree and is living across town with Don Leppke, the young fellow that manages the radio station.

I guess people in Holt didn't care much for that.

No, people didn't care for it at all. The station lost some advertising.

What became of her?

Her and Don went off to Denver. We'd hear her on the radio broadcasting from Denver now and then. She seemed to have a talent for it.

That happened after I left home, Lorraine said.

Yes. I think it did.

It had grown darker outside the house and suddenly there was a flash of lightning and it began to rain. The wind came up. Thunder rolled across the sky and there was more lightning flashing. In the living room they watched it out the side window. The rain came down hard at a slant.

Let's go outside and enjoy it, Lorraine said. Come on, Daddy.

They helped him move out to the front porch and stood watching the rain falling on the grass and out in the graveled street. There were already puddles in the low places and the silver poplar trees were dark, streaming with water. Lorraine held her hand out to the rain and patted her face and then cupped both hands and caught the overflow from the gutters and held her hands up to Dad's face. He stood leaning on his cane, his face dripping. They watched him, he looked straight out across the lawn past the wrought iron fence, past the wet street to the lot beyond, thinking about something.

Doesn't it smell good, Mary said.

Yeah, he said softly. His eyes were wet, but they couldn't say if that was from tears or rainwater.

16

THAT AFTERNOON, when the rains came, John Wesley was standing at the counter in the Holt post office mailing a package for his mother. When he was finished he went outside and stood next to an old woman who was waiting under the porch of the little entryway. Cars went by on Main Street splashing up wakes of spray, their headlights on, their windshield wipers going fast. The old woman was staring at him. You're that preacher's boy.

My father's a minister, yes.

I recognized you. She turned and looked out at the wet street. How about this rain?

I wish it'd quit, he said.

Oh no. You don't know nothing about rain out here. You haven't been in Holt long enough. You got to want it to keep on.

The rain came down hard and sheeted off the street, filling the gutters, running toward the town pond. Then as they were watching, it stopped as suddenly as it had started. The sun shone out from behind the racing clouds.

That's it. That's all we get, the old woman said. She stepped out briskly and walked away up the block.

He watched her. He moved out from under the porch roof and crossed Main Street and turned up Fourth Street. The trees were all dark and dripping, the sidewalk spotted with puddles. In the air was the sweet pure after-rain smell and the smell of wet pavement and wet ground. He was three blocks from his house when the two high school boys pulled up at the curb in a black Ford. One of them said, Hey. Come over here.

John Wesley looked at them.

We want to talk to you about something.

About what?

Something you need to know.

When he turned and went on along the sidewalk, they jumped out of the car and caught up with him.

Where you going? Wait up. Shake hands, son. The first boy put out his hand and when John Wesley only looked at it the boy snatched his hand and squeezed it.

What do you want?

What do we want. He turned to the other boy who was shorter but dressed in the same way, in long baggy shorts.

We want to help you.

That's right. Why don't we just walk along here and we can talk.

I don't think so.

No, let's just walk along here. He draped his arm around John Wesley's shoulder, moving him forward, and the other boy came along on the opposite side. They walked to the end of the block and crossed the street.

I figure you're headed home, aren't you. The bigger boy stared closely at the side of John Wesley's head. Am I right?

It's none of your business.

You're going back to your house. We know that.

He has to get himself ready, the other boy said. She'll be picking him up any minute.

How's she doing for you? the first boy said.

Who?

Genevieve. She's fucking you now, we know that too.

Shut up. He pushed the boy's arm off his shoulder.

Here now. Don't get upset. I was just going to give you a few point-ers. You don't want to make a mistake about this.

Leave me alone.

Now be nice. We're trying to be friends here.

We only want to give you some advice, the second boy said. Is she treating you right? Tell us that. John Wesley stepped off the sidewalk to move away but they moved in front of him now. I mean is she fucking you the way you want?

Fuck you, John Wesley said.

No, I can't do that, the boy laughed. I might like to.

She fucked you pretty good, didn't she, the second boy said. Like you told us she did for you.

Fucked me dry, the first boy said.

Shut your mouth, said John Wesley.

He don't like that kind of talk.

He's a preacher's boy. Course he don't. He don't appreciate bad language.

He still never answered you.

No, he didn't. Does she fuck you the way you want? Tell us the truth.

I said shut your stupid mouth.

Because she's done about twenty of us by now. She don't keep anybody for long, though. Fuck her while you can, is what I say.

John Wesley swung and hit the boy in the face. The boy coughed and bent over and spat in the grass. You little son of a bitch. I think you broke a tooth. He felt inside his mouth with his fingers and looked at the bloody piece in his hand. He grabbed John Wesley around the neck and hit him until his nose spurted blood and he fell down on the wet sidewalk. The boy leaned over him and wadded his shirt in his fist. I ought to beat the shit out of you. You little son of a bitch. He let go of the shirt and John Wesley dropped back on his elbows.

Let's get out of here. Come on. The two high school boys went back the way they'd come, looking around at the houses to see whether anyone was watching, and crossed the intersection and went on to the car.

John Wesley sat up and watched the Ford make a U-turn in the street and drive back toward Main. His nose was bleeding steadily. He wiped it on his shirtsleeve and lay back and looked overhead at the dripping trees. The sidewalk felt cool. He began to think of Genevieve. I fought for you. I'll tell you about it when I see you. They were bigger than me. There were two of them. I hit one of them for you. I hurt him and then he hit me and made me bleed. You can see the blood on my shirt. My blood was spilled for you.

17

ON THE FOURTH OF JULY, Lorraine went next door to Berta May's carrying an old blanket and came out with Alice, and then they walked out along the quiet empty street in the evening, heading toward Highway 34 and on to the high school football field to watch the fireworks. It was cool and fresh now after the heat of the day. Out beyond the town limits the combines were still running in the wheat fields, their lights turned on, bright in the fields, the grain carts and grain trucks parked off to the side, and above them the clouds of dust hanging in the air, carrying the smell of chaff and dust and cut wheat into Holt.

They walked to the highway and turned past Shattuck's Café and then south at the school grounds to go out behind to the football field. There were many other people walking along in the evening. They arrived at the field and went in through the gate at the chain-link fence and crossed the white-chalked lanes of the track and went out onto the grass. The lights on the tall poles around the field were burning fiercely, making a loud hum. The grass looked very green under the lights.

Let's go out there, Lorraine said. It's nicer. She led Alice out to the middle of the field where they saw the Johnson women seated on a blanket. Hello, Willa called. Over here. Come join us.

They walked up to their spot and Lorraine spread the blanket she was carrying and sat down beside them while Alice stood and looked all around at the grandstands filling up with people and the man up in the announcer's booth above the stands, a dangling lightbulb on a cord above him showing him there starkly, standing by himself, and she looked past the goalposts to the south end where the volunteer fire department was arranging the fireworks.

Do you want to sit down with us? Alene said, and Alice sat down between the Johnson women and Lorraine. Two boys her age came and sat in front of them. The boys turned to look at her and Alice saw them but pretended not to notice them. They sat with their arms wrapped around their knees. After a while the man up in the booth began to talk into the microphone.

Folks, I want to welcome you all tonight. Folks. He stopped. Is this thing on? His voice sounded loud and broken, scratchy.

Yeah, it's on, somebody called. Go on ahead there, Bud.

All right then. I guess you can hear me. Well. Good evening, folks, and some of the people sitting on the grass said Evening back to him, and he went on. This is a good occasion here tonight. Isn't it. We all know that. This is part of what makes us great as a country. This day, this celebration, this yearly event, commemorated here this evening. Now I'm going to start our program tonight by recognizing our armed service in this troubled time for our country. I want to request anybody here tonight who served our country to stand up. Army, Navy, Marines, Air Force. National Guard. All of them. It doesn't matter. They all count. Even the Coast Guard that in time of peace is under the auspices of the Treasury Department, folks, did you all know that? and under Defense in time of war. That's right. Stand right up. Let us see you.

Some of the men and a few women stood up in the grandstand and there was an old man who struggled up from a lawn chair near them in the football field.

Give them all a hand why don't you, folks, and all around them on the brightly lighted grass and in the grandstands people applauded. Alice watched Lorraine. She clapped her hands once or twice and then stopped, so she stopped too.

Now I want to make special recognition of one boy in particular here tonight, the announcer said. I won't say out his name because he said he don't want me to. But he's being sent over next week to the war over there. Helping to take our democracy across to the desert to those people they got there. Yes, that's him. I see him now. Down on the left side of the bleachers there. Stand up, will you, son? Yes, that's right.

A boy rose and looked out at the football field without making any gesture or turning around. A young boy, in his army uniform.

Give him a warm sendoff, people. Yes, that's the way.

Some in the grandstand stood up to applaud and some of the people out in the grass stood. The boy in uniform sat down beside a woman next to him and the man in the booth went on.

Now. We have us another treat here tonight. Big Bill Jones is going to sing a selection for us now.

Up in the booth a tall man took the microphone and began to sing "Some Gave All, All Gave Some" over an instrumental recording. When he was done singing people applauded. He had a good voice. Then the announcer said, Big Bill, wait right here if you would and get us started on "America the Beautiful." People sang along with him and they all sang the National Anthem. For that, people stood and men took off their caps. On the football field Willa stayed seated on the blanket. It's too hard to get up and down, she said. Never mind me. She smiled and looked around at them through her thick glasses.

They sat down again and the announcer said, Now will somebody shut off these field lights for us? They waited. Will somebody shut off these lights so we can start? Folks, we can't get started till the lights are turned off. After a while someone pulled the switch and they all sat in the faint light of the evening, the afterglow of sunset still showing to the west but everything dark now in the east. They waited and then suddenly the first rocket shot up and it broke overhead.

There was a loud explosion and strings of light spurted out and dripped down and winked out and white smoke drifted slowly away. Then another rocket exploded. The young boys in front of them named each one as it went off. Come on, bust, they said, and then the rocket burst and they said, Comet. Chandelier. Pixie Dust. Para-chute. Silver rain. Carnation. Chinese Night.

After a while, Lorraine lay back on the blanket. Then Alice did too, and presently the Johnson women stretched out on the blanket next to them and the fireworks fired up into the cool summer night and the ghostlike trails of smoke drifted away in the sky, the pure blue stars far over them, all shining, above the football field on the high plains. The boys went on with their running account. Alice slid over closer to Lorraine.

Are you doing all right, honey? Lorraine said.

The girl nodded.

Are you cold?

A little.

Lorraine pulled her closer.

I wish my mother could have seen this, Alice said.

Yes. Raise your head for a second, honey.

Lorraine laid her arm down on the blanket and Alice lay back and Lorraine pulled the loose end of the blanket up over them both. Alene looked over and watched Alice for a moment. A rocket went off and she could see the girl's face in the shimmering light. Her eyes clear and serious. Her smooth soft girl's cheeks. Alene's eyes welled up with tears, looking at the girl, but immediately she wiped the tears away. Next to her, her mother went on watching the fireworks.

At the end there was a long chain of explosions with a final cannon boom that echoed across the town out into the country. Then it was dark, the smoke drifting away above them, and then the high field lights came on again. Everything seemed brighter than ever.

The announcer came on again. That's it for tonight, folks. Take care going home now. Mind your step now.

On the field they stood up and folded the blankets and people came down out of the grandstands and they all went out slowly in a crowd, not talking much, tired now and satisfied, moving out through the gate.

Good night, dear, Alene said, and without prompting Alice went to her and hugged her and then she hugged Willa. Afterward she walked home with Lorraine, back on the west side of town along the gravel street under the corner streetlights past the quiet houses, a few of them with lamps on inside, and once they saw an elderly woman let a little white dog out and then she called it back in and shut the door.

18

IT WASN'T THE IMAGE of her naked beneath the thin raincoat standing in front of him in the back office of the hardware store that Dad Lewis remembered. It was the look on her face before she slapped him. And the pitch and the desperation of her voice on the phone three months later in the spring when she called, screaming that Clayton had killed himself in Denver.

When he had not stopped thinking about her a year later, he decided he had to find her. He drove to the town a hundred miles south of Holt where she had moved with Clayton and the two children to live with her parents. But she was not there now. The parents did not even live there anymore. A man with a beard was renting the house. I don't know, he said. I just moved in. I don't know anything about them. They left some stuff in the basement if you want that.

He drove to the post office and the police station and talked to people at both places. They didn't know anything either. He returned to the street where the house was located and knocked on the neighbors' doors, but it had begun to snow now and the few people who were home didn't want to stand there talking to him with the snow blowing in. On the opposite side of the street he finally found an old woman who told him the parents had moved back to a town in Nebraska and that their daughter had gone off to Denver with the two children. He thanked her and started driving back to Holt in the gathering storm. The wind was blowing the snow across the two-lane blacktop so hard that he had to squint to be sure that he was still on the road and he was forced to stop every five or six miles to scrape off the windshield.

Two weeks later he drove to Denver. It was on a Sunday and he told Mary that he had to pick up a special order. He didn't tell her then and he never did tell her nor anyone else what he was doing. The wind was blowing again but there wasn't any snow this time. He arrived in Denver in the middle of the afternoon.

From there it was almost too easy. Her name was listed in the phone book. She and the two children were living in a one-bedroom apartment in a run-down house in the middle of the city. He climbed the stairs and went back into the dark hallway and knocked. There was noise inside, a TV going. Then the door opened and she stood before him. She looked bad now. She had let herself go. She was barefoot and still wearing a bathrobe in the afternoon, made of some thick fuzzy material, dirty at the front and frayed at the cuffs. Her blond hair had grown out unevenly and she hadn't yet combed it for the day. She stood in the doorway staring at him.

You, she said. What are you doing here? Didn't you do enough already?

I wanted to talk to you, he said.

How'd you find me?

You're in the phone book.

Oh. Well, I don't have a phone no more. They shut it off. I can't afford it. What do you want?

I come to see how you are.

I'm here, look at me. Can't you see? What'd you think would happen?

Dad looked at her and looked away. He said, I'm sorry this happened. I'm sorry it turned out this way.

You're sorry.

I didn't mean for it to turn out like this.

Jesus Christ, she said.

Can I talk to you a minute?

What do you want to talk about? You want to take me up on my offer? Is that it? You changed your mind?

Your offer. What offer?

To let you fuck me. Pay off what he stole.

What? No. For hell's sake. That's not what I come for.

Well, I can't blame you. She pulled the robe tighter. The way I look now.

It's not that. Is that what you think? It's not about that. I come to help you if I can. Can I talk to you?

You just want to talk.

That's right.

You mean you want to come in.

Yes, so we can talk a little.

Come in then. It's a mess. But I'm not going to apologize to you. Why should I?

He followed her back through the dark living room, past the two children sprawled on the floor like some kind of little animals in front of the television, watching some animated movie.

Come out here, she said.

In the kitchen she removed dirty dishes from the table and put them into the sink which was already full of dirty dishes, and swiped at the table with a washrag. Sit down, she said. Don't be so polite. You don't have to wait for me.

He sat down. She dropped the washrag in the sink and sat across from him and lit a cigarette. He looked at her and watched her smoke. Then he removed the wallet from his back pocket and took out all the bills and stacked them on the table. He had five hundred dollars to give her. She stared at him.

What's that? she said.

For you, he said.

How come? Why are you doing this? I don't even understand why you're here.

I told you. I want to help you.

You're giving me this money.

Yes. That's what I come for.

You don't want nothing in return.

He shook his head.

She pushed the hair away from her face. I can still do things, she said. We could go in the back bedroom. I don't have no disease or nothing. She put out the cigarette in the ashtray on the table. I don't look like much but I could still give you a good time. You'd get your money's worth.

I'm not doubting that, Dad said. But that's not what I'm here for.

Are you a homo? she said. I wondered after that other time, when I was naked, when I still looked okay.

What are you talking about?

Don't you like women?

Of course I like women. I'm married. I'm still in love with my wife.

That don't have to stop you, she said. If you're not queer, are you just stupid?

Well, Dad said, I might be that.

She smiled for the first time and he saw she was missing a tooth. Jesus, I don't know about any of this, she said.

How much do you pay for this place? Dad said.

Why?

I'd like to know.

Four hundred dollars.

They pay the utilities?

He does. The old son of a bitch that owns the place.

Dad took out his checkbook. Who do you pay it to? What's his name?

She told him. He wrote the check in the owner's name and put it beside the cash. She watched him suspiciously. He wrote the owner's name in a little notebook. Then he told her what he was going to do. There would be a rent check every month and something extra for them to live on, and she could count on it, he would do these things without fail.

I still don't understand why you're doing this.

I told you.

They talked some more and he learned that she was working at night. The woman across the hall checked on the children after she got them to bed, after she left the apartment to start her shift. That isn't good, he said.

What else do you expect me to do?

You won't have to do that anymore.

He stood up and looked around the little kitchen and looked once more at her and went out past the two kids and walked out of the old house, and in the months following he sent her the two checks at the beginning of each month, and by the end of the year he decided to make a down payment on a little two-bedroom house in Arvada on the west side of Denver. After that he sent the house payment to the bank that held the mortgage, and she and the two children settled down in the new place. She got a daytime job and paid for regular child care. So things were looking up. She was thin again and her hair was cut nicely. He visited her once during that time but there was little now to talk about.

Two years later there was a letter, written on yellow tablet paper. I got married, I'm writing to tell you. He seems all right to me he's sixteen years older but that don't matter. I don't care about that now. Don't send the money for the house no more he wouldn't understand. He don't want somebody else's help. And don't contact me again. We're on our own now. Forget about me now. You done enough. I thank you for that, the last part of it.

19

IN THE NIGHT he lay awake next to Mary in the downstairs bedroom unable to sleep, remembering everything, taking all of his years into account. He decided he wanted to see the nearby physical world once more. He could let go of it if he saw these familiar places again.

They drove out on the Saturday morning in his good car, Lorraine behind the wheel, Dad in the passenger seat and Mary in the back. There was a robe over him and he was wearing his cap.

Now take it slow, he said. There's no rush about this.

A bright hot windless July day, and they put the car windows down. They began by driving past Berta May's yellow house and at the south end of the street where it met the highway they turned a block east and went down Date Street past the grade school and the playgrounds and the practice field and then up Cedar past the Methodist church and across to Birch where the banker lived and where the Community Church was located and then up Ash past the old white frame hotel that was only a broken-down rooming house now with a wide sagging porch and on past the Presbyterian church and the Catholic church and over to Main Street. They drove the length of Main without stopping, from the highway north to the juncture where you had to turn east or west. Which way now, Daddy? Lorraine said.

Go over here to the east, he said. I want to look at these streets too.

They went over a block and then south on Albany and over to Boston and Chicago where Rudy lived and onto Detroit where Bob's house was and then onto the state highway and back to U.S. 34.

You're going too fast, Dad said.

I can't go slow on the highway.

Let them go around. It don't matter.

Where to now?

Back up Main.

They went up the street again past the little houses that were built at the south end and the old water tower on its tall metal riveted legs and past the post office and then the three blocks of businesses.

Let's go back in the alley here, Dad said.

She turned slowly into the dark alley behind the stores. The mismatched backs of the buildings, the jumble of various things, and only a few cars and pickups parked along the way in the potholed gravel.

Stop here, please, Dad said.

She parked the car and they sat in the alley behind the hardware store. He looked at it all, the old brick wall with white flaking paint and the rusted Dumpster and the telephone pole black with creosote, the old rear entrances of the businesses on either side.

He shook his head. I should of painted that back wall again.

It looks about the same as always to me, Lorraine said.

That's what I mean.

Wooden pallets were stacked on one another, and there was the scarred wooden door with the window in it that peered out into the alley.

How many times I went in and out that door. Wasn't that the way, Mary?

How many times do you think, honey?

Fifty-five years times six days a week times fifty-two, he said. What's that come to?

It comes to a lifetime.

That's right. It amounts to a man's lifetime, Dad said. All right. We've been here long enough. Drive us around front now, please.

Lorraine started the car and they came out on Main Street. Should we stop?

Yes, pull in here at the store.

She parked at the curb in the middle of the block. The store was two old brick buildings side by side with high false fronts. Dad sat looking at the plate-glass display windows with the signs touting table saws and generators. The wide front doors propped open on the hot Saturday morning. The new lawn mowers and garden tillers wheeled out on the sidewalk with chains run through them to keep anybody from taking off with them.

A woman came walking toward them, she stopped to peer in through the window, cupping her hands beside her face to block the glare. She glanced up the street and looked inside again and went on.

What did she want? Dad said. We would of had it for her.

She's got to make up her mind, Mary said. She wants to take her time.

Let her come back then, he said.

From where they were sitting they could see Bob inside behind the front counter waiting on some man. The man paid, they watched him remove his wallet and put money out and Bob take it and ring the sale and make change and tear off the receipt. Then he ducked out of sight behind the counter and he reappeared with a brown paper sack in his hand and put the purchase—something silver, not shiny, a pipe wrench maybe—in the sack, slipping the receipt in with it, speaking to the man, thanking him, nodding his head, then something more, and the man saying something in return, and then the man swung around and came out through the open doors onto the sidewalk with the paper sack in his hand, coming directly toward them in the car, so near that they could see the buttons on his summer shirt, before he turned and went up the block in the bright sun.

Who was that, Daddy?

I can't think of his name. But I know him. I'll think of it, he said. His voice sounded odd and then suddenly he began to weep.

Daddy, what is it?

He covered his face with his hands, his shoulders shaking. Mary leaned forward and put her arms around him.

Dear, it's all right. What's wrong? What are you thinking? What happened?

He shook his head. He went on weeping as they sat in the car in front of the hardware store on the hot Saturday morning, with people going by on the sidewalk. Lorraine watched her father and looked forward toward the storefront and Mary kept her arms around him and rested her head against the side of his head. After a while he stopped and wiped his face.

Oh, Lord, he said. Well, we can go on now, if you want. I'm sorry.

Are you all right, honey?

Yeah. I'm going to be.

Where to now, Daddy? Should we go home?

No. Out in the country. Out south. I want to show you something. I was thinking about it last night.

They backed out into Main Street and went around the block and back to the highway, past the Chute Bar and Grill and the grocery store, and turned south on the blacktop. There was wheat stubble shining in the sun and waist-high rows of corn, very green, and then pastures with black cattle scattered out in the native grass and sagebrush and soapweed, and presently Dad said, Slow down. Turn here, please.

Lorraine steered them onto the unpaved road. They could hear the gravel kicking up under the car. There were barrow ditches on both sides and above them the long run of telephone poles and the four-strand barbed-wire fences.

Careful, Dad said. You don't want to go too fast.

She slowed down and they came to an old place set back off the road behind a front pasture. The road leading back to the house was closed off by a padlocked gate. Below were outbuildings and a horse barn and loafing shed and some stunted cedar trees. Everything looked to be in good repair but it didn't seem as if anyone were living in the house.

Stop here a minute, Dad said.

Lorraine shut off the engine and they looked out across the hot pasture at the old paintless house.

This here is where those old brothers lived, Dad said. The ones that had that high school girl come out and live with them. She was pregnant, then she had the baby and went off to college, and after that the one old brother got killed by a Angus bull in the corral back there with his brother right there seeing it all and not being able to do a goddamn thing to stop it. They're both dead now.

I didn't know this was their place, Mary said.

I knew them a little. They traded at the store. After the one brother got killed the other one went out with a woman in town and he and her stayed together till he died. I believe she's still in Holt. A nice woman, I understand.

I've known all that, Lorraine said. But I never heard what became of the girl and the baby she had.

They're up in the mountains someplace. The baby's grown up by now, of course. The neighbors look after the ranch.

Nobody lives here?

No. And she won't sell it or let anybody else operate it.

But what are we doing here, Daddy?

I just wanted to look at this place one last time. For sentimental reasons, I suppose. We can go on now. I'll show you where to.

They went farther east on the county road and then he said, Turn in here, if you would.

Right here?

Yeah.

It's not even a road.

It was no more than two tire trails in the sandy ground going out through pasture grass. After half a mile or so, the track began to rise and twist up onto a sandhill.

Daddy, I don't know if we should try this.

We'll make it. Just don't stop in this sand, you'll get us stuck. Somebody'll have to walk out of here and get help.

They drove on, the car bucking and rocking, the grass sweeping underneath, making a whispering noise. Once they got up on top where it was flat, Dad said, All right, we can stop now. This is it.

He opened the door and climbed out with his cane and Mary and

Lorraine got out, holding on to him, and the three of them walked away from the car and stood on the windy hill. There were more hills to the east and south, the town far distant to the north, with the grain elevators white above the green of the mass of trees, and elsewhere all the flat open space.

I wanted to tell you what I decided, Dad said. What I was thinking about. I'm going to ask you to bury something up here.

Bury what, honey?

It doesn't matter what it is. My cap or something. An old pair of my shoes. These eyeglasses here in my pocket if you want.

Why this place here? We've never come up here before.

I have. You can see this whole country from this place. I brought you both up here today to look with me.

All right, honey, we can bring something up here. I don't have any idea what it'll be.

They stood taking it all in, the wind blowing steadily, but it was still hot at noon.

It was only a simple little goddamn thing, Dad said. That's all it was.

What was, honey?

Me crying in town back there at the store. That's what set me off. It was my life I was watching there. That little bit of commerce between me and another fellow on a summer morning at the front counter. Exchanging a few words. Just that. And it wasn't nothing at all.

No, that's not right, it wasn't either nothing, Mary said. It was everything.

Well. It made me cry anyway, seeing it this morning. I cried like a baby.

Daddy, it's all right, Lorraine said.

I don't know, he said. I couldn't seem to help it.

She and Mary took his arms, standing in the wind, looking at the country. Then they returned to the car.

They were halfway back to town when Dad said, Darwin Purdy.

What's that, dear?

That fellow we saw coming out of the store. If I had a name like that I'd change it to Bill Jones or Bud Smith. He's a pretty decent fellow, though.

What about changing it to Dad Lewis? Lorraine said.

He smiled. No ma'am, he said. I wouldn't go so far as that.

Why not?

Look what become of him. Old man crying on Main Street, driving around out in the country making a nuisance of himself.

20

OH, I'VE BEEN TALKING TO Richard at night sometimes, Mom, after you and Daddy are in bed.

I didn't know you still had any feelings for him. I thought you weren't that sure of him.

I'm not. But there's nobody else right now.

All right. I just don't want you to be hurt anymore.

Haven't you been hurt yourself, Mom?

Of course, but almost all of my life here with Dad has been good.

You're lucky. Not many have had what you've had. Or we don't recognize it. Most of us just settle for some imitation of it so we don't have to live alone.

But I won't have him tire out your father.

I know.

He can come but he can't stay long.

He just wants to come in and say a few words.

Why does he?

He wants to see Daddy before he's gone.

They never cared for each other before.

It's how people are when somebody's dying. They want to forget the past. Forgive things.

Just so he doesn't upset him.

Richard drove out from Denver late in the afternoon and got out of his car and stretched and looked at the old white two-story house and came up to the door and Lorraine let him in. He kissed her. You taste good, he said. Is he sitting up?

No, he's in the bedroom.

Mary came out to the front room. He opened his arms to hug her but instead she only shook his hand. Now we need to be quiet. I don't want him disturbed.

How is he today?

He got up for a couple of hours this morning. He sat out here and slept and ate a little lunch and then went back to bed. He came out again for a short time this afternoon. He just now went back. I'll see if he's still awake.

While she was gone Richard kissed Lorraine again. That's enough, she said. Save it for tonight.

Mary returned and led them to the bedroom where Dad was lying propped up on a pillow. The window shade was pulled down and the room was dim and shadowy. Richard went over to the bed and sat down on a chair. How are you doing, Mr. Lewis? Dad looked at him. Do you remember me?

Yeah. I know who you are.

I'm sorry you're feeling so bad.

I'm not feeling bad. I'm dying.

Yes sir. That's what I meant. I'm very sorry.

Dad looked at the bar of light below the brown window shade and turned back. What do you want here?

Richard looked at Lorraine and her mother, standing near the door. I came to say good-bye to you. I wanted to get here before it was too late.

Good-bye, then.

Yes sir. I won't stay long.

Dad stared at his face, then shifted his eyes to Lorraine.

You don't need to worry, Mr. Lewis. I'll take care of her.

That's no comfort, Dad said.

Pardon?

I can't see why you'd think that would be good news to me. I never thought you was good enough for her.

Well. Hell. Goddamn. I'm sorry you think that way.

I'm sorry too, Dad said. I'm sorry I got to.

Richard stood up. I'll at least hope you're in no pain. I'm going to hope that much.

Not that kind I'm not, Dad said.

Richard nodded his head at this and looked once more at Lorraine and Mary and went out of the room.

Oh, Daddy, Lorraine said. What are you doing?

I'm too far down the road to soften my words now.

But still, Daddy. She came to the bed and kissed him and when she went out to find Richard her mother sat on the chair he'd been using.

Don't start lecturing me, Dad said.

I won't. I feel the same way.

Do you?

Only I wouldn't say it the way you did.

I felt like it, he said. What reason have I got to hold back now?

Well, you didn't.

Out in the living room Richard was standing at the window.

Do you want to go out, Lorraine said, and get something to eat? Then I'll meet you at the Chute after a while.

If you think I'm good enough for you.

I don't know if you are or not, she said.

At nine thirty when she got to the Chute Bar and Grill she saw that his car was there in the parking lot. She stood outside and smoked a cigarette as cars went by on the highway, pickups, loaded grain trucks. It was a warm summer night with only a hint of breeze.

She went inside and stood at the door, looking for him. It was cool in the air-conditioning and the jukebox was playing. Three men sitting at the bar turned to look at her at the same time as though they were linked together, one of them said something but she didn't hear it and didn't care. A few other people were at the bar, and a man and woman were sitting in one of the booths against the wall. From the doorway of the next room she saw that he was sitting alone in a booth, he had on a pearl snap shirt now and black jeans, and he was watching two women across the room playing shuffleboard at the long table with an electronic scoreboard nailed to the wall above it. The women looked to be having a good time, laughing and talking too loud, then one of them spilled the can of sawdust out on the floor and that seemed funny to them. They bent over to scoop it up.

You want some help over there, ladies? Richard said.

Come on over here, cowboy.

If you're not afraid to, the other woman said.

That was funny too, they sat down on the floor laughing.

Don't damage yourselves, he said.

Lorraine walked over and slid into the seat across from him.

You decided to join me after all, he said.

I was always going to be here, she said. What do you mean?

I couldn't be sure after the way your father was. What's he got against me?

He doesn't like you.

What's there not to like? He doesn't know me.

He thinks he does. Enough to form an opinion.

Of what? The kind of person I am? I don't need him to judge me. What does he know anyway?

He's been around for seventy-seven years. He knows a few things.

Because he's old and dying doesn't mean he knows anything.

In this case it might.

He looked around the bar. The two women were playing shuffleboard again.

You want a drink? he said.

Yes. I do.

He waved at the barmaid and she saw him at once and came over. She looked closely at Lorraine. Why, I haven't seen you in years. You're Lorraine Lewis, aren't you.

Yes.

Marlene Stevens, the woman said.

I remember you, Lorraine said.

I was two years behind you in high school. I used to be Marlene Vosburg.

How are you doing?

I'm here, so I guess I'm all right. I got two kids in high school now myself. What about you?

I had a daughter.

The woman's thin face flushed bright red. I'm sorry, she said. I knew that. She laid her hand on Lorraine's. I'm sorry for saying anything. Can I get you a drink?

I'll have another Scotch, Richard said.

You, hon?

A margarita. No salt.

I'll be right back.

They watched her walk away through the wide doorway into the front room. Little towns, he said. They all think they know you.

She does know me. Something about me anyway.

They know too much. I don't like it.

You don't have to.

He looked at her across the wood tabletop. Are you going to be like this all night?

Like what?

Like you got something up your ass.

That's a nice expression, Lorraine said. You didn't have to come here.

I wanted to see you.

You don't think so now?

He looked at the two women and looked back. Do we have to do this? Just tell me that.

Not if you can be nice, she said.

The waitress returned and set the tray on the table and set the glasses in front of them. Richard handed her a twenty-dollar bill on the tray and she started to make change. That's yours, he said. Keep the rest.

Well thank you. I'll be right in here if you need something. She went back out to the bar.

Was that nice enough? he said.

It's a start, Lorraine said. It was nice to her. That's all. It's not that much.

No?

You're no saint yet.

At midnight they left the bar and she followed him in her car over to his motel at the west side of Holt on the highway. He was still trying to be nice when they were in bed, and he slid down in the sheets and helped her to have her desire first.

When she woke in the morning she looked at his face and bare shoulders and arms and felt a little better toward him. They walked down past the row of parked cars to the motel café for breakfast. After they ordered he said, Come back to Denver, will you at least do that much?

I can't now. You understand that.

I don't mean now.

We'll see.

Are you thinking of staying here?

I don't know what I'm going to do. I can't tell yet.

After breakfast she kissed him and went home and he started back to Denver. When she got out of the car she saw that her mother had set the sprinkler going on the north side of the house and her father was sitting in his chair at the window.

Daddy, you're up already.

You're late, he said. It's the middle of the morning.

It's only eight o'clock.

You've been out all night with him.

What's wrong, Daddy?

He looked at the tree shade outside and she came across the room and sat on the arm of his chair.

I was worrying about you, he said. That's what it is.

What are you worried about? If I'll manage the store?

No. Hell. You will or you won't. That's not worth worrying about anymore. It'll happen or it won't.

What is it then?

He looked up at her face. I just was wanting you to tell me if you was happy or not. I'd like to know that before I'm gone out of here.

She rose and drew a chair close to him, facing him, and took one of his hands. No, she said. I'm not happy. If you want to know. Can I tell you that even now?

If that's what the truth is.

It is. Since Lanie died. I never have been what you'd call truly happy.

You don't get over it, do you. When a child goes. You never do.

I think about how we would be now. I want to talk to her. I want there to be long talks between my daughter and me. I have things I want to tell her. That boy that drove the car and killed her, I could do something terrible to him right now today. I swear I could.

Her eyes were shiny. Dad squeezed her hand and they sat quietly, both of them looking at the tree outside the window.

After a while he said, So what about this Richard?

I don't know, Daddy. He's okay. He's just wants to have a good time, go out drinking and take me to bed afterward.

I don't have to hear that part of it.

You asked.

Well, are you in love?

No. There's no one that way. I don't know if I'll ever find that kind. I'm too torn up inside.

I was hoping this morning you'd tell me you was happy.

I'm sorry, Daddy.

I'm sorry too. For you, I mean.

What about you?

Well, yeah, I been happy. Sure. Except for the one thing.

Frank.

Yes.

I know more about that than you think.

I figure you know a lot, Dad said.

I know what happened here with you. And other things that happened in town.

He told you.

Yes. A long time ago.

21

THE HIGH SCHOOL GIRL drove up to the house after dark. He was watching for her as always from the front room of the parsonage, his father and mother were back in the kitchen and didn't say anything to him anymore when he left the house. He went out across the porch to the car and got in beside her. She looked no different than she had the other nights, still dressed in black with the red lipstick dark on her mouth. He wouldn't have been able to tell that something was going to happen.

They drove for an hour up and down Main Street and along the residential streets of town and then turned out north on the highway. The farm lights were lit up in the night, the headlights of her car bright on the narrow highway ahead of them. Then she headed the car off on a gravel road and he sat looking at her with the air coming in through the open window, her music playing, she wasn't talking very much but sometimes she didn't, then before they got to the place where they had parked once or twice before under a cotton-wood tree she stopped the car and reached and turned off the music and they sat in the road with the engine running.

What are we doing? he said. Somebody could hit us here.

She was staring ahead over the steering wheel. I've decided it's time to stop this.

What? Why?

School's starting next month.

I know. But we can go on after classes start.

No. I'm going to have to work more than I ever have before, to get into a good college.

She wouldn't look at him. The headlights shone very brightly out ahead of the car on the gravel.

I don't understand what you mean, he said.

There's nothing to understand. Just accept it. We had a good time and now we're done. This is the last night.

You can't just do this, he said.

Of course I can.

No you can't. What about me, what I want?

I'm the one who started it, she said. Not you. So I'm the one who ends it.

It's two of us here now. Not just you.

You're such a child. She looked at him for a moment. Just a little boy.

I'm only two years younger than you.

Two years make all the difference at this age.

They were right, then, he said. They said you'd do this.

Who did?

The ones I fought you for. They told me.

You didn't fight for me.

I fought that one. I hit him.

You hit him once by surprise and then he knocked you down and pinned you down.

I protected your name. I spilled my blood for you.

What?

I saved your name with my blood.

Oh Christ. That's just bullshit. I don't need anybody to save me.

You don't believe me. I love you. And you don't even care.

Well, I'm sorry. She took hold of the steering wheel. That's how it is. This is the last night.

Why can't we still see each other once in a while? Can't we at least do that?

No. That never works.

You do this with all of them, don't you. You fuck them all. Then you quit them.

You stupid little shit, you're starting to make me sick. She jerked the car into reverse and roared backward, turning sharply to go back to Holt, and she ended up jamming them into the barrow ditch, the car suddenly stopped, stuck, high-centered. She raced the engine and the back wheels spun, throwing gravel up behind them, and the car sank lower.

Goddamn it! she screamed, racing the engine.

Quit doing that! he said. You're making it worse.

Shut up. Just shut your goddamn mouth.

She shoved her door open and they both got out. The back wheels were buried to the hubcaps and the rear end had settled into the broken ditch weeds. They went back up to the road and stood in front of the car. The lights of Holt were twenty miles away to the south and the lights of a farmhouse a half mile in the other direction. She shut off the engine and the headlights. It was all dark around them.

Are you coming with me or staying here?

Where are you going?

Over to that house.

I'm coming.

Let's go then.

What about dogs?

What about them?

She began walking toward the farmhouse and he followed a little behind her. The wind was blowing and whistling in the barbed wire fence and the only other sound was their shoes scraping in the gravel. They didn't talk. When they approached the farmstead they could see a machine shed and garage and a metal building and near the road the white house itself with a stand of locust behind it. A dog had started barking.

I told you there would be a dog, he said.

So there's a dog.

When they walked into the driveway the dog came out from the house barking at them. They could see him in the yard light, some kind of Australian blue heeler.

Here, she said. Here, boy.

The dog backed up and growled.

Now what? he said.

Wait, she said.

The porch light came on above the back door. A man stepped out and peered at them.

Who's out there? he called.

We're stuck, she called back. Up the road here.

What?

The dog kept growling.

We're stuck in the road up here.

Buddy. Hush up! Come here. The dog barked at them and trotted back to the house. I'll be out in a minute, the man said. Wait there.

I'll do the talking, she said, after he was gone. You don't have to say a word.

I don't intend to say anything.

That's good. Keep it that way.

The man came out of the house with the dog following close at his heels. They went out to the garage and when they came backing out, the dog was up in the rear of the pickup, riding on the toolbox. The pickup pulled up beside them in the driveway. The dog sniffed at them and the girl opened the passenger door and looked inside. Can we get in?

I think you better. Unless you plan to ride in back.

She got up in the cab and slid over to the middle and John Wesley got in next to her. The man was wearing his pajama top and he'd put on jeans and boots. Where's your car at?

Down here a ways.

To the south here?

Yes.

He looked at her. What's your name?

Genevieve.

You got a last name?

Larsen.

And you?

John Wesley Lyle.

The man looked at him. Your father's the preacher that just come to town.

Yes.

I see. Well, I don't guess I have to ask what you was doing out here in the country at night. I noticed the car stopped down here before. Your folks know about this?

John Wesley didn't say anything.

No, the man said. I don't guess so. Well, it's a nice night. A nice cool summer night and all these stars out.

That's the car, Genevieve said.

He looked at her. I figured it would be.

He pulled up to where it was pointed out crossways in the road. What were you doing, trying to turn around?

I was trying to back up.

You don't ever want to get off the road. That ground's pretty soft off in the ditch.

Can you get us out?

Oh, I imagine so. Don't you think?

She didn't answer.

What if I can't? What then?

I'd have to call somebody to tow it.

Maybe you wouldn't care to do that.

No, I wouldn't.

No, ma'am. I wouldn't if I was you.

They all got out of the pickup. The dog leaped from the toolbox onto the road and ran off into the dark field. The man walked over to the car and stood looking at the rear wheels.

Well, you tried, he said. You give her what for, didn't you.

It just dug in deeper.

It does that, he said. You get in now and start it up and turn your front wheels this way. I'm going to tow you out on the road and you want to be turned in the direction we're going. But not yet. Wait till I tell you.

He got back in the pickup and the dog came up running, panting.

I'm not going nowhere, the man said. Stay down. I'll let you know when I'm leaving. I ain't going nowhere without you.

The dog stared at him. It's all right, go on. The dog trotted out in the field again. The man backed the pickup in the road and came forward and backed again and came forward and backed up once more, until the rear almost touched the front bumper. He got out and brought the tow chain from the toolbox and crawled down in the gravel and hooked the chain underneath the car and stood up and brushed off his hands and knees and hooked the other end of the chain to the pickup hitch.

Now you tell me when that chain gets tight, he said.

Do you mean me? John Wesley said.

That's right. I'm talking to you. He turned to the girl. And you go ahead and get in and start your car now and put it in gear. When I start pulling, you ease it forward. Don't come racing out of there, you'll run into the back of me. He looked at the two of them. We all set?

She got in the car and the man stepped up into the pickup and eased forward very slowly, watching John Wesley in the side mirror. The boy gave him the sign that the chain was tight. It tugged against the pickup. Then the man drove forward gradually, steadily and the car came right up out of the ditch. When they were lined up on the road, he backed up to put slack in the chain, and got out and unhooked and dropped the chain back in the box.

Well. I imagine that's going to do it.

Thank you, the girl said. Thank you very much.

You probably don't want to do that again. He looked around at the fields and looked up at the sky. Well, like I say, it's a pretty night. He gave the boy and girl a long look. Then he whistled. Here! Buddy! Come here. The dog raced up out of the dark. Get up, the man said. The dog leaped into the back of the pickup onto the toolbox and they drove away, the man's arm out the side window, casually, as if it were the middle of the day. They watched the red taillights disappearing. Dust rose up from the road and hung in the night air.

This doesn't change what we talked about, she said. Don't think it does.

They drove back toward town on the county roads. He could see the lights of town ahead, the streetlights and the red warning lights on the grain elevators and the light at the water tower, and all around them the farm lights dotting the countryside.

What are you stopping for now? he said.

I'm going to do this last thing for you. She slid out from behind the steering wheel and began to unbutton his pants.

Don't.

Yes, she said. You know you want me to.

No. Leave me alone.

She brushed his hands away and finished with the buttons and pushed his underwear down.

Put your head back, she said.

No.

Do what I say. Lay your head back. You want to remember this, don't you? He shut his eyes and leaned back against the seat and she bent over and put her head in his lap. He began to cry. She went on anyway and after a little while it was finished. She sat up and wiped her mouth on the sleeve of her black shirt. There, she said. Remember I did that.

Then she drove them into town and stopped at the parsonage.

There's nothing more to say, she said. Go on. Get out.

I don't care. I still love you, even if that doesn't mean anything to you. I want to kill myself.

No, you're not going to do anything like that at all. You're going to get out. That's what you're going to do.

He opened the door and stood at the curb, watching her drive away, then went up the steps to the house. It wasn't late. His mother was still sitting in the living room, reading a book. He started past to go upstairs.

You're home early, she said. What's the matter? Did something happen? Stop there a minute.

She rose from the chair and came to look at him. She raised her hand and turned his face to the light.

Why, you've been crying. Did she make you cry? Are you all right?

After he went up to his room she went upstairs and woke Lyle.

Are you awake?

What's wrong? he said. What is it?

Go talk to him. He's been crying. He won't talk to me.

What happened?

That girl doesn't want to go out with him anymore.

Then he won't want to talk to me either.

He hates it here, she said. This will only make it worse.

It would help if you tried to like it here yourself.

I am trying. You have no idea.

He got out of bed in his pajamas and T-shirt and went down the hall to the bedroom and stood listening and then knocked on the door. Son. Can I come in?

No.

I'd like to talk to you.

Let me alone.

I'm coming in. He opened the door and found John Wesley slumped over his computer, writing. Your mother says you had some trouble tonight.

I don't want to talk about it.

Did the girl do something? Is that what happened?

She broke up with me. She breaks up with everyone.

Is that what she says?

She goes out with them all and screws them all and then she leaves them.

She told you this?

They told me.

Who's they?

Some of the assholes she went out with.

Now she's broken up with you?

Yes. But leave me alone. I don't want to talk anymore.

You loved her, I guess, didn't you.

I still do.

It feels like hell, doesn't it.

You don't know anything about it.

I've had some bad nights. Some bad times.

Don't tell me about them. I don't want to hear about it. I know about you and Mom.

I know you think you do. But you don't know all of it. Only your mother and I know all of it, and we each know parts the other doesn't know.

Let me alone, Dad. Please, I want to be alone. I hate it here. Why did we have to come here?

You know why. This is where the church sent us.

I want to go back to Denver.

I know that. I'm sorry you feel so bad.

Well, just don't tell me I'll get over her.

No. That doesn't help, even if it's true. I could help you. I wish you'd let me.

Just let me be. Please.

He put his hand on the boy's shoulder. Try to get some sleep. Then he went out and shut the door and went back to the other bedroom.

Would he talk?

No. Not much. Just what you already know.

Did you find out anything more?

She's evidently done the same thing with other boys. He said that much. It's her pattern apparently.

What else did he say?

He wants to leave. Go back to Denver as we've heard before. He wants us to let him alone.

22

ALENE AND HER PRINCIPAL came out of the beautiful old redbrick hotel with carved stonework onto the street a block east of Union Station in downtown Denver. This was in the following winter now. They had seen each other for a year whenever they could. It was late in the afternoon, almost evening, the light beginning to change along the street, darkening, a soft winter twilight. People were walking along the sidewalk, going home or heading to the taverns for a drink. She walked with her arm in his arm, a tall thin young woman still, pretty, still dark haired. Snow was piled up at the curbs but it didn't feel cold out. They crossed the street and walked down to the middle of the next block and stopped in front of the restaurant. It was all brightly lit inside.

You're sure about this, he said.

I want her to meet you.

She's not going to like it. You know that. How could she?

Yes, but I want her to know that I'm not alone.

If that's what you want.

He opened the door and they stepped into the warm café. The headwaiter met them at the front. Two? he said.

We're meeting someone, Alene said. She may be here already.

Yes, she said you would be coming. She's back here. Will you follow me?

He led them through the big room of dining tables that were set with clear water glasses and shining silverware and white napkins on the white tablecloths. They followed him into the next room to the table where Willa was seated near the wall. She looked well dressed and sure of herself, a woman in her early fifties then, iron gray hair and the eyeglasses that were not bifocals yet. The waiter led them to her table. Here you are, madam.

She looked up at them. The waiter left.

Mother, this is John Kelly. This is my mother, Willa Johnson.

How do you do.

The principal held the chair for Alene and she sat down beside her mother and he sat across from her.

I hope you haven't been waiting too long, he said.

No. Not very long.

The waiter, a different one, came to the table with menus and asked if they wanted to order drinks. Willa ordered white wine and Alene and the principal each asked for red wine. The waiter wrote in a little pad and went away.

I believe I've been told that you're a high school administrator, Willa said.

Yes. That's right.

Where is the school?

North of here. In a little town along the Front Range.

I notice you don't say the name.

I could tell you, he said. But it won't matter.

To me or to you?

I was thinking it wouldn't matter to you and might only cause problems for me.

Because you're married.

He looked at Alene then at her mother. Yes, he said. That's right. Because I'm married.

At least you don't hide it anyway, Willa said.

Do you mean from your daughter?

From her. Or from me.

I don't think I would do that. I might do other things. But I wouldn't keep that from Alene. There are enough secrets already.

Your wife doesn't know, of course.

No. She doesn't. I wouldn't be here if she knew.

Do you have children?

Yes. Two girls.

How old are they?

They're ten and eight.

Just young girls.

Yes. Innocent young girls, if that's what you mean.

Do you love them?

What do you think?

The waiter came with their drinks on a tray and a plate of bread and butter and set them out on the table and took their dinner orders.

I was a teacher myself, Willa said. A long time ago, before I married Alene's father.

What did you teach?

This was out in a country school in South Dakota. I had five grades all at the same time, all subjects. Then I fell in love and after I got married I found out that my husband didn't want me to work outside the home. He wanted me there with him. I hadn't understood that before I married him. People didn't divorce then, so I gave up my career. I never went back.

I'd guess you were a good teacher.

Yes, I was. I was very good.

Why are you telling all of this now, Mother? Alene said.

Because it's true. I want your friend to know. It was after the Depression. We were lucky to have survived.

You're exaggerating now, Alene said.

Do you think so? There were people out on the plains who canned thistles to eat. People died of lung disease because of the dust. You might not believe me. But it's true.

The man passed the plate of bread around.

Do you intend to leave your wife? Willa said.

He put his roll down. We haven't decided that yet.

When will you decide?

Mother, now what are you doing?

I'm trying to ask the questions you need answered.

You don't know anything about this.

Don't I?

No. Please stop it.

The man laid his napkin down and rose from his chair. He took out his wallet from a pocket of his trousers and placed money on the table beside his plate.

This isn't doing anybody any good.

I think I would like you under different circumstances, Willa said.

Probably not, he said. Good-bye.

Alene got up and went with him out through the café to the sidewalk. The sky was darker now, the streetlights had come on and people were hurrying. It was cold now outside along the street.

I'm sorry, she said. I didn't expect this.

It was a mistake. We shouldn't have done it. This was too much to expect her to accept.

Will you call me?

Yes.

When?

In a few days.

He kissed her quickly and walked away around the corner out of sight and she went back inside and sat down beside her mother. The waiter had brought their entrées and the plates of food were steaming at the table.

What were you thinking? Willa said. Why would you want me to know about this? I thought we were just meeting for supper. Just a friend of yours.

I wanted one person to know, Alene said.

You should have told a girlfriend, one of your young friends. Not me.

I thought you'd want to know. For my sake. Because I'm happy when I'm with him. There's some pleasure in my life that I've never had before.

He's married. He has children to think of. Nothing good can come of this.

Don't say that, Mother. I thought it would be all right if I could tell one person. I wanted you particularly to know.

You were wrong, Willa said.

Why did you tell him about teaching and the Depression? And my father. You didn't have to say all that.

Because things don't often turn out the way we think they will. I wanted to be sure you knew that.

I know that too well, Mother.

23

WHEN FRANK WAS FIFTEEN and Lorraine eighteen and they were both attending Holt County Union High School, he came into her bedroom late one night. She was in her winter pajamas reading, listening to the radio turned down low. He stood in the doorway looking at her. What's wrong? she said. He came in and shut the door. Come over here, she said. He went to her bed and stood there. Tell me.

They did it again, he said.

Oh no. What was it this time?

He told her. After football practice that afternoon some seniors and a couple juniors jumped him when he came out of the shower and held him down on the floor in the corner while he was still wet and naked and rolled him over and slapped him hard on the butt and the back of the head, laughing and calling him what they always called him, and then turned him faceup and one of the naked boys sat on him. Look at him. He likes that. One of the boys grabbed at his dick and hit it back and forth, cursing him, while the others pinched and gouged at him. One boy had an arm pressed against his throat and he could hardly breathe.

Then the coach finally heard the shouting and noise and came down the hallway. What in the goddamn hell? You boys get the hell out of here. Go on now. Goddamn it, get out of here.

They jumped up and grabbed their clothes from the metal lockers and put them on and ran out. He was still wet and naked, where they'd left him in the corner. He got up and stood shivering, shaking uncontrollably, turned sideways away from the coach, hiding himself.

What was all that? the coach said. What in damn's name is going on here?

He wouldn't speak. He stood shaking, burning all over.

The coach looked at him for a long time.

You better go on home. I don't like this. Go on now.

I'm going.

What did you do to them? You must of done something.

I didn't do a goddamn thing to those sons of bitches.

Well. I don't know. You think you're all right? Are you hurt?

I'm all right.

Get dressed then. Go on now. The coach watched him a while longer and shook his head and turned and went back to his office down the hallway.

He went into the toilet stall and blew his nose on the paper and washed his face at one of the sinks and got dressed and left.

I'm never going back, he told his sister now. I'm done. I'm quitting them all. I don't care.

You don't have to go back. You shouldn't go back.

The goddamn assholes. He began to cry, his shoulders shaking.

She got up and drew him down on the bed and they sat together with her arm close around him. It's all right now. It's okay. Oh, Frankie.

He cried for a time and then stopped.

Are you going to tell Dad and Mom? she said.

No.

Then I'll tell them.

No. Don't say anything about this.

They'll know something's wrong if you come home early from school. And if you're not suited up for the games.

I'll tell them. I'll make something up.

He began to cry again and she held him tighter.

Those sons of bitches.

Don't, she said. They're not worth it. Not one of them is worth it. You're here. It's okay now.

No, it isn't, he said.

She held him as close as she could and pulled the blanket over them both. Later in the night he went back across the hall to his own bed.

24

THE QUESTION WAS how to make it seem acceptable to Berta May. I've known her for more than sixty years, Willa said. She was just a young woman only a little younger than I was when I moved here to marry your father. I met her at church. And then that man she married turned out to be no good and he left her and their daughter, and then her daughter married someone like her father and now she's dead from breast cancer and Alice is sent here, for Berta May to raise at her age. I won't have her troubled anymore, even a little, for anything. We have to be careful how we do this.

We can tell her it's for us, Alene said.

That's exactly what it is. It is for us.

We'll tell her she would be doing us the favor.

That much is true.

Even if she doesn't believe it.

We can hope she wants us to think she does. Will you call her or shall I?

You've always known her better, Alene said.

So the next day in the middle of the afternoon Berta May sat in the living room of her house in her housedress and apron and then the girl came out with her hair brushed and her face freshly washed.

Come here, honey. Let me look at you.

The girl stood in front of her.

You look just fine, Berta May said. Now be nice to them. Like you were when they took you out to eat. Do you know why?

No.

Because they're lonely. They want to do something with someone young. They chose you.

But why?

I don't know. They don't know other young girls, maybe. Just be grateful for this.

But Grandma, I don't need new clothes.

Yes, but they need to give you some. It's for them. They need to have a reason to be with you and this is how they do it. It's all right for you to receive this.

You said it was better to give than receive.

Now you're letting them give. You're giving by letting them.

When they drove up in front of the house, Berta May and Alice came out and stood at the door and looked out at the old woman and her elderly daughter waiting in the car and Berta May said, Now have a good time. That's allowed. And you remember to thank them.

I will.

Good. I know you will. Go on then.

The girl walked down the steps and out to the car, not in a hurry but steadily, and got into the backseat behind Willa. Alene was driving.

Hello, dear, Willa said.

Hello, she said.

Alene turned and smiled at her and she smiled back. They drove over to Main Street and parked in front of Schulte's Department Store at the intersection of Main and Second. Inside the store it was warm and not very brightly lighted. The big ceiling fans were spinning, making a clicking noise. They went back toward the rear of the old store with its narrow creaking wood floors to the girls' section and Alene and Willa began to consider the selection of shorts and T-shirts. Alice hung back and then the clerk came, a high school girl working in the summer, and the Johnson women explained to her what they had in mind and she began to show Alice different outfits and combinations and to hold them up against the girl's thin bony chest to size them. Alice watched the two women, to see what their reaction might be, and then she went alone into the small boxy dressing room against the wall where there was a full-length mirror and locked the door and took off her clothes and set them carefully on the bench and put on the new clothes, looking at herself in the long mirror, turning to view herself sideways, and unlocked the door and came back outside to the aisle where the women and the high school girl were waiting.

Well yes, Willa said, you look very nice.

Alene came forward and adjusted the shirt a little. What do you think, honey?

I like them all right.

Just all right?

They're okay. They're nice.

But you don't really like them.

She shrugged.

What do you like better?

I don't know.

Would you want to look at these over here? the high school girl said.

Alice went back to the dressing room and took the new clothes off and came out again in her own clothes and then they went to another section even farther back in the store and Alice stopped to look at some black shorts and black tops with long red sleeves.

Aren't they too hot for summer? Willa said.

If it's what she likes, Alene said, that's what matters. Do you like these, honey?

If you don't care.

No. Now it's not if we care or don't care. It's what you want. You have to say.

I like them, Alice said.

That's better. Let's have a look.

They took the shorts and shirt and another set of the same style, together with matching socks, and she tried them on in the back dressing room and came out carrying them to the register and the high school girl folded them neatly on the counter and put them in a store bag and rang them up. Alene paid for them while Alice watched and didn't say anything or even smile and then the high school girl handed the bag to Alice and they went out into the sun on Main Street. The light glinted sharply off all the windshields of the cars parked along in front of the stores.

Thank you, Alice said. Thank you for these clothes.

You're very welcome, Willa said.

A few cars were moving along in the afternoon, a few people walking in the crosswalk and on the wide sidewalks before the stores.

Well, Willa said. What shall we do now?

Let's go across the street, Alene said.

What's over there?

I'll show you. Alice, would you care to go to the hardware store with us?

If you want to.

Do you want to put your things in the car first?

She set the bag in the backseat of the car and then together they crossed the street at midblock and entered the hardware store through the big open doors.

What are we doing? Willa said.

I was in here a few days ago, Alene said. Come back here. I want to show Alice something.

They followed her back to the far corner of the store through the aisles of paint cans and the display of paint chips and paintbrushes, past the cartons of washers and screws, little boxes of bolts and nuts, the bins of nails, and came to the bicycles. Five of them. One with training wheels and one full-size and three for young people. All hanging from hooks suspended from the ceiling, looking as if they would pull loose and crash and hurt somebody. They stood back looking up at them.

You don't have one, do you? Alene said.

No, Alice said.

Would you like us to get you one?

I don't know. She kept looking at the bicycles. I don't know what Grandma would say.

What do you think she would say?

She'd say it's too much.

What do you think yourself?

Maybe it is too much.

Do you want to call her and ask her?

Yes.

So the two women and the girl went back to the front of the store. But when they got there no one was at the counter.

I'll find someone, Alene said. She disappeared into a nearby aisle and came back with Rudy.

You're asking to use the phone? he said.

It's not for me, Willa said. It's for this young lady.

I hope it's not long-distance, Rudy said. He winked. The store can't pay for no long-distance calls.

It's my grandmother, Alice said. I need to talk to her.

Then that'll be okay. Just go right ahead. She lives in town here, doesn't she.

He handed the phone to Alice and she looked at the three adults watching her and then made the call. She stood up straight and spoke into the phone very quietly, almost whispering. Grandma, it's me, she said softly. They want to buy me a bicycle. The ladies do. I told them I'd have to ask you. I don't know. No, I didn't say anything. I didn't even know they had any bicycles. Yes. Here. She wants to talk to you. She handed the phone to Willa.

Willa carried the phone out of their hearing, into an aisle of electrical supplies, and stood and talked. Yes, this is Willa, she said. Yes, we do. Well, it was Alene's idea. Your granddaughter selected a few clothes and then Alene brought us over here to the hardware. Well, Alice said we would have to speak to you first, to see what you thought. It is a lot, yes. But we would like to do this if you think it's all right. Oh, I don't think she will get the wrong idea. She's such a nice girl. You've done so well with her. I just think she's very dear. Well, Alene seems to want this very much. Yes. Well, all right. Thank you. We'll be there soon. You're welcome. Oh, Alice said so too, of course.

She came back to the front counter and handed the phone to Rudy. The other clerk, Bob, was there now too.

She said it would be all right, Willa said, if that's what we want to do.

They looked at Alice. She wouldn't look at them.

Let's go choose one, Alene said.

They followed Rudy back to the corner of the store and stood below the suspended bicycles and watched as Bob stepped up on a stool and handed down the bicycles from the chained hooks, the three that would be the right size for her, and Rudy stood them on their stands on the old scarred wood floor.

Here you go. Now take a good look. You can't go wrong with none of them. Any one of these here will do good for you. Which one do you like?

Don't rush her, Bob said. Let her take her time. Nobody likes to be rushed.

I'm letting her. That's what I'm saying. Take your time, honey.

Alene put her arm around Alice and they stepped forward and the girl touched the rubber handgrip of the handlebars of the one purple bike and Rudy said, You go right ahead and try the seat there. And that seat's adjustable.

She sat on the seat and gripped the handles and gazed forward as if she might be riding, going someplace, and didn't show a thing on her face.

You prefer this one? Rudy said. You don't want to change your mind and try this red one?

I think she's made up her mind, Alene said. Haven't you, honey.

Yes.

She climbed off the bicycle and Rudy wheeled it up to the counter through the aisles, all of them following again in single file, as in a ceremony, without talking, and then Alene paid and they all went out to the sidewalk in the brilliant hot light of midday and crossed the street and put the bike in the trunk of the car and Bob tied a piece of twine to the trunk lid to hold it down. The two store clerks shook hands with the Johnson women, in a formal way, and shook Alice's hand too, and then went back to the hardware store and the Johnson women and Alice drove back to the west side of Holt to Berta May's house and lifted the bicycle out onto the street.

Berta May had been waiting for them and had come outside now and was watching from the porch.

Is that it? she said.

Yes, Grandma.

Who's going to teach you how to ride?

I don't know.

I'm going to help, Alene said.

Why, do you know how to ride a bike?

They say you don't forget. I used to ride out in the country on the roads.

Then I bet you do remember, Berta May said.

We're just going to try anyway.

She and her mother held the bike and Alice sat down on the seat.

You know these are the brakes.

Alice squeezed the handles.

And this is how the gears shift, by twisting.

I know.

Okay. I imagine you do. Probably more about it than I do. Let's give it a try.

Alice pushed off, pumping the pedals, and the two women stepped along beside her, walking fast, starting to trot, fumbling their hands out to touch her, and she went pedaling on, they couldn't keep up and then she wavered and leaned sideways and tipped over but caught herself. She stood the bike upright. They tried again, Willa leaning and trotting alongside, Alene a little faster, their faces red and flushed by the hot day and the excitement, hurrying along in their soft summer dresses and summer shoes. The girl went a little farther and wobbled again but caught herself before she fell. Behind them, Lorraine had come out from the Lewis house and Berta May was still watching from her porch.

Do you need a hand? Lorraine called. Maybe I can help you.

Would you, please? Alene called back.

The two Johnson women fell back and Lorraine walked alongside as Alice began to pedal and then Lorraine ran beside her, steadying the bike. All right, go on now. Go on. You're on your own. Don't stop. You're doing fine.

Alice went ahead, wavering in the gravel road, pedaling, the tracks of her tires making long teetering lines in the dirt, and went up a hundred feet and made a wide turn and came back, then Lorraine began to trot along beside again. Put on the brakes, she said, and Alice stopped too fast, tipping forward, but Lorraine caught her.

Not so hard next time. Not so sudden.

The Johnson women came hurrying up, flushed and sweating, panting.

That's really good, Alene said. How did it feel? Let's see you go again.

I'm going to.

They gave her a little push and she went back the other direction to the north and before she reached the railroad tracks she made a sweeping turn and came back. She pedaled up to the women and stopped by putting her feet down in the road.

Wonderful, Alene said.

Alice looked at each of them. Thank you, she said, her eyes were shining, the hair around her face was sweaty and dark.

How about going again? Lorraine said.

Did you see me, Grandma? she called.

Yes. I did, Berta May called back. Good for you.

She rode off toward the highway. A car was coming but she saw it and veered to the side and the car passed by, and then farther away they watched her turn and start back to them. When she was in front of Berta May's house she stopped and stood the bicycle at the curb and grabbed the store bag from the backseat of the Johnsons' car and ran past her grandmother on the porch and into the house.

Presently she came back out. What are you doing? Berta May said.

I'm riding. She had put on the new black shorts and black shirt with the red sleeves and the black socks and she rode back and forth in the gravel street in the late afternoon while the women all gathered in the shade and watched her.

In the evening, after the Johnson women went home, Lorraine brought a table from the house and set the supper dishes on it out on the porch, and Berta May and Alice came across the yard carrying bread and garden beans and radishes, and they sat all out in the cooling air and sat Dad Lewis up at the table with a blanket over him.

After supper Alice got on her bike to ride in the street.

Dad watched her from the porch. I hope she don't get run over out there. You better pay good attention to her.

The light had gone out of the sky by now and the street lamps had come on and she rode, going back and forth, from pool of light to pool of light.

25

AFTERWARD IT WASN'T CLEAR what Lyle expected the sermon to accomplish. But he wasn't even half-finished when some of the congregation, men mostly, hurrying their wives and children with them, but some women too, began to rise up from their pews and glare at him and walk out of the church.

The sermon came after the call to worship and the first hymn and after Wandajean Hall sang "Softly and Tenderly Jesus Is Calling" as a solo anthem in her thin sweet wavering soprano, and it came after the reading of the Bible text but before the offering and the doxology and the Lord's Prayer and the benediction, because they never got that far in the normal order of worship. By that time the people who were so angry and outraged that they felt they had to leave had already marched out the big doors at the back of the sanctuary, leaving Lyle's wife Beverly and their son John Wesley and the two Johnson women and the old usher and the remainder of the small congregation still sitting in the church, still looking around at one another in embarrassment and disbelief, many of them just as angry and outraged as the others had been but unwilling to make any display or public objection in church on Sunday morning, still waiting along with the pianist who was still seated down front at the piano.

It began simply enough. He gave the reading. He took up the Bible and stood out at a little distance from the pulpit. He didn't often do that. But he had done it once or twice before so people were not immediately bothered or surprised by it. So he began to read to them without benefit of the barrier of the pulpit between him and them. Just his reading and the Bible. He didn't wear a suit or suit coat this morning, not even a light summer suit. Instead he was wearing a white shirt open at the neck with the sleeves rolled up and a pair of black slacks and a black belt with a silver tip, his dark hair fallen as usual across his forehead. He looked good. There were women who came to church for that reason though they would never have said so.

The text was from Luke.

But I tell you who hear me: Love your enemies, do good to those who hate you, bless those who curse you, and pray for those who mistreat you. If anyone hits you on one cheek, let him hit the other one too; if someone takes your coat, let him have your shirt as well. If you love only the people who love you, why should you receive a blessing? Even sinners love those who love them! And if you do good only to those who do good to you, why should you receive a blessing?

He went on reading and came to the end of the text.

Love your enemies and do good to them, lend and expect nothing back. You will then have a great reward, and you will be sons of the Most High God. For He is good to the ungrateful and the wicked. Be merciful just as your Father is merciful.

Then he stopped and stood quietly and looked out at the congregation. The sanctuary was hot. The windows were open but it was a hot day and hot inside. Women fanned at their faces with the church bulletin. A car drove by in the street. There was birdsong from a nearby tree. He turned and set the Bible on the pulpit. Then he began to talk.

This passage, he said, is usually referred to as the Sermon on the Mount. Augustine first called it that. It appears in the Gospels of both Matthew and Luke but the texts differ somewhat. Matthew's is over a hundred verses long. Luke's is only some thirty verses. Matthew says Jesus sat and spoke to the multitudes and his disciples from a hill, a mount. The writer of the Gospel of Luke tells us that Jesus stood on a level place and spoke there. Both Gospels begin with the Beatitudes. The Blesseds. In Matthew there are nine and in Luke four. But the most important of these Bible texts say essentially the same thing. These are the ones I've read just now. The crux of the matter for us. The soul of our lesson and the very essence of the teaching of Jesus.

Love your enemies. Pray for those who harm you. Turn the other cheek. Give away money and don't expect it back.

But what is Jesus Christ talking about? He can't mean this literally. That would be impossible. He must have been speaking of some utopian idea, a fantasy. He must be using a metaphor. Suggesting a sweet dream. Because all of us here today know better. We're awake to reality and know the world wouldn't permit such a thing. It never has and never will. We can be clear about that right now.

Because here we are at war again. And we know the inescapable images of war and violence so well. We've seen them all too often.

The naked young girl running in terror toward us, crying and screaming, away from fires behind her.

The boy in the hospital room with his little brother and their frightened mother. He's been blinded, his face is scarred. Am I ugly now, Mother? he says.

We see the pictures of the headless body dumped out beside the road in a ditch.

We've seen the soldier, the black stiff grotesque thing that once was a man, burned now and hanged, dragged through the streets behind a truck.

We've watched in horror the human figures leaping out of the windows of the burning towers.

And so we know the satisfaction of hate. We know the sweet joy of revenge. How it feels good to get even. Oh, that was a nice idea Jesus had. That was a pretty notion, but you can't love people who do evil. It's neither sensible nor practical. It's not wise to the world to love people who do such terrible wrong. There is no way on earth we can love our enemies. They'll only do wickedness and hatefulness again. And worse, they'll think they can get away with this wickedness and evil, because they'll think we're weak and afraid. What would the world come to?

But I want to say to you here on this hot July morning in Holt, what if Jesus wasn't kidding? What if he wasn't talking about some never-never land? What if he really did mean what he said two thousand years ago? What if he was thoroughly wise to the world and knew firsthand cruelty and wickedness and evil and hate? Knew it all so well from firsthand personal experience? And what if in spite of all that he knew, he still said love your enemies? Turn your cheek. Pray for those who misuse you. What if he meant every word of what he said? What then would the world come to?

And what if we tried it? What if we said to our enemies: We are the most powerful nation on earth. We can destroy you. We can kill your children. We can make ruins of your cities and villages and when we're finished you won't even know how to look for the places where they used to be. We have the power to take away your water and to scorch your earth, to rob you of the very fundamentals of life. We can change the actual day into actual night. We can do all of these things to you. And more.

But what if we say, Listen: Instead of any of these, we are going to give willingly and generously to you. We are going to spend the great American national treasure and the will and the human lives that we would have spent on destruction, and instead we are going to turn them all toward creation. We'll mend your roads and highways, expand your schools, modernize your wells and water supplies, save your ancient artifacts and art and culture, preserve your temples and mosques. In fact, we are going to love you. And again we say, no matter what has gone before, no matter what you've done: We are going to love you. We have set our hearts to it. We will treat you like brothers and sisters. We are going to turn our collective national cheek and present it to be stricken a second time, if need be, and offer it to you. Listen, we—

But then he was abruptly halted. Someone out in the congregation was talking. Are you crazy? You must be insane! A man's voice. Deep-throated. Angry. Loud. Coming from over on the west side of the sanctuary near the windows. What's wrong with you? Are you out of your mind?

He stood up, a tall man in a light summer suit, staring at Lyle. You must be about as crazy as hell! He turned fiercely and grabbed his wife's hand, pulling her to her feet and gesturing angrily at their little boy. They came out of the pew and went hurrying back up the aisle through the doors and out of the church.

The congregation all watched them leave. Then they began to look around at one another. They looked again at Lyle.

What do the rest of you think? Lyle said. What do you say? He was standing next to the pulpit now.

I'm not afraid to say, a man said. You're a damn terrorist sympathizer. He rose up in the middle of the sanctuary, holding on to the pew-back ahead of him. A big heavyset man. We never should of let you come out here. You're an enemy to our country.

The old usher who had been sitting at the back stood up now from his customary chair and came rushing, limping down the aisle. Wait! Stop! You can't talk that way in church!

The big man in the pews turned and looked briefly at the old man in his dark suit, shiny with age. Go back and sit down on your chair there, Wayne. I'm not talking to you. But I'm not staying in here. No by God, I don't have to listen to this damn fairy tale on a Sunday morning. He looked around the room. And if the rest of you know what's good for you, you won't either. He shoved out of the pew and went out.

The two Johnson women were sitting down front. Willa stood up, her white hair pinned in a bun, her eyes glinting behind her thick glasses. Let them go, she said. If that's how they are, let them leave and good riddance. We have to listen to what the minister is saying. Even if we don't agree with him, we need to listen and consider. We have to be civil to one another.

No! a woman cried from the back. You be quiet. You shut your mouth.

What? No. I won't be quiet, Willa said. She turned all around, looking at the congregation. I'm going to speak. Who's talking to me back there?

Nobody answered her.

Then Alene stood up beside her mother and looked around at the people, but now there were others who had begun to rise and glare at Lyle, and these people started to slide out of the pews and to turn up the aisles to go outside. At the back of the church one of them, a man, stopped and turned back. Go to hell! he shouted. You go to hell!

Still, most of the congregation, more than half of the people in attendance that morning, stayed seated in the pews yet, waiting in shock and disbelief, and curiosity too, for what Lyle would do now. The pianist was still in her place down front and Beverly Lyle and John Wesley were still seated in the middle of the sanctuary, and the two Johnson women, and the old usher remained standing, outraged, in the aisle. Lyle looked out at them all. After a time he spoke. May we have the last hymn now?

You mean you still want to sing? the pianist said. You still want to?

Yes, would you play the hymn, please?

Yes. If that's what you want.

She began to play the introduction out loudly, with a kind of flourish. It seemed a sort of madness, a kind of miscalculation of the tone and temper of the moment. Lyle began to sing. He had a good voice. It was one of the old hymns Charles Wesley had written two centuries ago. A few of the others gradually, falteringly joined in. They got as far as the end of the first verse and the first refrain, then Lyle stopped singing and the Johnson women and the old usher and the others ceased—his wife and son had never been singing—and the pianist played a few more measures and then she stopped too.

Thank you, Lyle said quietly. Thank you for that much.

He stepped down off the dais and walked back up the aisle, staring straight ahead, looking at none of them, while in the pews they followed him with their eyes, turning their heads as he passed, then he stopped at the rear of the church and raised his hand in the ancient gesture of benediction.

The Lord bless you and keep you; the Lord make His face to shine upon you and be gracious unto you; the Lord lift up His countenance upon you and give you peace; both now and forevermore. Amen.

Then he turned and opened the big oaken doors behind him and stood in the doorway. A hot wind blew in from outside. At the front of the sanctuary the pianist closed up the piano, folding the lid over the keys, and slipped out a side door. The old usher limped up.

Should I close up now?

Yes, if you don't mind.

This won't last. People get upset.

Yes. I know.

They shouldn't be saying what they said. That kind of language in church. That's not right.

They weren't prepared for it.

It won't last. I've seen worse, the old man said. He turned and went back down an outer aisle and began to shut the high windows with his long pole with its hook at the end.

The congregation began to shuffle out. Sullenly, uncomfortably, not talking to one another, moving in an uneasy mass. A few of them stopped to look at the preacher, a few said a word or two but most of them didn't, and went silently out. The Johnson women stepped up and shook Lyle's hand.

It's always this way in time of war, Willa said. It was like this in the 1940s. And during Vietnam. This mix of nationalism and hate and fear.

What will you do now? Alene said.

I'm not sure, Lyle said. This doesn't change what I believe.

No. Don't be disheartened.

You won't be, will you? Willa said. They shook his hand again and went on outside.

The usher had shut all the windows and had gone down the back stairs to close up the basement. Lyle's wife and son, the last in the church, came toward him, John Wesley in front, taller than his father. Lyle reached to take his hand.

Don't, the boy said. Don't touch me. God, how I hate you

when— He broke off. How could you? He swung violently away and rushed down the concrete steps to the street, running past the Johnson women and all the others going to their cars, running on toward the parsonage and his bedroom two blocks away.

Lyle's wife stepped up. At first she didn't speak, she seemed quite calm. Slim, smooth haired, wearing a summer blouse and skirt. You've ruined this too, she said, haven't you. What did you think people would do? Did you actually think they'd agree with you? Be convinced by your eloquence and passion? My God.

No. No, I didn't think that. I had to say it anyway.

Why? For what earthly reason?

Because I believe it.

You believe it. You take it literally, you mean?

Yes. It's the truth. It's still the only answer.

Oh my God. She shook her head and looked away. You're such a fool.

He watched her descend into the bright day. The sun was directly overhead now. He pulled the big doors shut again and stood alone at the back of the church looking at the dim and silent and empty sanctuary.

26

THERE WERE OCCASIONS when Dad Lewis and Mary went together to Denver to see Frank after he left home and never came back. Once was when he was nineteen and waiting tables in a downtown café, just before Christmas. It was not an expensive or sophisticated place where he worked, but more than a hamburger joint, more of a steak-and-potato and deep-fried-fish sort of place, in a one-story building that ran all the way back to the alley.

They drove in from Holt on a bright cold Sunday afternoon. They were only a middle-aged couple then, Dad still had most of his hair and Mary's face was not yet wrinkled and lined. Along the highway snow was drifted in the fields of corn and wheat stubble and cattle were humped up in the freezing air. When they got to Denver they found the café on a corner of Broadway.

You think this is it? Dad said.

It must be, Mary said.

It doesn't look like much.

Now don't start.

I'm not starting anything.

Then don't use that tone.

What tone is that?

She looked at him. And don't be stupid.

What if I can't help it?

Just don't be stupid on purpose, she said. Be nice. I want this to be nice. I've been looking forward to it. And you have too, only you won't admit it.

You know a lot, Dad said, but you don't know everything.

He parked the car and they went inside. The café was not busy, it was too early for the supper trade and they had stopped serving lunch two hours ago. At the front counter was a sign that said Please Seat Yourself. They took a table by the windows overlooking a side street and a used-car lot with a long cord of white lightbulbs that drooped above the hoods of the cars. The lights were already switched on in the late overcast winter day. The interior of the café had a lot of black and white. The stools at the counter were all black plastic and the tables had checkered tablecloths matching the black-and-white tile on the floor.

I don't see any waiters, Dad said.

Somebody'll come.

I thought he was supposed to be working now.

This is his shift, she said. That's all I know.

A man with a flattop haircut came out from the kitchen over to their table. I'm sorry, we're not open for supper yet.

When will you be? Dad said.

Another hour.

What can we get now?

Whatever's not listed on the supper menu.

We don't have any menus at all yet.

The waiter went to the register and brought back two plastic-covered menus.

We were really just wanting to see our son, Mary said. Is Frank here?

Do you mean Franklin?

Frank, Dad said. Last name Lewis.

Well, there's a Franklin Lewis here.

Is he nineteen years old? Mary said.

Maybe. I'd guess about that.

Could you tell him we're here?

He's out back in the alley on break.

You think we could have some coffee while we're waiting? Dad said.

Of course. I should of offered. He went behind the counter and returned with a coffeepot and two white mugs and poured the coffee and went behind the counter again and through the swinging door into the kitchen.

Franklin, Dad said. Is that what he's calling himself?

I don't know, she said. Do you want some cream?

He didn't bring us any.

I know. She got up and looked at the tables, then leaned over the counter and found a little metal pitcher.

This looks fresh, she said.

She sat down again. Dad poured cream into his coffee and looked in his cup and sipped at it.

Is it all right?

He nodded.

Then Frank came out through the kitchen door. He saw them and came over and stood beside their table. He was tall and very thin, his hair grown out long. There was a bruise on his cheek.

Well, you made it, he said. You're too early for supper though.

That waiter let us know, Dad said. He called you Franklin.

That's what I call myself now.

Why would you do that?

Because. I'm making changes. That's part of it.

Changing your name.

That's right.

It isn't what you were born with.

I know. That's the point, Dad.

Dad looked out across the street at the used-car lot.

How long will you be here? Frank said.

We have to go back tonight, Dad said. He turned back.

Lorraine's at home on Christmas break, Mary said. We don't want to be away while she's there.

We don't close till eight and I have to help clean up. So it'll be late.

We can wait for you, Mary said. She looked at Dad. Can't we.

They won't let you off any earlier? he said.

They might but I don't want to lose this job. I've just had it a month. Do you want anything to eat?

I guess we can get some hamburgers, Dad said.

You want some chips too?

You don't have any fries?

Not yet.

Frank left and went back to the kitchen.

He looks too thin, Mary said.

He always was thin. He's probably always going to be thin.

You saw that bruise on his cheek?

He must of got hit, Dad said. In a fight or something.

Why would someone want to hit Frank?

I advise you not to ask him.

I know. I don't intend to.

Maybe it wasn't too bad, Dad said. Maybe he didn't get the worst of it.

Frank came back carrying two thick crockery plates with the hamburgers and chips, lettuce and tomato and onion on the side. He stood for a while next to the table, talking. Then a boy about his age came out from the kitchen and stood beside him.

This is Harlan, Frank said. He wanted to meet you.

How do you do, Mary said.

The boy reached and shook her hand. His hair was long too.

This is my dad, Frank said.

He shook Dad's hand. You're from here in Denver? Dad said.

Yes, sir. I was working here before Franklin ever started.

Then you've been here a while, Mary said.

Too long. He looked at them. Well, it's good to meet you. I've got to get back to the kitchen. He popped Frank on the back of the head and Frank turned and said, You better be careful, you might get in trouble, boy. The boy laughed and went back through the door. Frank watched him until he was gone and then looked at his parents. They were looking at each other. Then two women and a man entered the café and Frank went to meet them. They watched him and it was clear that he was good at meeting people, and soon the café got busy. Outside the light began to weaken along the street and Dad and Mary ate their food and when Frank came back they ordered pie and presently he brought the pie and set it down.

I asked Howard. He said I could get off at seven thirty if we aren't too busy.

A half hour earlier than usual, Dad said.

Yes, plus missing out on cleanup. What do you want to do?

We'll meet you out front, Dad said.

When they finished eating they left money on the table and went out to the car and drove to Civic Center. Colored lights were shining up from big lamps, flooded onto the fronts of the government buildings. Dad parked and they walked along the sidewalk in front of the buildings with other people, the families and their kids in heavy coats and caps. The buildings were all lit up for the holiday and the trees had colored lights strung in the bare branches. They walked by the museum and the public library and back to the car. They were sitting on the side street near the café for an hour before Frank came out. They waited and looked at the car lot and watched the diners through the big windows and saw Frank working at the tables. Everybody was eating and talking and they could see Frank talking. They all looked festive and happy.

It's after seven thirty, Dad said.

He's still busy, Mary said.

Then Frank finally came out. He was only wearing a thin jacket with a long dirty scarf wrapped around his neck, he got in the backseat and they drove over to his apartment.

The street was dark with old tall wooden houses. One of the street lamps was broken out at the corner. They got out and Frank used his key and they climbed the stairs to the third floor, where there was a wide bare hallway with a single shared bathroom. Frank's apartment was just one room looking out onto the dark street, with a narrow bed and a chest of drawers and a curtain hung across the corner for a closet, with an electric hot plate on a stand and a half-size refrigerator, a bare table and two chairs. A poster of the night lights of New York was taped on the wall. Opposite was a poster showing an Indian girl above a caption that said Better Red Than Dead.

Sit down, Frank said. I can make you tea or coffee.

Tea would be good, his mother said.

They sat at the table and Frank put a pan of water on the electric burner and got out tea and sugar, then stood and waited for it to boil. Dad was looking at the poster across the room. You believe that? he said.

What?

What that poster says.

I don't want to kill anybody, Frank said.

That's not what I'm talking about.

Don't worry, Dad. My lottery number's a low one. They're not going to call me.

When did you hear that? Mary said.

A couple months ago.

You didn't tell us. We've been worried.

I got lucky.

The water boiled and Frank poured out three cups and they made their tea. He took his across the room and sat on the bed.

It was warm in the room. They looked around at the spare furnishings.

Have you seen your sister lately? Mary said.

She came down and stayed a weekend with me. And I went up to Fort Collins.

She seems to be doing all right. Don't you think?

Yeah. She's good.

Have you decided if you're coming home for Christmas at all? We'd like to see you.

I have to work, Mom.

You can't get off for even one day?

Maybe. I'll have to see what he tells me. We'll see.

That means you won't, Dad said.

It means I don't know, Frank said.

He got up and carried his cup back across the room.

Are you done?

He took their cups and stacked them in the little sink in the corner.

I've got you something for Christmas, Mary said. I didn't know what you needed. She opened her purse and took out an envelope, she'd written his name on it in red ink and handed it to him and he opened it, a Christmas card with a fifty-dollar bill inside.

Thank you, Mom. He bent and kissed her. You too, Dad.

You're welcome.

I'm sorry I didn't get you anything.

It doesn't matter, honey.

I think I'll go down and get the car warmed up, Dad said.

Do we have to go so soon?

It's late. We still have two and a half hours of driving ahead of us.

Dad looked at Frank. I'll see you, he said, take care of yourself, and he went out the door and they heard him going down the wood stairs.

After a while Mary stood up and buttoned her coat and hugged Frank.

You know that money was your dad's idea. It was from him even more than me. I want you to know that.

I appreciate it, Mom. I know that.

Can I tell him?

Whatever you want.

But are you all right here, honey? I need to know. I never hear anything from you.

Yes, I'm all right.

You're telling me the truth.

Of course.

You know that every time I call you, Dad wants to know what you said. He wants to know how you are too.

I'm doing the best I can, Mom. That's all I can say. I'm getting along the best I can. You can tell Dad that much too.

She went out to the hallway and down the stairs. Frank followed her and she hugged him again on the sidewalk, holding him tight, and went on to the car at the curb. She got in and looked at him standing there without a coat. She rolled the window down.

Go back in, honey, she told him. It's cold out here.

They drove out of Denver and out onto the plains going east toward Holt County.

I wish I was a drinker, she said. She was peering out the side window at the country going by, at the dark clear sky.

What?

I wish I drank. I wish I was a drinker. I never cared for it though.

Are you sick? You want me to stop?

This would be a good time for it.

To start drinking.

Yes.

What's wrong? I don't understand what you're talking about.

What did you think would happen today? she said.

I didn't think much of anything would happen today.

You were right about that. It didn't.

You sound upset.

I am upset. I'm disappointed that we don't have anything to do with him. Anything more than this. Than what happened back there. You give me money to give him and I put it in an envelope for Christmas and he hasn't even thought to have anything to give us in return. We see him working at the café and we follow him up to his dirty little apartment room in a dirty old house and we drink tea and we talk for five minutes, then you go outside to warm up the car and that's it.

What did you expect?

I wanted it to be nice. I told you that. Something present there between us and our son. We're going to lose him, she said. Don't you know that?

We lost him a long time ago.

You lost him. I didn't.

Dad pulled out on the highway to pass the truck ahead of them and they went around its long high length in the night and sped on faster. He looked at her. You wish I was a drinker too?

No, I wouldn't wish that on us, she said. We have enough already.

She dozed the rest of the way, until Dad pulled up in front of the house and stopped the car. The house was all dark, Lorraine was not home yet. She was still out somewhere in town with her friends. It was almost midnight, the latest they'd been awake for a long time. They sat for a while looking at the unlighted house and then Dad shut the engine off and they went inside and fell to sleep beside each other in their familiar downstairs bedroom at the back of the house.

27

THE HOSPICE NURSE had come and gone. The same small quick efficient woman with the beautiful smile. It was late morning now on a hot July day toward the end of the month. She had arrived just after nine o'clock and Dad was back in bed when she came. He had gotten up for breakfast, had drunk his morning coffee and eaten a little piece of buttered toast, dunking it in the coffee, and afterward he had sat for an hour at the window in the living room looking out at the green lawn and the shade tree, then he had gone back to lie down in bed in the back room. The nurse had attended him there.

She checked his blood pressure and pulse and temperature and asked how he was and he said he was a little worse maybe, he couldn't tell but felt he might be slipping faster now, and she asked about his pain, and if he was taking the medication regularly, and he said it was all right, he could live with it, and again she told him he didn't have to just live with it but could have relief, and he looked away and said he knew that, he understood that, then she checked his pills, to see if he had enough, and asked was there anything else, and he said he couldn't think of anything, but he wanted to thank her for coming and looked at Mary and Lorraine who were standing at the foot of the bed watching and listening to it all, and then the nurse leaned forward and took his hand and pressed it warmly and said she'd be back, to call her if he needed anything, anytime day or night, and then she packed up and left.

Mary and Lorraine walked her outside and stood in the shade of the silver poplar trees. How long do you think now? Lorraine asked her.

Two weeks maybe. Sometimes they surprise us. Maybe ten days.

Is there anything more we should be doing?

No, I don't think so. He's lucky to have such good care. A lot of people don't. But you need to be sure to take care of yourselves too. You must know that.

We can rest later, Mary said.

Yes, the nurse said.

She got in the car and drove off up the street. The street looked hot and dry. A dust rose up behind her.

When they went back into the house Dad was asleep again. Later in the morning they woke him when Rudy and Bob came to show him the store accounts, knowing he'd be disappointed if they didn't.

The window was open in the bedroom and there was a warm breeze blowing in but even so Dad lay in the bed with the blanket pulled up over him. Now he propped himself on the pillows and Rudy and Bob carried two chairs into the bedroom and Lorraine followed them and sat in the big chair that was always in the corner. Dad looked at the two men.

Lorraine's going to join us here, he said. I mentioned that the last time.

We know, Dad, said Rudy.

Okay. I didn't know if you remembered.

Yeah. We remembered.

Well. How you doing? How's it going these days?

We're doing good. And you, Dad, that's what we want to know.

I'm going down, I guess, he said. I can feel it.

Are you hurting?

Not very much.

He is, Lorraine said. But he won't take all his pain pills.

You ought to take your pills there, Dad, said Bob.

I will when it gets bad enough. I want to be awake as much as I can. I don't want to faze out.

Yeah, but if you're in a lot of pain, Dad. We wouldn't want to think you was hurting too much.

I appreciate that. That's what they keep saying too.

He won't listen to us, Lorraine said.

No, he always had his own mind, didn't he, Bob said.

And I still got it, Dad said. What's left of it. You sound like I'm not here already. I don't want no pity either. You remember that. He looked at the two men and looked at Lorraine. All right, will you show me the accounts? You better do it soon. I seem to sleep all the time now. I seem to want to sleep.

Rudy stood and laid the store accounts in their folder on the bed beside Dad and he picked them up. Hand me my glasses there will you, honey? he said. Lorraine gave him his glasses and he looked briefly at the papers and then pushed the folder across the bed to her. You look at them, he said.

I will. Can they be left here?

We have other copies, Bob said.

I'll look at them later.

So, Dad said. Everything's all right down there?

Yes sir. No problems to talk about this week.

I don't guess I'd much care if there was. I'm too tired.

You need to rest. That's the best thing. Leave this to us.

He studied them for a while. I was thinking about that old spinster lady again after you left the last time. She come to my mind. When I was laying here. What's her name?

Miss Sprague, Rudy said. The old lady with the freezer, you're talking about.

Yes, her.

Did you change your mind? You want us to repossess it?

No. But she's all alone, isn't she.

There's nobody over there except her, that I know of. Never has been. So far as anybody else knows either.

I want you boys to help her.

How do you mean?

I don't know. But I want you to find some kind of help for her. Somebody to look in on her.

You mean hire somebody.

Something like that. You figure it out. Lorraine can help you. I don't want her left alone over there in that house of hers.

Yes, we can do that, Lorraine said.

You can pay for it out of the store. Get some kind of caretaker for her. Some older woman or somebody. But it needs to be taken care of.

We will, Rudy said.

And another thing. I was remembering that fellow Floyd down there in Oklahoma.

About his story, you mean?

The one that drowned, Dad said. That's not funny no more. The man went over the side of that boat into the lake and didn't come up. He was alive, then he died and his life has to mean more than just a story some guy that comes up here from Texas tells us that's on some combine crew.

You want us to do something there too? Rudy said. I don't see what we can do about that.

No. I'm just saying. Telling you what I've been thinking about while I'm laying here. It's not funny to me no more. Not this morning, anyway.

If that's how you feel, Bob said.

That's how I feel.

Then we don't have to mention it again.

Dad lifted one hand from the bedsheet and inspected it front and back and let it fall back down. I don't know if I'm going to see you fellows again, he said. I got a idea this might be it. But I want both of you to know how much I appreciate all the days and years we've been together at the store. I trusted you. I believed in you. You two fellows—you've been more to me than somebody I just hired. You were friends to me. I want you to know that. Dad's eyes welled up as he was talking.

Thank you, Dad, Bob said. We feel the same way.

Well, I wanted you to know. I wanted to have it said out.

The two men were teary eyed now too. They sat side by side, tall and short, on the two hard wooden chairs in the hot room, their hands in their laps.

So, Dad said. All right. Lorraine's going to be the store manager. Like we talked about. For a while anyhow. And you two fellows are going to still be assistant managers together.

They didn't say anything.

You understand me, don't you.

We understood this was coming from what you was saying before, yes sir.

And I want you to get along with each other. Put aside any bad feelings.

We don't have no bad feelings, Rudy said.

Good. Then I'm going to say one more thing. I want you to pay yourselves a ten-thousand-dollar bonus, each one of you.

What's this, Dad? We don't expect nothing like that.

Now don't interrupt me. You don't need to say nothing about it. I've been laying here thinking and that's what I want. He paused to study them. Now I'm wore out. Come over here, if you would.

The two men looked at him.

Come over here, please. I'm asking you to come closer. They slowly rose from the chairs and stepped up beside the bed. Dad reached and shook Rudy's hand and then Bob's. I thank you for all these years, he said, for what you done for me. Good-bye, you fellows.

Good-bye, Dad. We'll be thinking of you.

They glanced across the bed at Lorraine, sitting on her chair in the corner crying quietly. They went out to the living room and stood looking toward the kitchen. Mary noticed them and came out.

Would you let us know if we can do anything? Rudy said sadly.

Was he able to talk a little?

Yes. He was able to talk a little. He said some things to us. We're sure going to miss him. That's all there is to it.

In the bedroom Lorraine moved onto the bed and lay beside Dad.

Are you all right, Daddy?

Yeah, I am.

She took his hand.

That went pretty good, don't you think it did? he said.

Yes. You know how much they think of you.

Well, I think a lot of them too. But they never say much, do they. They never say much to me.

You don't let people, Daddy. You never have.

You think that's what it is?

Yes, I do.

Well. I don't know about that. I couldn't say.

28

IN THE DAYS FOLLOWING the sermon Lyle began to wander in the town. After supper with his wife and son, he'd put on a jacket and cap and begin to walk—after the sun was down. It was usually nine or ten before he began.

He stayed away from the center of Holt and the bright streetlights. When it happened that he had to cross Main, he waited until the street was empty and then he crossed and went on walking up and down the dark sidewalks and passed over the tracks to the north side where the houses were small and meager, with empty weed-filled lots. At the end of town, he looked out at the starlit windblown fields, and then turned back into the neighborhoods.

He stood in front of houses in the shadows of trees and looked in through the windows opened to the summer nights, watching people. The little dramas, the routine moments. People moving about in the rooms, people eating and getting up from the table and crossing in the flickering blue light of television and at last turning out the house lights and going out of the darkened rooms, while he stood outside waiting to see if they would come back.

Once he saw a man in his undershirt kneel down before a woman in a robe sitting on a sofa, his face raised up to her, and the woman leaning forward, drawing him to her, running her fingers through his thin hair and taking his face in her hands and kissing him a long time, and then the man rising and rubbing his back while she sat still and watched him walking away with his hair all mussed up.

One night he stood so long in front of a house that a man called the police. He actually watched the man on the phone having the conversation.

A police car pulled up at the curb and the officer put on his cap and got out.

What do you think you're doing here? he said.

Just standing here, Lyle said.

These people said you were looking in their window.

I didn't mean to disturb them. I'm sorry if I have.

Let's see some identification.

Are you charging me with something, Officer?

Let's look at your driver's license.

Lyle took out his wallet and handed the license to him. The man examined it under his flashlight, then put the light up into Lyle's face.

Rob Lyle. That's you.

Yes.

The preacher.

Yes.

Is there something wrong with you? What are you doing out here?

I'm just walking. Having a look around town.

Your family knows where you are?

They know I'm taking a walk.

It doesn't bother you to look in other people's houses? You think that's all right.

I don't think I'm doing any harm. I didn't mean to.

Well, these people don't like it. This man called you in.

What did he say?

That you were looking in his house.

Did he say what he was doing in his house?

Why would he say that?

People in their houses at night. These ordinary lives. Passing without their knowing it. I'd hoped to recapture something.

The officer stared at him.

The precious ordinary.

I don't know what you're talking about, but you'd better keep moving.

I thought I'd see people being hurtful. Cruel. A man hitting his wife. But I haven't seen that. Maybe all that's behind the curtains. If you're going to hit somebody maybe you pull the curtains first.

Not necessarily.

What I've seen is the sweet kindness of one person to another. Just time passing on a summer's night. This ordinary life.

Well, people are pretty good, generally. Most of them. Not all of them. I see the other side.

Lyle looked around at the houses. The officer watched him.

You'd better go. People don't want you looking in their windows, good or bad. I'll wait here till you leave.

On Saturday night he was walking on the east side of Holt a block off Highway 34 when two men rode up in a pickup.

Is that you, Reverend?

Lyle looked at them. Yes, it's me.

We thought it was. Just stay there a minute.

They got out and came over to him.

What are you doing out here, Reverend? Taking the night air?

Yes.

It's pretty late. Why would you be out here now?

Did you want something? Lyle said.

There is something, the first man said and he slapped Lyle across the face. Lyle fell back and the other man moved closer. What did you think of that? the first man said.

Lyle didn't say anything.

Tell us about love, the man said. Turn us the other cheek now.

That's what this is about, Lyle said. I see.

What did you think it was about?

I didn't know.

You forgot already.

No.

No, he didn't forget, the second man said. He still loves them desert sons of bitches. He still has that on his mind.

The first man said, You believe all that, I guess, don't you.

Yes.

He slapped Lyle again. Lyle faltered backward. He wiped his hand across his mouth, smearing blood on his cheek.

Now what do you say?

I ask you to stop this, Lyle said. It won't get you what you want.

He thinks he's proved something.

Do you?

No.

But you hate me now, don't you.

I don't hate you. I don't like you very much.

If I slap you again, you'll start to hate me then.

Let's go, the other man said. Somebody's going to see us.

All right. We're done here. But you need to watch what you say, Preacher. You better mind your mouth, you're about to get yourself in real trouble.

They went back to the pickup, the headlights came on and they drove off toward the highway. Lyle watched them until they'd disappeared around the corner, then he looked at the houses along the street. No lights had come on. He looked up at the sky, all the flickering stars, and started back toward the parsonage, crossing Main Street and going on into the sleeping residential neighborhood, and at the parsonage he stood at the bathroom sink to rinse his face with water. His wife appeared in the doorway.

What happened?

He turned toward her. His face was bruised and swollen.

Oh no, she said. Now what?

A couple of men stopped me. One of them slapped me.

Why? What did you do?

It's because of what I said in church.

How did they know that? Were they from the church?

No. But they didn't need to be. Everybody would have heard.

You don't have any idea who they were?

I've never seen them before.

What will you do?

I'm going to clean up my face, he said, then I'm coming to bed.

You won't even inform the police?

No.

But why not?

Because this isn't about the law. Or police protection.

She looked at his swollen face and the blood on his shirt. I don't think I'm going to last here much longer, she said. I'm going back to Denver. This is too much.

We can talk about it in the morning.

No. I'm done now. I can see that.

She turned and went back to bed. He looked at himself in the mirror and bent over the sink and began laving cold water onto his cheeks again.

When he got into bed, she was still awake.

Are you all right? she said. Are you badly hurt?

No, not badly.

I never thought our lives would turn out this way, did you?

No, but you can go back to him and be comforted again. Is that your plan?

I don't have a plan. Except to leave here. And find a job.

What about him?

Who? John Wesley?

Him too. But I meant your friend.

I haven't seen him in over two years.

You haven't talked to him?

When would I talk to him?

Anytime. Whenever I'm out of the house.

No. I told you I was finished. There's nothing more to us.

But you'll pick up if you go back.

I don't have any interest in that. I'm too tired. I feel like somebody slapped me too.

29

A LITTLE WHILE before noon on a day earlier in that same week, Lorraine went next door to Berta May's and then she and Alice came out and drove east on U.S. Highway 34, then south on the gravel to the Johnson house.

When they turned in at the country house and got out of the car, the Johnson women stepped outside and stood together on the back porch waiting for them. The two women had on thin cotton sleeveless dresses and looked cool despite the noontime heat. Come in, Willa called. Come in.

Here we are, Lorraine said.

How's this sweet girl? Willa said when Alice came up on the porch.

Pretty good, Alice said.

Hello, sweetheart, Alene said.

They hugged her and hugged Lorraine. I brought this too, Lorraine said. She brandished a bottle of wine.

They ate lunch in the yard on the north side of the house under an elm tree. They carried the food out and set it on the old wood picnic table. Somebody needs to paint that, Willa said. Look at it. The table was paint-flaked and dry.

We'll just cover it up, Lorraine said.

They brought the food out in dishes covered with white dish towels, chicken salad with fruit and country potato salad and dinner rolls. Alice carried out the plates, the old thin delicate ones, hand-painted with blue grapes.

They're too good for a picnic, Lorraine said.

No. I'm going to use them. What else are they for? My mother gave them to me for my wedding a long time ago. I'm missing two of them.

They brought out glasses and silverware and salt and pepper shakers and a dish of pickle relish and pink cloth napkins and iced tea in a glass pitcher. All was arranged on the table. Alene and Willa sat on one side, taking their time getting seated, Willa particularly, swinging her old bare legs over the wooden seat. Lorraine and Alice sat on the opposite side.

Over them lay the shade of the tree, dappling and swaying when there was a breeze at this noon hour.

Alice watched them, no one spoke nor began to eat yet. Then Willa said, I know we can't all think alike, but I want to say something that resembles grace.

They looked at her. She shut her eyes behind the thick glasses, and they closed their eyes.

We're grateful for this summer's day. We're grateful for this beautiful food. We want to be thankful that we are here in this particular place on this particular day together. We want to acknowledge these our many blessings. And we're so thankful for this young girl here with us. May she be filled with joy all her life. And may there be peace in the world.

Then she ceased. They opened their eyes and looked at her. Amen, she said. Let's eat.

They passed the dishes around. Alene had made the chicken salad with mandarin oranges and olives and slivered almonds, and Lorraine said how good it was and Alene said how good her potato salad was too and she said it was just potato salad but Alene said it wasn't.

Alice watched them talk, watching each speaker. The chicken salad was served on opened lettuce leaves. She watched what they did. Lorraine cut hers as she ate and Alice did the same.

The women drank some of the chilled wine and made a toast. The tree shade moved, and there were birds calling from the lilac bushes and from the trees below the house.

After a while Alice leaned over to whisper in Lorraine's ear and Lorraine said, It's back through the kitchen, I think.

Is she wanting the bathroom? Willa said.

Yes.

Excuse me, Alice said.

She got up and went to the house. It was cool inside, the kitchen very clean and neat. There were starched curtains at the windows. The little bathroom was off the kitchen, it was clean and neat too, with a picture of a red flower framed on the wall. She washed her hands and looked out the kitchen window into the yard, they were still sitting at the picnic table. She looked through the doorway of the dining room, at the wood table and matching chairs and matching buffet, and farther back was the living room with the window shades drawn down for coolness.

When she went outside, Alene asked her, Are you okay, honey?

Yes.

Did you get enough to eat? Do you want some more iced tea?

Okay.

Lorraine said, I'm so satisfied and full. I could nap right here.

Well, we could, Willa said. We could just lie right down on the grass here in the shade.

I'll get some blankets, Mother.

Alene went in the house and came back with two old chenille bed-spreads and laid them out on the lawn.

What about the food? We don't want it to spoil.

I'll just put it in the refrigerator, Lorraine said. Alice can help me.

They lay out on the ground in the shade of the tree, with dinner napkins draped over their faces, to ward off the flies. Alice shut her eyes. She could still see light through the napkin. It was nice under the tree with the women.

We need a little music, Willa said.

Something soft and slow, Alene said. Piano or violin.

Then no one said anything for a while. Alice lifted the napkin from her face and looked at them, the three women lying on the ground with the pink napkins over their faces. Then she lay back and shut her eyes.

I wanted to play the piano, Willa said. I've told you this before, Alene.

Yes.

We were speaking of music. I wanted to play the piano and my mother bought lessons for me when I was a little girl younger than Alice here. I walked once a week across the field and paid a quarter per lesson. I walked half a mile across a plowed field to the teacher. I could do the right hand but couldn't seem to make the left hand play in time, and after a month or two the teacher said to Mother, She doesn't seem to be making much progress. Doesn't she practice? Mother said, I don't believe she does. Then Mother told me, Willa, you either have to practice or give up your lessons. I went out to the barn and just cried. A quarter was a lot of money then, like a dollar is now. Oh, more than a dollar, much more. So I told Mama I'd stop, I wouldn't waste any more money. I've criticized and rebuked myself a hundred times since. I do so like music. I used to dance too.

I never heard you talk about the dancing, Mother.

Yes. I did tap dance with shiny shoes.

Then no one said any more. After a while Alice heard Willa begin to snore and then the softer snoring of Alene and the breathing of Lorraine right beside her. She opened her eyes once more under the cloth, the warm daylight was there, and she shut her eyes.

When she woke she was surprised that she had been asleep. The women were sitting up, not talking, only looking out toward the barn, waiting for her to wake. It was very hot now in the afternoon, with only a little hot wind blowing.

———

We ought to go swimming, Lorraine said. I wish there was a creek out here.

I used to dunk my head in the stock tank on a hot day, Alene said.

The cattle are there now, Willa said.

They wouldn't bother us.

It's so dirty out there.

It's not that bad.

We don't have any bathing suits.

Oh damn the bathing suits, Mother.

They looked at each other and laughed.

All right then. But we do need towels.

I'll get them.

And we can take out the lawn chairs, Willa said. I'm not sitting in the dirt. I don't care what you say.

The three women and the girl walked out to the barn carrying the towels and the lawn chairs and the leftover wine and went in through the gate and crossed the hot empty corral, going out into the pasture through the far gate, and walked along the path worn by the cattle alongside the fence and stopped at the stock tank. There was a pad of concrete laid around it, with dirt and manure below it and mud on the low side of the tank where the tank overflowed, the mud pocked with the deep split hoofprints of cattle. The tank was brimming full. Behind it, the windmill ran water whenever the wind gusted up, the pump banged and clanked, the rod jerked up and down, then the cold fresh clean water spouted out through a long pipe.

They set the lawn chairs in a line back from the tank. Alice stepped up on the concrete apron and looked in and felt the cold water. On the bottom was a bed of mud and there were strings of green moss around the edges. She could see black tadpoles squirming away into the mud. She went back to the women.

Lorraine said, Well. Then she just proceeded to take her clothes off and laid them out on a chair. She was white as cream and full breasted with blue veins in her breasts with a swatch of dark hair below her stomach to match the dark hair on her head. They looked at her. She raised her arms. Oh God, what a beautiful day. She stepped toward the tank in the hot manurey dirt and stepped up onto the concrete and leaned over and cupped her hands in the water, her bare back and legs shining in the sun, and doused her face and hair and her breasts and gasped, Oh God! Dear Lord! She lifted one foot onto the rim of the tank and brushed her foot off and stepped over into the water, her body halved, all of her full-fleshed body in the bright sun, and then lowered herself into the water and cried, Goddamn! Oh Jesus! and lay out in the water and disappeared and came up all white and shining. Jesus! Jesus! Then she stood up and turned to them. Come on, all of you, she called. Get in.

Well then, said Alene.

And she took her clothes off too. She was pale and thin, a little bony, a little sallow, with small breasts and thin arms and thin thighs and graying hair below. She walked over to the tank and splashed herself and climbed in and squatted down and rose up streaming. Oh Jesus! God bless us! Oh come in, Mother. Alice, come on.

Alice removed her clothes then. She had a girl's flat chest and flat stomach, the points of her backbone showed and her shoulder blades were sharp edged and she had no hair there yet, her legs were tanned up to her thighs from wearing shorts and her arms were tanned. She went to the stock tank and dipped her fingers in the water. Lorraine and Alene held out their hands to her and she stepped over into the cold water and caught her breath.

Honey, Lorraine said, go ahead and yell. You have to.

Oh Jesus, she said softly.

They laughed. Yes, Lorraine said. But yell this time. Yell.

Oh Jesus. Son of a bitch.

They laughed again. Where in the world did you learn that?

At school.

Well. That's the way then. Let it out. Yell now.

She yelled a little bit.

That's better.

Now they looked at Willa still outside the tank.

Mother, come on now. You must.

Oh. I don't know.

Yes. Come on.

Well. Damnation. All right, then.

She took her glasses off and set them on a chair and removed her dress and removed her bra and her white old lady's underwear, she was flat chested with soft pale flaps for breasts, the nipples pointing down, and had a sagging stomach and wide soft hips folded a little and loose thighs and almost no hair below her stomach, almost as unhaired in her old age as Alice was in her youth, and she came over and they held out their hands to her, and she sat sideways on the rim and swung her legs over. Mercy heavens! she cried. Mercy! She cupped water onto her face and chest. Lord! I'm an old woman and I've never been naked outdoors before. Look at me. Have you, Alene?

No, Mother.

At least you didn't wait till you were this old.

Alene leaned forward and kissed her on the cheek. We're out here now, Mother.

Lorraine pushed off and swung her arms and swam a few strokes across the tank, the water was deep enough, and crossed to the water pipe. She stood up half out of the water gleaming wet and spun around making a wave with her cupped hands and then came swimming back. She stood up again. Then without a word Willa just lay out and began a surprising backstroke that made her appear to be a kind of delicate white bird in the water and went a little ways across the tank and stood up. Her hair had come loose from its pins and was long and full and shiny, then she floated back to them and stood again.

Your hair is so beautiful, Lorraine said.

Oh. Thank you. I've always been too vain about my hair. I'm afraid I still am.

It's beautiful, Mother. I've always wished I had your hair instead of mine.

But you've always been so pretty, dear. So tall and graceful.

Oh no. That's not true.

It is, dear.

Then Lorraine said, Alice, do you know how to swim?

No.

Can you float?

I don't know how.

It's time to learn. Come out here into the middle. Alene, will you help?

The two women held her as she lay back.

Now just breathe. And spread your arms out.

When she began to sink they lifted her up, and after a while she was able to stay up and they stepped back and she lay out on the water, half-submerged, her blue eyes open to the blue sky.

After a time they got out and sat in the lawn chairs, facing the sun. It was past middle of the afternoon now. The women put on their sunglasses and drank the chilled wine that had been set in the tank and gave Alice a little to taste. They sat naked, drying in the sun. Willa's long white hair hung down over the chair back.

Then some of the black cows in the pasture began to come cautiously up to drink. The cattle snorted and switched their tails, looking at the women, until one of the older cows came up and halted and advanced and came on, still watching them, and stepped heavily up onto the concrete and shoved at the stock water with her black rubbery muzzle and drank and afterward stood dripping, looking at them, and drank again. Then the other cattle came up and drank, their young black calves with them.

The women and the girl watched one nearby cow with a calf beside her.

That calf will want to eat when they go back out to the pasture, Willa said. You know how they butt and pull on their mothers.

Yes, but it's nice to nurse, Lorraine said. You feel the world might be all right then. And you can feel it down inside you too.

What if you had to be butted like they do? Willa said. What if you were a milk cow with that great bag hanging down? Think of that between your legs, the way milk cows have to trot with that full bag.

I know, Lorraine said. But think of a man washing your tits with warm soapy water, fondling you twice a day.

She and Alene laughed.

Or a woman, Alene said. Women milk cows too.

Or a woman, Lorraine said.

Now you're going to embarrass Alice and me, Willa said.

Are you embarrassed, Alice?

No.

No. She's not embarrassed.

I'm going to get back in, Alice said.

The women watched her move to the tank, this young thin quiet girl, naked out in the country in the broad daylight. The cows looked at her. She climbed into the tank and lay out flat and floated and paddled her feet and came to the other side and stood. A brief gust of wind rose up, the water spouted from the pipe, and she turned her head and drank.

The women climbed into the tank with her and squatted down and lay back and floated and stood streaming. Their faces and bodies shining. Later they got out and dried off and put on their clothes and carried the lawn chairs and the empty wine bottle and walked back through the corral and across the hot gravel drive to the house. Their hair was still damp. It felt heavy and cool on the backs of their necks.

30

Two months after Alene introduced the principal to her mother in a Denver restaurant, she was buying groceries on a Saturday morning in the little town where she taught school. She was standing in the produce section when a short black-haired woman in nice clothes came up to her and without warning reached up and slapped her in the face.

Wait! Alene said. What are you doing?

But she recognized the woman. She'd never met her before, but she'd seen her picture in the newspaper once, showing the principal with his wife and their two children.

The woman began to scream. You're filthy! You're just a whore! I won't let him go! I won't ever! She raised her hand again, but Alene caught her wrists and shoved her away. The woman fell back in her high-heeled shoes and good dress against the stand of oranges and knocked some of them rolling out across the floor.

Oh! You shoved me! You can't do that.

People were watching them now. Housewives, old single men, the stockboy. The woman rushed at Alene and tried now to hit her with her purse, swinging it. Wait, Alene said. Stop it.

Oh, don't speak to me. Whore!

Then the grocery manager came hurrying up. What's going on here? What's this?

She's sleeping with my husband. She wants to steal him. She's a whore.

Here now, he said. Stop this. Let me help you. He put his arm around her and she tried to slap him too, but he caught her arms and pinned them to her sides. Whoa, he said, let's just go outside. Come with me.

He held her tight and half carried her out the door. Alene and the others watched them out in the parking lot. The manager opened the car door and she got in. She appeared to be calmer now, as if she suddenly were exhausted. He stood talking to her, and then he shut the car door, she started the engine and drove off. The manager came back in the store and walked up to Alene. Aren't you a teacher in the grade school?

Yes.

What are you doing? he said and shook his head.

I'll just go, Alene said. She left her grocery cart and went outside to her car into the cold day. She drove home and on the following Monday she returned to her classroom of young children. Everyone in town knew what had happened in the grocery store and nevertheless there she was, still teaching.

The principal of her school called her into the school office and said they could not have this behavior, she'd have to be on probation now, and one more thing like this, if anything happened again, they'd let her go. She was a good teacher, he said. They didn't want to lose her. But they couldn't have this.

In the other town the man, the principal, almost lost his job too. The district school board met with him in executive session in the school's library. The board chairman, a retired insurance agent, said, In the name of Jesus, what were you thinking of? Didn't you know you can't do that?

Yes. I knew.

Then why did you?

Oh, we all know why, said one of the other board members, a young man. Why did you think you could get away with it? That's what I want to know. I thought you grew up in a place like this.

Yes. It was about this size.

Then you would know you can't do anything without everybody else in town hearing what happened before you even got home. Whether you broke your leg or your thumb or some woman's heart on the other side of the county there.

I know that, the principal said.

So what were you thinking of? Tell us.

He didn't answer. He looked around the room at them, in the school library with the reference books collecting dust on the shelves and the school librarian's desk located in the place where she could keep watch on everything, and the bright posters on the walls.

He wasn't thinking, one of the others said. That's the point of all this. You weren't thinking, were you. It wasn't about thinking. Thinking didn't have a thing to do with it.

He didn't answer that either.

All right, the old chairman said. You can never mind that. You will have to at least answer this, though. Are you done with her?

The principal looked at him for a moment. I am, he said.

You're finished.

Yes.

You promise us that.

Yes.

Never mind what you promise your wife. You have to be sure, what you tell us. We won't put up with this kind of thing. We're not like your wife might be, we won't take you back.

I said it was over.

All right. The chairman looked around the room. Anything else concerning this issue here today?

None of them spoke.

All right then. I don't like this way of doing things. Talking out here in the open about what ought to be kept back secret behind closed doors. This isn't good. I don't like it.

———

She never met the principal again. She did not even have a final talk or a final hour with him in a café or a last night in a rented bed in a hotel room. She only ever saw him once again, and that was from a distance at a meeting when he crossed in a hallway fifty feet away, wearing a suit and tie. Then in the summer she heard that he and his wife and children had moved to Utah.

She phoned three times during those months, but he couldn't or wouldn't take her calls. She wrote him a letter but she never knew if he received it, or if he simply refused to answer. She decided finally that he was a kind of coward for that. That was the word that came to her mind. She herself stayed and taught for years in the same little town. She believed she had to do that. It took a kind of courage. She was marked and known. It was how you paid for love. But over time that was lost too. She became part of the history of the town, like wallpaper in the old houses—the aging lonely isolated woman, the unmarried schoolteacher living out her days among other people's children, a woman who'd had a brief moment of excitement and romance a long time ago and afterward had retreated and lived quietly and made no more disturbance.

The principal only ever came to visit her in dreams that were never satisfactory and from which she woke in tears, with an ache that wouldn't be healed or soothed.

She had a picture of him that she had taken herself. And one of them together in the hotel lobby that the desk clerk in Denver had taken that first winter. A black-and-white picture which didn't show how red their cheeks were, coming in off the cold street, before they rode the elevator up to the room to undress and lie down in bed together.

31

HE WAS SITTING in his chair at the window after breakfast when he
saw Alice go out the front door and retrieve her bicycle from the back
porch and then push it along the side of Berta May's house and begin
to ride in the street. He watched her pedal out of sight. He looked the
other way to the west where the barn and the corral were. He hadn't
got the barn painted and the weeds in the corral were as tall as the
top of the fence. Then Alice rode back into view and he watched her
pedal out of sight in the other direction.

He drifted off to sleep. When he woke it looked hot outside in
the yard. He couldn't see the girl. He pushed against the arms of the
chair and stood a while to steady himself. All was quiet. He took his
cane and began to walk, shuffling, and looked out to the kitchen. He
called, Are you there, Mary? He shuffled on and entered the bathroom, looking at his face in the mirror, an old man with a day-old
grizzled beard, looking angry and puzzled at the same time. He stood
his cane against the wall and pushed down his sweatpants and sat too
hard. After a while he tried to get up. He called, Mary, come here,
will you? He sat. He called again. Where in the hell? And dozed off.

Then she had come in. You're in here, she said.

He opened his eyes. Where were you? I called for you.

I was outside talking to Berta May in the backyard.

I couldn't find you.

I'm sorry. Are you done here?

As much as I'm going to be. Now I can't get up.

Let me help you.

Wait. Maybe you better get Lorraine.

She's downtown shopping.

I don't want you to hurt yourself.

I'll be careful.

She lifted under his arm and he gradually rose up and stood, his legs shaking, quivering.

Honey, are you all right?

He looked straight ahead. Yeah.

She drew up the diaper inside his sweatpants. This one's still good, she said. We don't need to change it.

I'm about like a goddamn baby, he said. It's a damn nuisance.

It's time for your pill. Let's get you in the bedroom.

She held his arm while he used his cane and they went into the room and he slumped on the bed, then he lay back and she lifted his legs over in place.

I don't like you lifting like that, he said. You're going to hurt your back.

Are you all comfortable now?

I'll take that pill, please.

She put the pill on his old parched tongue and gave him the water glass. He raised his head to swallow.

Okay?

Yeah. He closed his eyes.

Can I get you anything else?

No, thanks. You do too much already.

I don't mind at all. You know that. Would you like me to sit here with you?

No. I'm all right now.

When he woke an hour later the room seemed too dark. He hadn't slept so long, it wasn't the end of day, night wasn't coming on yet. He peered at the ceiling. Then he felt there were people in the room. He had visitors. But she hadn't wakened him. It wasn't like her letting people come in when he was asleep. He didn't like anyone seeing him asleep unless it was his wife or his daughter, and he didn't want even them to sit and wait for him to wake up.

He looked around. There were four of them, two sitting on chairs in the corner where the room was darker, and two more in chairs near him. The closest one was sitting straight up, a man. He was watching him. He was smoking a cigarette.

You shouldn't be smoking no cigarettes in here, Dad said. Didn't she tell you that? I got cancer of my lungs. I can't breathe good.

I'm almost done with it.

Dad looked at him closely. I know you, he said.

You ought to. I haven't changed that much.

Frank. Is that you, Frank?

Yeah, it's me.

You lost your hair on top. Most of it. I didn't recognize you.

Isn't that the berries?

Yeah, I guess. But what do you mean?

I end up looking like you.

You don't look like me.

Yeah. I do. Have you looked lately?

Well. If you mean you look like I used to. Not now. Maybe back then.

When you were in your fifties.

I guess so.

Well. That's where I am. I'm in my fifties.

Dad looked at him sitting there, smoking. I know you now. I'm glad you come.

Are you? Why would you be?

I want to talk to you.

Go ahead. Talk.

Dad looked around at the others. I don't like to talk in front of these other people here.

They won't mind.

Who are they?

Don't you know me? The woman in the chair behind Frank moved so he could see her. A blond woman about thirty, ripe-looking with a big chest, wearing a low-cut blouse and shorts. Her legs looked white and plump. Don't you know my voice too?

I never thought I'd see you again, Dad said.

Here I am. I came to visit you.

Do you want something?

Maybe I do.

What is it? I thought you told me you never wanted to see me again. That it was enough. You wrote that letter.

I know. That's what I'm talking about. I want to catch you up. Tell you all that's happened.

That's fine. Go ahead. But just a minute. Who's these others here?

You know us too, Dad. Hell, you ought to recognize us.

Is that you, Rudy?

Nobody else.

And Bob?

Yeah. It's me, Dad.

I don't understand this. Aren't we done with the store?

Yeah. About done.

He peered at them. Then he studied the other faces, one after the other. Well, do you want some coffee, all of you? He looked toward the open doorway.

No, Rudy said. We wouldn't want to bother Mary.

I never got to meet her, Tanya said.

Didn't you?

I used to see her in town on Main Street when we was still living here before we moved away. Before you made us get out of here. Before you told Clayton what you told him.

What was I supposed to do? Dad said. He stole from me.

You say. There might of been different ways though.

What ways?

You might of let him work it off. Pay down his debt that way.

I didn't want that, Dad said. I couldn't have him in the store. I never wanted to see him again.

Yeah. Clayton told me that's what you said.

Dad looked at each of them again. You don't want any coffee, Rudy?

No, sir. I'm okay. Doing fine.

You neither, Bob?

No, thanks.

I don't know if you even drink coffee, Frank.

Don't you remember?

No. Should I?

You would have, if you were paying attention.

What does that mean? Dad said.

I drank coffee all the time when I was still here. When I was going to high school. You don't remember that, do you.

No. That's just a little thing. Why would I think of something like that?

No reason. You're right, it doesn't amount to anything if I was drinking coffee and sitting at the same table with you every day, you and Mom, for however many years I was doing it before I left and went to Denver.

We come to see you in Denver, Dad said.

And stayed one hour. That was all.

We had to get home. It was wintertime. They said it was going to snow.

It didn't snow, Frank said.

It was going to.

They were still with him when Dad woke once more in the darkened bedroom.

Does your mother know you're here? he said.

Mom?

Did you see her? Did you tell her you were here, that you come in? She would want to see you. He didn't answer. Dad looked out through the window toward the barn and empty corral, the tall weeds growing up.

Never mind Mom for now. We'll get to Mom.

What are you talking about? Dad said.

You don't understand, do you.

You ought to have more respect, Tanya said. He's your father. You shouldn't treat him like that.

I have respect for him. For some aspects of him.

You don't show it. He's going to be gone anytime now and then you'll wish you'd of done him different.

Like you and Clayton, you mean, he said.

Clayton don't have nothing to do with this.

He's why you're here, isn't he?

Not like you're talking about. I loved Clayton.

Okay. Good, said Frank. You loved him.

I loved that man and then he goes to Denver and shoots himself in the head. How would you like that?

It seems like as good a way as any, Frank said.

But how would you like to have to look at that thing there, to say that's him. That thing used to be my husband and now I got two little kids that don't have no daddy no more.

It's tough shit, isn't it, Frank said. It's life. Maybe they were better off without him.

She looked at him. Oh, you got hard, she said. Didn't you.

I had to.

They turned toward Dad lying propped up in bed watching them talk. Gray and yellow-looking, with parchment skin, sunken eyes, hair shoved up awry on the sides of his head.

That's life, isn't it, Dad. Isn't that what you would say?

I don't know.

You would if you were thinking right.

I'm thinking okay.

It's life, Frank said. It's the way it goes, it's how shit happens. I used to want you to do something.

What are you talking about now? Dad said.

Do something. Show something to me.

I don't know what you're talking about.

I waited for you for years and nothing happened. You never did anything, did you.

I did things, Dad said. I did a lot of things.

Not like what I'm talking about. You didn't.

Dad stared at him. After a while he glanced toward the window again.

It's tough shit, isn't it, Frank said. It's just life.

I helped her. This woman here. I did things for her, Dad said.

He give me some money, Tanya said. He did.

For quite a long time too, Dad said.

After you killed her husband, Frank said.

What are you talking about? I didn't kill him. You just heard her say he shot himself.

How come, though? Who caused that to happen?

You can't blame that on me.

I don't have to. You blame yourself.

Dad peered over into the corner. The two familiar figures, one tall, one short, were still sitting there, listening to everything, picking at their big hands. I treated you all right anyway. Isn't that true? Dad said.

I was going to be manager, Rudy said.

You still are.

No. She is. Your daughter is.

Someday you will be.

Which one of us?

I don't know. That comes later, after I'm out of this.

Who's going to decide that?

That ain't for me to say. I gave you each a bonus.

We appreciate that.

Ten thousand dollars, Dad said.

For twenty years.

But you acted like it was a good thing I did. I believed you.

We know.

He turned to Frank. Does your mother know you're here? Did you tell her? I need some water. I don't see no water here. I need some water.

Honey, who are you talking to? Mary said.

He looked up and she was standing beside the bed now.

You were talking out loud. Were you dreaming, honey? Were you having a kind of dream-like? Here's your water. Your water's right here. She gave him the glass and he took it but didn't drink.

They're right here, he said.

There's nobody here.

Frank is here.

Frank. You saw Frank?

He was here. I didn't get to talk to him enough. I wanted to talk to him.

I wish he'd talk to me, she said.

Did he drink coffee? Dad said.

Who?

Frank. Did he drink coffee when he was still living here? When he was a boy?

Yes. Of course. He always drank coffee. Frank loved his coffee.

32

ON THAT NEXT SUNDAY there were only a few of the congregation waiting for him in the sanctuary to begin the service. His wife was there and their son, sitting beside her, looking bored and angry already, and the old man, the old usher, standing in the back with a handful of bulletins to be distributed, and the Johnson women sitting where they always sat, and a dozen or more others, mostly women, and the pianist at the piano down at the front of the sanctuary, playing the invitation to worship over and over until the preacher should arrive and they could begin.

Then he came in, entering from the side door and crossing the carpeted dais to the pulpit. He was dressed in black pants and the long-sleeved white shirt, open at the neck as before, but with the sleeves buttoned this time, and this time he stood behind the pulpit according to custom.

He stood there for a time not speaking, looking out at them. They waited. It was very quiet. The pianist had stopped playing, finally making an awkward end to the music in the middle of a passage.

Then he began to speak, in a quiet voice. Go home, he said. You might as well. I have nothing more to say. You don't need me or whatever I might think of to say to you. You know yourselves what you should do. Now or at any other time. Go home. You might as well. I don't take any of it back, I don't retract it. But you don't need to hear it from me.

He stopped. They waited for more, not moving. His face was swollen a little from the previous night. He looked at them over the pulpit. There was a long silence. The congregation waited, but he said no more, except to say: Thank you for coming back this morning. I want to say that. Perhaps there's a kind of hope in that. I choose to see it as such. But you can go home now. Be at peace. I have nothing more to say.

He looked at them for a moment longer. Then he turned from the pulpit and crossed the dais to the side door and was gone. The congregation glanced around at one another. Finally an old lame woman stood up and came out of her pew and started toward the back. They watched her. She stopped midway. That's it, she said. Don't you see? It's no point to sit in here waiting for nothing. The rest of you can sit here all you want. I never expected to see such a thing in church in my life. I never hope to see it again. She hobbled slowly back up the aisle past the usher standing at the back and went out.

Then it was just quiet again. Then Lyle's wife rose from her pew and walked down to the front of the church and turned at the communion rail to face the congregation. She looked tired but still attractive in a nicely tailored summer dress. I came down here to say something, she said. I felt I should make some kind of amends here this morning. After what my husband said last week and what he did just now. She stopped. Except I don't know what to say. Why it should be me to say some conciliatory apologetic thing, I don't know. I haven't done anything wrong. It wasn't me. She stopped again, turning slowly to look at them. I only know I've had enough. I'm saying this publicly, I'm worn out. This is very similar to what happened in Denver. People thought he was wrong then too. Now he's wrong again and people have turned against him once more and it's no surprise that they have. So I'm going to leave. That's what I see I will have to do. I must save myself at least, and my son.

No. You should support him, Willa Johnson said. She and Alene were sitting not far from her.

What did you say? Are you talking to me?

You should stay here and help him. This is your place. I thought that was what you came forward to tell us. I was thinking, good for you, I was thinking that you were brave, more than I knew.

No. Don't you see? That's not it. What can you know? How can you understand what it's been like for me?

I don't care what it's been like for you. You're his wife. Your place is with him.

Have you ever been married?

Yes, of course. I was married for a long time. This is my daughter here with me.

All right, Lyle's wife said. I will admit that he has principles. I am aware of that. I used to admire him for his principles and his generous intentions. But what good are they, finally? You can't eat them. You can't depend on them. There's no security in principles.

You should be proud of him, Willa said. So few of us have the beliefs he has. And fewer still act on them.

Then the boy John Wesley stood up in the middle of the sanctuary, where he'd been sitting in embarrassment staring at the floor, his face in his hands. Now he was angry. Shut up! he shouted. Shut up! You don't know anything, you stupid old woman! Be quiet! Leave my mother alone.

Then, as on the previous Sunday, the usher came hurrying down the aisle. Stop it! We won't have this again! We had it once, but we won't again. This is the church.

You shut up too! the boy cried. All of you! Everyone stop talking! Leave us alone! And he turned out of the pew and ran back up the aisle and out the big doors.

They watched him, in shock and amazement, and then they turned once more to look at Lyle's wife. She appeared to be crying now—her hands over her face. She started to move slowly, gropingly up the aisle, her head lowered, following her son, then near the back of the church she dropped her hands and began to hurry and she rushed out. The usher came all the way down to the front. He looked all around. What should I do with these? He held up the church bulletins.

Never mind, Willa said. We don't need them anymore, Wayne.

We got so many, he said.

Yes, she said. Thank you for taking care of them. Maybe you'd better shut up the church now.

She and Alene went out and the woman at the piano closed the lid over the piano keys and walked away and the rest of the small congregation filed out of the church, not talking any more than they had the previous Sunday, moving quietly. The usher began to close up the high stained-glass windows with his hooked pole.

When Lyle left the church he went home to the parsonage and walked directly through the house and out the back door to the garage and climbed in the car and drove out on the narrow blacktop to the south, driving fast but slowing after a few miles and turning east on one of the county roads. He drove without motive or destination and after a while he came to the sandhills and stopped to look at three horses standing in a pasture. He got out and walked down through the ditch weeds and stood at the barbed-wire fence. The horses watched him, two red mares and a colt. One of the mares came forward and he held out his hand and she nuzzled it and backed away. Then the mare and the two others turned and walked off. He went back to his car and drove on along the section roads, all running north and south or east and west, straight and surveyed and exact, and after an aimless hour of driving he came to the Johnsons' place.

They were already home from church, not having wanted to see anyone or talk to anyone, and at home they'd taken their Sunday dresses off and changed into soft worn housedresses and had sat at the kitchen table and had eaten tomato sandwiches, the tomatoes from their own garden, and had drunk iced tea. They'd spoken only a little about what had happened at church. Then they heard the car on the gravel coming up to the house. Alene got up and looked out the kitchen window. It's him, she said. Reverend Lyle.

Oh good Lord, Willa said. What would he want?

Let's find out, Alene said.

He'll want to talk, Willa said.

Maybe he will. That's all right if he does.

They went to the porch and stood waiting as they had when Lorraine and Alice had come to visit in the previous week. Lyle climbed out and looked over the roof of his car at the women and at the barn and corrals and pens and the windmill and the outbuildings and sheds. He turned back to the women again and walked around the rear of the car and stopped. Would you mind if I rest a moment?

No. For goodness' sake, Willa said. Come in. Won't you?

I'd like to.

Yes, Alene said, do please come in.

He came up the little sidewalk in the yard and followed the women into the kitchen.

This is pleasant in here, Lyle said. It's very cool and peaceful.

It always stays cool in this part of the house, Willa said. Because of the shade trees and the porch.

And you keep the windows open, Lyle said.

We almost never close these windows in summer. There's almost always a breeze. Will you sit down?

I'd like to wash my hands first, if you wouldn't mind.

The bathroom's there, Willa said.

He went inside and shut the door and when he came out Alene was clearing the table.

Do you prefer to sit here or in the living room? Willa said.

This is fine here, Lyle said. Don't you think?

Have you had anything to eat?

No.

We have cheese and tomato for sandwiches, Alene said. Or I could make you a bacon lettuce tomato sandwich.

Thank you. I'd like that.

Please sit down. We don't stand on any formalities here.

He sat down at the table and Willa seated herself across from him.

Alene brought the iced tea and began frying bacon in a black iron skillet.

I saw the name on the mailbox, Lyle said. That's how I found you. I thought it must be you.

Yes. We've been here a long time. My husband grew up on this ranch and then we lived here after we were married and then Alene came. After she went away to college and started teaching, it was just the two of us again until he died.

When did he die?

It's been thirty years now, Willa said. I've been without my husband for thirty years. He had a heart attack out in the calf pen at night checking for new calves. I was the one who found him. I went out in my nightgown and overcoat with a flashlight and there he was on the ground with his eyes staring up.

I'm sorry. That must have been hard.

Yes, it was, she said softly. I've often wondered, is it better to have these years with someone you love and then have to remember and compare ever afterward and feel the lack of him. She glanced at Alene. Or never to have had that other person so you don't have to keep remembering what it used to be.

I'd have to say it's better to have loved that person, Lyle said.

Alene brought the sandwich to the table on one of the delicate old plates with the blue grapes painted on it and poured a bag of potato chips into a bowl and refilled Lyle's iced tea glass.

Can I get you anything else?

No. But thank you very much.

She sat down next to him across from her mother. He began to eat. They watched him, he ate in big bites, they wouldn't have guessed that he would. There had not been a man eating in their kitchen for a long time.

He ate half of his sandwich and began on the other. His face looked sore and swollen. I saw you at church, he said. Did anything happen after I left?

Yes, Willa said. You may not want to hear about it, though.

What was it?

Your wife got up and came down front, Alene said, and spoke to us.

What did she say?

She said she admired your principles, but she said you can't eat principles.

He smiled. She's right there.

Can we tell you what else she said? Willa said.

Of course.

I'm afraid she said she would have to leave now. Leave Holt, she meant.

I'm not surprised at that. She's talked about it before.

She mentioned Denver and what happened there. Your son was very angry.

Did he say anything?

He shouted at us and ran out. I don't blame him.

What will you do? Alene said.

He wiped his mouth on the napkin and looked out the window above the sink. I don't know, he said. I think I'm done.

You don't mean that, Willa said.

Yes. I'm finished as a minister. I haven't done much good.

But people will get over this.

Probably they will. But I won't. People don't want to be disturbed. They want assurance. They don't come to church on Sunday morning to think about new ideas or even the old important ones. They want to hear what they've been told before, with only some small variation on what they've been hearing all their lives, and then they want to go home and eat pot roast and say it was a good service and feel satisfied.

But you shouldn't make up your mind yet, Willa said. I hope you won't.

I think I already have, he said.

People make things unhappy, Alene said.

I would guess you know something about that.

A little, she said. All life is moving through some kind of unhappiness, isn't it.

I don't know. I didn't used to think so.

But there's some good too, Willa said. I insist on that.

There are brief moments, Alene said. This is one of them.

They looked at Lyle sitting quietly, his swollen face shining in the sun coming in the window.

I'll have to meet with the assembly director and the ministerial relations board. They'll want there to be some kind of a meeting about this, to make it all official.

33

THEY DIDN'T EVEN KNOW she was gone until half the morning had passed. Dad woke late and turned his head on the pillow and saw she was not in the bed, though that was not unusual, she often was up and dressed and out in the kitchen working by the time he woke. He called for her. Then he tried to push out of bed but was too weak and called again. Finally he couldn't wait any longer. He wet the diaper he was wearing and he lay there wet and sopping under his pajamas, feeling angry and uncomfortable.

After a while Lorraine came in. Where's Mom?

I don't know. I been calling for her.

She's nowhere in the house, Lorraine said. I can't find her.

Is she over next door?

Maybe. Can I help you, Daddy?

I made a mess of things.

Did you?

I'm all wet down here on myself. Some of it might of come out. I got to get out of bed but I can't without somebody helping me.

Will you let me change you and put some dry clothes on?

I want Mom here.

I know. But Mom isn't here right now, Daddy.

Where is she?

I'll have to find out. Let's get you cleaned up first.

She helped him from the bed and he hobbled into the bathroom in his sagging pajamas and stood like a child at the hospital commode while she peeled off his pants and the diaper. She handed him a washcloth to clean himself and afterward she washed his skinny behind. He was shaking. Goose bumps appeared on his flanks and legs.

Do you want to sit down here for a while? she said. See if you can go some more?

Yeah. I better.

She went out, giving him his privacy, and looked out the front window to the street and came back and helped him put on a new diaper and clean sweatpants and a cardigan sweater. He came out of the bathroom shuffling, sliding his feet in his slippers, using his cane, and moved to his chair by the window.

The car isn't here, Lorraine said. I just looked. She must have gone to the store.

She's been gone too long for that. You want to ask Berta May if she knows where she is? You'll have to go over there. She don't answer the phone every time.

Next door Lorraine stood on the front porch and when Berta May came to the door they went inside the house and Berta May said she hadn't seen her mother this morning. Then Alice came in and they asked her and she told them she was riding her bike when Mrs. Lewis came up in the car and said, Now you be careful out here. Are you watching for cars? And I said I was watching.

Then what?

Then she drove away.

Do you remember what she was wearing? Lorraine said.

She had a dress on.

You're sure.

Yes. A blue one.

Back at home Lorraine began to look around more carefully and she found the note now that had blown off or fallen off under the little stand where the phone was located.

It was written in brief neat script, with no salutation and no closing, just the one line. I went to find Frank.

———

She had gotten up early from the bed when it was just turning light outside. Dad looked gray in the dim light, breathing slow and hard, his mouth belling out when he exhaled, making a rattling kind of noise. She removed her nightgown and pulled the dress off the hanger in the dark closet where she'd hung it the night before, and put it on and carried her shoes out to the kitchen, turning the light on there, and sat down on a kitchen chair to tie her shoes. She put bread in the toaster and started coffee, then went back into the bathroom to wash her face and apply a little lipstick to her mouth, watching herself in the mirror, her deeply wrinkled face, and brushed her thick short white hair. When she went back to the kitchen, the coffee was ready and she filled a thermos and spread butter on the toast, put it in a plastic bag, and took the thermos and her purse and went silently out the front door into the beautiful cool Sunday morning.

In the street she stopped to talk to Alice on her bicycle and then headed west on U.S. 34, toward Brush, and passed Fort Morgan on the interstate and went on toward Denver. Along the way she drank the coffee and ate the toast.

She was all right until she got to Denver. But then there was a lot of road construction and they had the men at work even on a Sunday morning. She got lost in the detours and roadblocks and ended up in the north side of the city. It was half an hour before she had any idea where she was at all.

She pulled into a corner gas station. There were no other cars at the pumps or parked at the cinder-block office but she could see an old man sitting behind the counter. She got out and locked the car and looked all around and went inside. The man looked up. He wasn't as old as she had thought. It was just that he had gray hair, which was combed back on both sides of his head, with a wave pulled up above his face in the way the boys used to do when she was young. He'd been reading a newspaper spread out on the counter.

Good morning, she said.

Yeah. Morning.

I'm just going to tell you right out. I'm lost. All that construction turned me in the wrong direction. I'm trying to get downtown.

Lady, he said, you don't ever want to tell people you're lost. You don't know what they might do to you.

Oh, I don't think people would do anything to me. Look at me here. I'm an old woman. She stood in the middle of the little room watching him.

You never know, he said. You can't tell.

All right, I won't say it again. But can you help me or not, do you think?

Yeah. I can help you.

He got up and went over to the rack on the wall next to the entrance and took down a map of Denver.

Oh, she said. Do you have to do all that?

What else am I going to do?

He went around to his side of the counter and opened the map and showed her where she was and pointed out the streets to take downtown.

But I can't drive according to maps, she said.

He looked at her. Why not?

I don't know. I just can't. It's the way I look at things and the way my mind works.

Well, can you just remember, if I tell you?

No. Not like I used to.

I don't know what I'm going to do then. What do you want me to do?

I want you to tell me slowly and I'll write it down. I'll take the turns you say, left or right, from off the paper.

But I got this map here for you. It'd be the same thing.

No, a map wouldn't do any good.

Well, he said. If that's what you want.

Then he told her very patiently and she wrote on the blank side of a flyer for a car auction all the directions he gave her, and folded the paper and put it in her purse.

How's the gas in your car? he said. You don't want to take any chances.

Thank you for asking. I'm all right that way. But I wonder if I could use your restroom.

Go ahead. It's right there.

The restroom wasn't very clean. She put paper down on the toilet and afterward washed her hands thoroughly, and looking in the mirror she applied some new lipstick, and she thought her red mouth and her white hair looked striking together, then she came back out to the office where the man was. Thank you, she said. I feel like I ought to buy something, for all your trouble.

Is there something you need in here?

No. I don't think so.

Then you don't need to buy anything. It's no trouble. Just don't tell nobody else you're lost.

I'm not lost now, she said. Aren't these directions good?

Yeah, they'll get you there.

Thank you, she said. You're a good man.

No, he said. He looked out toward the gas pumps. I don't know if my wife would agree with you.

Why not?

All the water under the bridge.

You mean something happened.

Yeah.

But you're still together.

As of this morning we are.

Do you still want to stay with her?

She's the one I want. Always has been. There's no mix-up in that direction.

Then you've got to make her see it that way.

Doing what?

I don't know. That's for you to know.

I'm pretty sure she's give up on me.

No, she hasn't. I doubt if she has. You wouldn't still be in the house.

No. I think she has. She's give up. It's over for her. She don't feel the same way no more.

But you're a good man, I can see that. I could write her a note as a testimony.

Oh lord, wouldn't that be something.

Do you want me to?

Yeah. Sure. Why not? Hell, what harm's it going to do?

You have any more paper to write on?

Sure. Write on this.

He gave her another flyer with a blank back.

What's your name? she said.

Ed.

She started to write, then stopped. Your wife's name?

Mary.

That's my name, she said.

Glad to meet you, he said. He stuck his hand out above the counter and they shook hands. She wrote, Dear Mary, you don't know me but I met your husband Ed this morning at the gas station and he was very kind to me. I have the feeling he's a good man. I have a good one at home myself so I know, even if some people might not think so but I've known him for fifty years. I wish all happy days for you. Signed, Mary Lewis, your friend (unknown). She folded the paper. Don't read that till I get away from here, she said.

Why's that now?

It wouldn't be any good then. It would jinx it.

I won't, he said. You take care of yourself now.

I'm on my way to see my son, she said, and went out and got in the car and drove away.

———

In downtown Denver there wasn't much traffic yet since it was still only midmorning on a Sunday, and by sheer luck and instinct she drove to the street where Frank's apartment was located and parked and locked the car doors and walked up the sidewalk to the porch of the old run-down frame house. It had not been painted in the years since she and Dad had been there. She knocked and waited. She looked at the next house and it looked just like this one. She tried the door. It was unlocked. She stepped into the dark hallway which ran back to two closed doors the way she remembered, and she went quietly up the stairs to the apartment where Frank had lived. A short Mexican woman came to the door. A program in Spanish was playing on the TV behind her. Is Frank here? she said.

What?

Does Frank still live here?

Is no Frank here.

Mary looked at the other doors. Have you been here a long time?

Me?

Yes. How long has it been since you moved here?

I don't know.

You don't know?

Not very long.

Is anybody else here?

My husband is sleeping.

She looked past the woman into the apartment. I'm looking for my son. I'm looking for Frank Lewis.

I don't know this man.

We haven't seen him for a long time. I don't know where he is. He wouldn't talk to us.

No? Why?

Because of him and my husband. What happened between them. And all of us.

Did he hit him?

No. It wasn't like that.

Oh, I'm sorry for you.

Mary looked at her, and her eyes smarted with tears now. Thank you, she said.

I'm sorry you can't see your son.

Thank you for your kindness.

Then the woman suddenly reached and hugged her and Mary held the woman tightly in return and stepped back and thanked her again and managed to smile a little and went down to her car. She sat a while. Then she drove until she found Broadway and the corner café that Frank had worked in and parked where Dad had parked when they had come looking for Frank on that winter evening when the floodlights were all lighted up at Civic Center.

The inside of the café wasn't black and white anymore, but all yellow and brown. There were a lot of people out on Sunday morning eating brunch. She stood at the door waiting until someone would come to lead her to a booth or table. She couldn't see Frank among the waiters hurrying in the room.

Then she was seated at a small table near the back and she ordered a breakfast of eggs and toast and coffee and sat watching the people with their families and their friends, they all had someone to dine with and talk to. The waitress who came was a young girl. Later when she brought the bill Mary said, You don't know anybody by the name of Frank do you?

You mean here?

Yes. Somebody who works here.

There's nobody by that name here.

He might have been called Franklin.

You could ask Janine. She's worked here the longest.

Where is she?

That's her over there.

Would you ask her if I could talk to her?

We're pretty busy.

Just for a minute. Would you ask her, please?

The girl went over to the woman wearing red-framed eyeglasses, she looked too old to still be working. The girl said something to her and after a while the woman came over. You're looking for somebody?

I'm looking for a young man named Frank. Or he might have called himself Franklin.

Franklin Lewis? He used to be here. When I first started he was working here. That was a long time ago.

I know. It would have to be. He's not here now?

He's been gone for years. And he wouldn't be very young now. I'm lucky I even remember him.

Where did he go?

No idea. Him and his boyfriend took off someplace together.

His boyfriend.

That younger kid he was with.

Why did they leave?

The waitress looked at her closely. Ma'am, how much of this do you want to know?

Whatever you can tell me.

All right then. The owner found Franklin with some of the café's money. I heard he'd been taking it for months.

I don't believe that.

You said you wanted to hear this.

I don't believe Frank would steal.

He had some of the money, that's all I know. I don't remember how they discovered it but the owner gave him a break, told him he could just give it back and leave.

He must have had a reason, Mary said. Her eyes filled with tears again.

I'm sorry. Can I get you something?

No. I'm all right. I just need to sit a minute.

The old waitress moved away and Mary sat still for a while and then stood up and placed money on the table and went out to her car. It was a little past noon.

———

She was four hours driving home. She drove cautiously getting out of Denver and went too slow on the interstate so that cars and trucks racing past honked at her. By the time she reached Brush she was so tired that she stopped in the parking lot at McDonald's and put the seat back and rolled the windows down. She went to sleep at once. An hour and a half later when she woke she was sweaty and hot.

She started the car, turning the air-conditioning on, and ordered a large cup of iced tea at the drive-up window and then drove back to Holt through the wide-open flat country and the mile roads and the pastures and the stubble. In town she turned north on her own street and looked at all the houses and then parked at home. She took her purse and the empty thermos and passed through the wrought iron gate and on up to the house. It was quiet inside. As soon as she stepped through the door Lorraine came out from the kitchen. Mom. Are you all right? You look tired. You had us scared.

I'm all right.

You shouldn't take off like that all alone.

Well, I did.

And you're all right. Nothing happened.

I'm worn out, that's all.

Did you find him?

No. He wasn't at the café.

That was so long ago, Mom.

I had to look somewhere. I tried his apartment too. I don't know where he is. He's disappeared. He's out in the world someplace, in thin air. He's not coming back.

No. I don't think he is, Mom. He doesn't want to be found any-more.

I can't just forget him. I can't.

I know.

Well, she said. She put her purse and the thermos on the table and looked around. How's Dad?

About the same. Maybe a little worse.

What did he say about me leaving?

He didn't know what to say. Neither one of us did.

Well, I'm back now.

She walked into the bedroom and he was lying on his back, the sheet over him. He turned to see her. His eyes looked dull. Is that you? he said.

Yes, honey. I'm home now.

Did you find him?

No. I never found him. She came close to the bed. How are you this evening?

Not much good.

34

THEY MET IN THE BASEMENT of the church in what was called the fellowship hall. A big open room with a kitchen at the back, with the smell of mold rising from behind the trim at the edges, and long folding tables and metal chairs stacked against the wall, and an old upright piano in the corner.

Outside the church the light was beginning to fade, and there was a little breeze. But it was dark down in the basement and the recessed ceiling lights had been switched on.

The five members of the ministerial relations board were there along with the assembly director from Greeley, a middle-aged man with bifocal glasses. He was wearing a white shirt and tie but it was a warm evening and he had draped his coat over a chair. They all sat around one of the long tables that had been unfolded and set up.

The director had opened the meeting with a prayer and then they had begun to discuss Reverend Lyle. The board wanted to put this outrage and unhappiness and disruption behind them, they wanted Lyle to be replaced, to be discharged and not to be allowed to preach in Holt again.

Maybe he doesn't even want to, one board member said. He wasn't here this last Sunday.

No, he was here, one of the others said. He just didn't do any preaching.

Would you be willing to allow him to stay, the director said, if I talked to him and he agreed to avoid this kind of controversy?

I don't want to take the chance, the first man said. There's no knowing what he'll say when he gets up in the pulpit. You can't trust him. He could say anything.

But I think he would be willing to make some kind of promise if I talk to him.

I don't even want to try.

What about the rest of the board here?

They looked back at the director, in his tie and white shirt, and didn't say anything.

I've spoken to him by phone, he said, but I haven't seen him yet. Does he look pretty bad? I understand he was attacked.

Attacked. I wouldn't call it that, another man said.

What would you call it? I heard two men stopped him at night and beat him.

He was out wandering around town at night, looking in people's houses. What would you expect? After what he said in church.

And you think that justifies what those men did. Settling the score for the whole town, so to speak.

I'm not saying that. Did I say that?

But they did hurt him.

A little. Not much. I don't think he was hurt very bad.

That makes it all right then.

No. Somebody roughed him up. We know that. But nobody knows who. If anybody knows who it was they aren't saying. And he never made any complaint or accusation to the police. It wasn't much anyway.

So he's all right now. He's not seriously hurt.

He's able to talk at least, the first man said. Like we said, he came to church last Sunday and spoke a little.

What did he say?

I wasn't there. I heard he just said that he didn't have anything more to say. He told people to go home. It wasn't a sermon.

It was then that Willa and Alene Johnson opened the basement door and looked in at the board members and the director.

Yes? the chairman said. We're meeting here, Willa. This is a board meeting.

We know you're meeting. That's why we're here.

But you're not on the board. This is a private conference.

I know, Tom. I've been on the board myself. Before you were even a member of the church, when you were still just a little boy scurrying around here in the basement bothering people.

She and her daughter stepped into the room and shut the door. Willa was carrying her purse. Otherwise they had nothing with them. They came up to the table where the five men and the director were sitting, watching them.

I want to talk to you, Willa said.

But you shouldn't even be here, the chairman said. I've already told you. You must see that.

I know what the rules say, but we're here nevertheless.

Let's let her speak, the director said. If you don't mind, I'd like to hear her.

But this isn't the normal way, the chairman said. This isn't official now. We're going off record now.

Have we met before? the director said, looking at Willa.

Yes, but you don't remember. I'm Mrs. Willa Johnson and this is my daughter Alene Johnson. We're both longtime members of this church.

It's good to see you. Will you sit down?

I don't think so. I don't expect we'll be here long enough to bother with chairs. We know what you're doing here.

We're talking about your minister.

You're talking about removing him. About refusing to let him stay here and preach to us anymore.

That's still under discussion. We haven't decided that yet.

You will, she said. Before you do, I'm going to say something in his behalf. She looked at Alene. We're both going to say something.

That would be appreciated, the director said. If you can help us be fair and just, we'd like to hear from you.

Oh, we don't expect you to be fair, Alene said. That's not going to happen. That would be a shock to everybody here.

Wait now, the chairman said. That's too much.

No. It's not, she said. He was trying to remind us of the truth. The real truth. To help us to think bigger than we do. We need to listen to him. But we're not. Not enough of us.

That wasn't the truth, one of the men said. That was just insanity. Craziness.

It's in the Bible, Willa said. Do you think the Gospel of Luke is craziness?

That was out of context. He takes it literally.

Don't you? Aren't we supposed to? At least that passage?

Not here. Not now. Not like that.

Yes. Right here, right now.

My God, are you that ignorant, woman? There's a war going on.

There shouldn't be, she said.

Wait, the director said. That's not the issue. Let's just calm down. This isn't helping. Let us pray again. I think we should. He looked at them. Will you all pray with me? He bowed his head and folded his hands on top of the table.

So they prayed again, but it didn't change anything. Afterward they would not allow the Johnson women to say whatever else they had come to say and the chairman led them each by the arm across the room to the door and went up with them to the street. It was dark now and the corner lights had come on.

I thought better of you than this, Tom, Willa said. I thought you were a better man.

You shouldn't have come here.

We had every right to come here. We're members of the church.

No. You didn't have the right. We're the duly elected board. But I'm not getting into that again. Is your car here? Will you be all right? Watch your step in the dark.

You need to watch your step too, Tom. And don't ever touch me again, please.

Good night. He went back to the basement.

———

In the basement they went on talking.

Do all of you want Reverend Lyle to leave? the director said. You don't seem to have given him much chance and opportunity to prove himself. Have you already made up your minds?

Is he kind of stupid? one man said. Is he slow? Is that the trouble with him?

Maybe he's having a breakdown, one of the others said.

He's like some kind of ignorant and dangerous boy. Wanting the world. Wanting what's on the other side of the store window and making trouble for everybody around him.

What is wrong with him anyway? the board chairman said. You know him.

Nothing's wrong with him, the director said.

Something is. Look at what's happened here.

And Denver too. Or he wouldn't have been sent out here. We wouldn't have got him. He wouldn't have been given this charge. We all know that.

You shouldn't have sent him. This isn't a good place for someone like him. With his ideas.

It wasn't only my decision, the director said. Others help make these choices.

Then those others screwed up.

Here now, the director said. We don't need that kind of talk.

But it was a bad mistake. Say it how you want to.

I think he's a good man, one man said who hadn't spoken yet. I can see that. That's not in question. He's someone with a vision of how it could be.

Not here though.

Maybe not here, maybe not now. But it could be. It's like what the Johnson women were saying.

Never mind that, the first man said. Let's get this over with. Let's vote.

———

Afterward the director stayed behind. He called Lyle on the phone. Will you come over now? We're finished talking. I'd like to speak with you now.

Where are you? Are you still in the church?

Yes, in the basement.

We could go upstairs and talk in my office.

No. I have all my materials down here. This'll be fine.

Lyle left the house and walked out in the mild evening and went down the steps to the basement hall where the director was waiting at the long table. The director had gotten himself a glass of water in the kitchen and he was sitting with the half-empty glass and his notes and papers in front of him. He had put his suit coat on again. He stood up when Lyle came in and they shook hands. Lyle was wearing old jeans and a T-shirt. He sat down on the same side of the table as the director with three of the empty chairs between them.

You didn't bother to dress up tonight, I see, the director said.

No. I assume the decision has been made already.

I thought you might have put on appropriate attire out of respect for the greater Church, if not for me.

Does it matter?

The formalities matter.

It still comes out the same.

The director took a sip of water from his glass.

So. Is this what you want? What's happened here tonight?

It wasn't. But it is now.

You've done what you could to make it come out like this. Haven't you.

How much time do I have? I will need some time to move my family.

You don't even ask if you can be reassigned.

No.

Don't you want to be?

No. I'm done. I'm finished with all of this.

We could probably reassign you as associate pastor somewhere. If you agreed to cooperate.

No, I don't think so.

It doesn't have to be this abrupt, so all-of-a-sudden.

Yes it does, finally. It was headed this way for years. It's just taken this long to get to this day.

The director stacked the papers on the table in front of him. You don't understand, do you?

What don't I understand?

How to make changes. How to transform things and move people in God's direction gradually. It doesn't have to be fire and brimstone. Bombast and arm waving.

I'm sure I never waved my arms.

But you take my point. Changes can be made by slow accretion.

Not in my experience. I don't see it.

Well, you didn't, and you haven't. That's true. Still, I want to give you time to reconsider. To sleep on it and reflect and pray over this tonight.

I'm not changing my mind.

It wouldn't be official until the decision had gone through the formalities and the appropriate channels and the church hierarchies, then they would talk again. The director insisted on shaking hands once more and gathered up his papers, put them in a briefcase and went out the door. Lyle stayed behind and carried the water glass the director had used to the kitchen and washed and dried it and put it away in the cupboard and stacked the chairs against the wall and put away the table. He turned the lights off and went back up to ground level. A car was going by on the dark street. He walked home in the quiet night.

———

At the parsonage he called his wife and son into the kitchen and they sat at the table looking at him. Is it over? she said.

I'll tell you.

Then he told them: the board had made its decision tonight, he was being discharged and they'd have to leave. But they had time to consider what to do, until the end of summer. They could stay in the house in the meantime while they decided.

I'm going now, she said. I'll leave tomorrow. I won't wait. It was bad enough coming to a place where they didn't want you in the first place, but the shame of being dismissed . . . I can imagine the glances and the whispers now. How people will act in the stores. I won't endure that.

It's not shame, he said. That's not what this is. It's something different from that. I don't feel shame.

Well, don't tell me about it, she said. I don't want to hear it.

Mom, John Wesley said, I'm going with you.

Oh, you poor boy, she said. What a hard time for you. She lifted her hand to his face but he pulled away.

I'm coming with you.

No. You can't. Stay here with Dad. For a while longer. Just for a while. Wait till I have a job and a place for us. We don't even have a place to put our heads down in Denver. You can come when I find something.

Yes, that's better, Lyle said. Your mother needs time. Stay with me, son. He turned again to his wife. You're sure this is what you want to do? Or should you stay until we figure out what we're all going to do?

It'll be a relief. .

You don't think about me, the boy said. He was close to tears. Neither one of you does. You never do.

He stood up shoving the chair out of the way, it fell over backward, and he ran out of the room.

Let him go, she said. He needs a chance to take this in.

They stayed in the kitchen talking and afterward she went upstairs and began to pack.

35

WE HAVE TO GO over there a last time, Berta May said. I want to tell him good-bye. I want you to come with me.

Why?

Because he likes you so much.

He's never told me.

He wouldn't. But he does, I know that. It will be good for him to see a young person again.

I don't want to, Grandma. He scares me.

He's just an old man. He might be in bed or he might be sitting up in his chair by the window. It doesn't matter. We'll just stay a little while.

I don't want to go back in his bedroom.

He won't hurt you. Now don't you make a fuss. Do you hear?

Yes.

All right. Now take the scissors out to the garden and cut some flowers so we can take them to him.

She went out to the garden and cut a red zinnia, leaving the stem long with the leaves on it, and brought it inside.

You only cut this one?

Yes.

How come?

I just wanted one. I thought he'd like it.

All right. Go wash your hands and brush your hair, then we'll go.

Berta May telephoned next door. Is this a good time to come over for a minute to see Dad?

Yes, Mary said. He's sitting up if you'll come now.

We're on our way.

They went out across to the gate under the trees and up to the house and Mary let them in. Dad was at the window in his pajamas, a blanket spread over his legs, looking gray and thin. He stared at them when they entered the room and Berta May came over and he slowly lifted his hand and she took it and held it and then she gestured for Alice to come. The girl walked across the room, holding the flower in front of her, and presented it to Dad. He looked at her and his mouth moved in a whisper. Thank you. Mary took the flower and Dad said in the same whispery voice, Put it in a vase.

I will, honey.

And bring it back.

Yes.

Berta May patted his shoulder and turned and sat down on the couch, and Alice sat with her, next to Lorraine who pulled her close and kissed her cheek. Mary came back with the flower in a glass vase half-filled with water and put the flower on the windowsill and Dad looked at it and turned to look at Berta May and Alice. Every time Alice looked at Dad he was watching her. She couldn't tell what he might mean by looking at her in that way.

Mary, Dad whispered. Bring me my box from the bedroom.

Your cedar box?

Yes.

She stood up and left the room and the others sat looking out the window. Another hot day, Lorraine said. You can see the way the tree leaves look so limp already.

We can be glad it cools off at night, said Berta May. I don't know what we'd do otherwise.

Live with it, Lorraine said. Or get air-conditioning.

Mary came back with the red cedar box that had a lid that closed with a brass fastener. She set it in Dad's lap on top of the blanket. He tried to open it but his fingers couldn't manage the small lock. You do it, he said.

She lifted the lid and he looked across the room at Alice. Would you come back here? he whispered.

Do you mean me?

Yes. If you would.

She looked up at her grandmother.

Go ahead, Berta May said. There's nothing to be afraid of.

She came across the room and Mary put her arm around her and then sat down in her chair.

Take something, Dad said.

What is it?

Look inside here. It's just old things.

She moved closer and began to look at things and put them back. Arrowheads, snake rattles, wartime tokens from the 1940s, a pocket-knife, a ruby ring, a thick pocket watch, old silver dollars, a little box of wood matches.

You see anything you want? he said.

But these are your things, she said.

I want to give you one.

You don't care?

Whatever you want.

She picked a snake rattle.

That's not much, he said. Take something more.

She held up one of the arrowheads.

He fumbled in the box and brought out two of the old smooth silver dollars and handed them to her and shut the lid.

Then without warning he reached up to touch her face. She jerked away. He let his hands fall and he looked at her, his eyes watery and staring.

What do you want to do? she said. I don't know what you want.

I wanted to touch your face, he whispered. That's all.

She looked at him. Go ahead, she said. She leaned over closer to him.

He raised both hands again and held her face in his old loose-skinned hands and shut his eyes. She watched him, she could see his eyes moving beneath his closed eyelids. His hands felt papery and cold on her face. Then he released her. She looked at him. Thank you for these things, she said softly, and turned and went to sit again with Berta May and Lorraine and showed them what she had. Dad stared out the window. Soon he was asleep.

When they got up to leave, Berta May said, Don't wake him. We'll just slip out.

Thank you for coming, Mary said. I know he wanted to see you once more.

That afternoon when Lorraine came in to his bedroom he was asleep under the sheet in the new pajamas they had bought in the department store on Main Street. His mouth was open, his closed eyelids fluttering, and his hands were rested over his chest. She thought at first that he had died and she came to the bed and bent over his face, then she could feel the faint air he blew out and could smell his sour breath.

She sat down in the chair next to the bed. The window was open overlooking the backyard, the brown shade was pulled down to keep the sun out. It was dim in the room and the air was warm but not hot.

Dad woke and opened his eyes. He stared at Lorraine and she smiled at him. He lifted his hand toward her and she held it, looking into his eyes.

Hello, Daddy, she said.

Yes. Hello. He spoke very quietly, slowly.

Daddy, when you were touching Alice's face, what were you thinking?

That was this morning.

Yes.

I just wanted to touch a girl's soft face again.

Did you touch mine like that when I was little?

He stared at her for a long time. I don't think so.

Why didn't you?

I was too busy. I wasn't paying attention.

No, she said. You weren't. She lifted his hand to her cheek now.

Forgive me, he whispered. I missed a lot of things. I could of done better. I always loved you.

You never told me that when I was her age.

Can you forgive that too?

Yes, Daddy.

I want to tell you now, he said.

She watched him, his watery eyes staring at her.

I loved you, he whispered. I always did. I approved of you completely. I do today.

She kissed his hand and put it back on his chest and leaned far over and kissed him on his cracked lips.

Thank you, Daddy. I feel the same way. I hope you know that.

He shut his eyes, the tears squeezed out onto his cheeks. She stayed next to him, not talking anymore, and when he went to sleep again she went out and climbed the stairs to her room on the second floor and lay down in the bed in the hot afternoon while the wind blew the curtains in and out at the window.

36

AT THE PARSONAGE John Wesley used most of that same long hot summer afternoon to clear everything from his computer. Then as the day stretched toward the end, when the sun had moved far westward, he came out of the bedroom and walked down the hall to his parents' room at the front of the house and looked in the drawers in the walnut bureau that had belonged to his mother, but she had taken all her clothes and makeup with her to Denver. He drew the curtain back from the window and looked out at the corner of the street and into the high branches of the trees. The late-afternoon light in the street had a slanted look. He walked back down the hall and searched the upstairs bathroom in the cabinets and chests, but there was none of her mascara or lipstick on the shelves or in the drawers.

Downstairs in the kitchen he took out the box of wood matches from the junk drawer together with a flat dish from the cupboard and carried them into the bathroom. He struck a match and smeared the charcoal end on his fingers, it made a black stain. He lighted a dozen more matches and set them in the dish. Then he began to blacken his face. When he was finished he stood looking at himself in the cabinet mirror, all his face was dark now, and he shut the light off and dumped the match ends in the trash can and rinsed the dish and put it away and drank a glass of water at the sink and went out the door to the garage.

There was a long narrow driveway running alongside the house to the garage. Grass had grown up in the gravel. In the garage he pulled the overhead door shut and locked it and locked the side door. Light filtered in from the small windows at the sides.

From the rear of the garage he brought out an old wood chair and set it in the middle of the floor where the fine dirt was black and shiny with oil leaks from the car. Then he brought out the wood box from under the workbench. On the bench were a steel vise and cans of nails and old hammers and wrenches all coated with oily dust. He set the box on the chair.

After that he got out the cotton rope he'd bought at the hardware store on Main Street and hidden in the corner by the workbench.

Then he stood next to the chair and threw one end of the rope over a rafter, making the fine dust from all the years sift down and hang in the air, and tied a knot in the rope and pulled it tight. He leaned against the rope to test if it would hold.

Then he walked over to the window and looked out at the back-yard where his father had started a garden. He looked past the yard to the neighbors'. Through the trees he could see the town water tower, with Holt spelled out in red, at night it was always lit up but he wouldn't see that anymore, and he crossed to the other side and looked out west across the street. Nobody there. Nothing happening.

He came back and climbed up on the box and immediately he lost his balance and had to step off. The box tumbled down. He brushed the dirt off and set it back on the chair and stood up on it slowly, carefully, leaning and tottering, then stood still. He reached around behind and brought the rope over his shoulder so that it hung in front of him. He held it for a moment, looking at it. Then he tied a slipknot and fit the loop over his head and drew it tight around his neck, with the knot at the back of his head just under the bulge of the skull, and let the loose end fall behind him. Then he lowered his hands and arms to his sides.

For a long time, for maybe twenty minutes, he stood without mov-ing. He turned once and looked out the window at the day and all the nearby world. The light was lower now. In the garage it was darker than it was outside.

———

Out on the high plains the sun went down and disappeared beyond the low flat horizon. The boy still stood on the box with the rope around his neck.

He hadn't been able to make himself kick the box out from under his feet. Then he discovered that he couldn't untie the knot behind his head without moving the box. If he moved at all the box tipped. He began to cry, without daring to move, as the room darkened. The tears left runnels in the charcoal on his face. He watched afraid, as the light seeped out of the room. He couldn't hear anything outside.

It had been completely dark for an hour when his father came home and the headlights of the car came tipping and rocking up the gravel drive. Then the headlights went off and he heard the car door shut and heard his father going up the back steps into the house. He called to him, but there was no answer. Then after a while Lyle came back out of the house to the garage and tried to open the door. He peered in through the window.

Dad.

What's going on? Are you in there?

Help me, Dad.

Why? What are you doing?

Help me.

Lyle smashed the window with a rock and reached in and unlocked the door and stepped inside.

Dad, don't touch me.

What is this? What are you doing?

You can't touch me. You might push me off.

My God.

Help me get down. You'll have to cut the rope.

I'll turn the car lights on.

No, don't. Somebody might see me. Just get a flashlight. Please.

Lyle stood looking up at his son's dark face. I'll be right back, he said. Don't move.

He rushed into the house and came back with a flashlight and a kitchen knife and played the beam over the boy's face, blackened and smeared, tracked by tears.

God Almighty, son. Oh my Lord.

You can't tell Mom. You promise?

What do you mean? She has to know.

I don't want her to know. Promise me, Dad. Nobody else either.

I have to get you down from there first. He got a stepladder from the side of the garage and stood it next to the rope.

Dad. Don't bump me.

I know, son. Be quiet.

You can't even touch me.

Stay quiet now. Hush.

He climbed the ladder slowly and shone the flashlight up and down the rope and over the boy's frightened face and cut the rope loose with the knife. The end fell away. The boy began to cry, and he stumbled off the box and fell down in the dirt. Lyle climbed down and pulled the rope from his neck.

You're all right now, honey. He held him tight. It's all right now.

I want to go with Mom.

Yes, you can go with her. You're safe now.

But you won't tell her.

No. Not if it's important to you.

37

IN THE EVENING, on the following day, Dad lay awake with the window open, the smell of dust and mowed grass drifting in.

Mary came in the room with a pan of hot water and set it on the chair next to the bed and brought in a second pan and set it on another chair and went out again and returned with towels and washcloths. She switched on the bedside lamp and got Dad out of his pajamas and his diaper and covered him with a flannel sheet. Are you ready to get cleaned up, honey?

That water isn't too hot, is it? he whispered.

No. But I don't want you to get chilled.

She began by washing his face and head with a soapy washcloth and rubbed his face and head with a washcloth from the rinse water and dried him with a towel. She washed his chest and arms and hands and rubbed him dry, and pulled the flannel sheet up, covering his upper body to keep him warm, and washed his wasted legs and feet and rinsed and dried them. Roll over on your side now, honey. Hold on to my hand. He made a little moan in pain and turned slowly to his side and she washed his back and his gaunt behind and cleaned him thoroughly and dried him, then he turned back and she washed between his legs.

Nothing there, he whispered.

There used to be, she said. We had us some fun, didn't we.

She put a new diaper on him and helped him into his pajamas and drew up the sheet and summer blanket, then he lay back and looked at her.

I appreciate all this, he said.

You're welcome.

I wish I could do something for you.

You have. All these years. I'll just clean this up and come back and lay down with you.

She took the pans to the bathroom and wiped them clean and put the towels and the flannel sheet in the laundry and washed her hands. She put on lipstick and brushed her hair, then came back and switched the lamp off and lay down beside him.

He had dozed off but he woke now. He drew his hand out from under the cover and reached for her.

I don't have long to go, he whispered.

Oh, honey, don't you think so?

I'm tired. I want to go on. I need to let you be. So you can have some peace and rest.

Oh, don't say that. I'm still all right. I just want you to be comfortable. Are you hurting?

Yeah.

She got up and got him another of the pills and a sip of water, then got back into the bed and took his hand.

Everything's taken care of, isn't it? he whispered.

Yes. Everything's fine. Nothing to worry about.

The store and the money?

It's all done. You've done everything. We're all right. You can rest about that. Are you worrying, honey?

I been thinking about Frank.

I miss him, she said. I want you to see each other before you go. I wish he'd come.

He wouldn't come even if he did know. Maybe you won't see him now either.

I refuse to think that, she said. I won't. She sounded close to tears.

Dad turned his head to look at her. Then maybe he'll come. After I'm gone out of here.

At least Lorraine's here, she said. That makes a difference.

I wish she had a different choice of men, Dad said. I don't care for the one she's got now.

It's not our decision. It's up to her.

I know.

They didn't speak for a while after that. She thought he'd gone to sleep again. Then he whispered, You've been everything to me. All these years. Everything. I want you to know that.

I know, honey. You've been good to me.

He breathed quietly and she lay for a long time holding his hand. The room was all in darkness now, all was shadows. She got up and came around the bed and kissed him in his sleep and went out to the kitchen and turned the light on and made coffee. Lorraine came in from outside.

How's Daddy?

I gave him his bath. He's sleeping.

When Dad woke he was alone in the dark, the only light in the room was the light coming in under the shade from out at the barn, from the big yard light. The window shade breathed in and out, a little movement. Not much. There was not much of a breeze this night but still there was a little cool air coming in.

He turned in the bed and looked toward the window, then he saw he was not alone, people were already sitting here in the room looking at him, waiting on three wood chairs at the side of his bed. He knew them all. Frank. And his own old mother and old father.

His father was as he looked and dressed in the Great Depression and during the war. Sitting on the hard chair, patient, leaning forward a little, his hands holding his hat, wearing his old brown suit with the wide lapels, a stain on the lapel and another one at the old fly of the suit pants, the crotch so long that he always pulled the pants up practically to his chest, his hard-won gut paunch rounded out below the belt at the top of the pants, so that he looked short bodied, foreshortened, misshapen, all long thin legs with only a little upper half to him above his belt, like some comic figure out of a vaudeville show. Sitting with his hands idle, loose, not even turning the hat but just sitting motionless, patient, in the old-fashioned brown suit just as Dad remembered him. No hair on his head to speak of. His face burnt red, from working out in all the weather. Outside all day. Down at the hog pen and the cow barn and scooping grain in at the narrow slat-wood door of the granary and digging postholes in the ground, and every year planting dryland wheat back in Kansas and every year harvesting what meager crop there was. Working all the days of his life and never enough to show for it, never enough to get ahead.

And next to him, on her chair, his mother. The silent woman. The uncomplaining unexpressed uninflected woman. Gray hair pulled back in a tight bun. Her Sunday dress, old pearl-colored gabardine buttoned to the neck, shiny in places. Too loose, irreplaceable, out of poverty. And her long thin hands, bony red hands, and red bony wrists. With the scrap of battered adhesive tape wrapped around as guard holding the worn-out wedding ring on her bony finger. Her face wrinkled and lined. Her wire glasses on her nose that was too thin and pinched. Sitting here looking at him. His mother and the old man together just sitting, looking, quiet, as patient as some kind of old work-exhausted animals, waiting.

Beside them Frank was smoking a cigarette again. He looked worn out this time, tough, ragged, disheveled, unhappy.

Dad peered at them for some time. What do you want? he said. What have you come for?

We can't stay long, his father, the old man, said. We got to be getting on here purty soon now.

We come to see you, his mother said. We come to see how good you're faring, son.

Frank smoked and looked at them and looked at Dad.

I'm not too good, if you want to know, Dad said. I'm about finished. I'm going down now.

We come to see you, before you do, she said. We'll be waiting for you.

We got to go purty soon, the old man said.

Where is it you're waiting for me? Dad said.

Oh you know, she said. Don't be worried.

He turned toward Frank. What about you? You won't be waiting for me.

No, I won't wait for you. I'm still here. I got things to do yet. He exhaled smoke and then dropped the cigarette on the wood floor and twisted it out under his shoe.

So how you figure you're doing? the old man said to Dad.

I just told you. Not very good. I'm going down.

Well, you sure got you a real fine nice big house here. You done all right that way, didn't you. This is a real nice big pleasing satisfying house you got here.

I worked for it, Dad said.

Well sure. Of course. I know, the old man said. Had some luck too, I believe.

I had some luck. But I worked hard. I earned it.

Yeah. Sure. Most people work hard. It's not only that now, is it. You had you some luck.

Goddamn it, I had some luck too, Dad said, but I earned the luck.

Some people got to stay back in Kansas out on the dry prairie, the old man said.

What are you talking about? This is dry prairie. It isn't much different. No trees. Dryland farming except where they found water underneath.

We never had none of that in our piece of Kansas. No sir. We wasn't so lucky as that. No sir, we never was that lucky where we was.

That's all right, Papa, the old woman said. Let it be now. Don't you fret yourself.

The old man looked at her. We better get on purty soon. We can't stay here much longer.

Do you know my son here? Dad said.

Of course. Yeah. We know him, the old man said. We met him just now. He takes off of you, don't he.

I guess he does, Dad said. I don't see it myself.

Well, course he does. You ain't looking right. You never brought him to see us, did you. Never once.

No. I didn't want to.

No. You never did. Out of spitefulness, wasn't it. Out of meanness.

We better go, Papa. It's getting late. We just stopped in to see how you was faring, son. Don't be afraid.

I'm not afraid, Dad said.

Don't be afraid, son.

I'm not.

It's not like folks think, she said.

Is it all right though?

Don't worry about it, son.

I'm not worried about it.

We'll be a-seeing you, the old man said. You just take it easy here now. That's all you got to do.

Enjoy all of it while you can, she said.

Take her good and easy, boy. We got to go on.

When Dad woke again the old man and the old woman in their old Sunday clothes were gone. Frank was sitting next to the two empty chairs in the low barn light coming in from under the shade.

They left, I guess, Dad said.

They said they had to go, Frank said. They weren't so bad. Not like you said. You always made them sound like they were terrible people.

You never met them before now.

No. When would I?

Well, you saw them now.

They weren't so bad. They didn't bother me.

It was because he wanted to beat me again, Dad said. I wasn't going to have it. I was fifteen and I run away. I never went home after that.

History repeats, Frank said.

What?

I'm saying I know that story. A version of it, anyway.

Maybe so, Dad said. He looked at Frank for a while. Goddamn it, I didn't even know how to cut my meat or eat my potatoes right, I chased my peas around the plate with a knife. I come out of that kind of life, out of their house, knowing nothing but hard work and sweat and paying heed and dodging cow shit and taking orders. I cut my meat about like it was a piece of stove wood.

None of that matters, Frank said.

No. That don't matter, Dad said. But it matters what it stands for. He talks about luck. Your mom was my luck. I was lucky in your mom.

I know, Dad.

Your mom helped me change.

Well, I don't like to tell you, but you're not all that sophisticated yet, Dad. If that's what you're talking about.

What?

Never mind. That doesn't matter either.

Wait now. I know what you're talking about. I know what you mean. But you don't know where I come from. I wanted more. I wanted out of that. I wanted to work inside someplace. Talk to people. Live in a town. Make a place for myself on Main Street. Own a store, sell things to people, provide what they needed. I worked hard, like I told him. It wasn't just luck. Your mom was my luck. I know that but I worked hard too.

Dad, who are you talking to? Don't you know who you're talking to? I know all that. I was here, remember?

Dad stared at him. All right. I'll pipe down. He looked around the shadowy room. You want some coffee? I know you drink coffee.

No. Not now.

Go ahead and smoke if you want. I don't care. What difference does it make now.

All right. I'll do that.

Frank took a pack from his shirt pocket and lit a cigarette with a match and blew smoke toward the window. The smoke was sucked out by the night air.

Your mom went to find you in Denver, Dad said.

I know she did.

How do you know?

They told me.

Who?

At the café.

I thought you weren't there no more.

I'm not. But I drop in.

They didn't tell your mom.

I drop in once in a while.

What are you doing now?

I've been out in California where most of us end up. Where else?

I guess it's nice and warm all year long out there, Dad said.

It's warm. Yeah. But we're out there in numbers. That's what I'm talking about.

You mean others like you.

Yeah. Other weirdos and cocksuckers.

Don't talk like that about yourself, Dad said.

It's the truth, isn't it. Isn't that what you think?

I did once.

What do you think now?

Not that.

What then?

I don't know. I don't understand it. I'm too ignorant. I don't know nothing about it. I told you, I come off a farm in Kansas. That's all I knew where I come from. It took all I had to get this far, a little plains town, with a store on Main Street.

You did all right, Dad. You've come a long way.

Not far enough.

No. That's true. Not yet you haven't.

Dad looked at him, his eyes watering again.

What's wrong? Frank said.

Nothing.

I thought you were going to cry.

That's the first kind thing you've said to me in forty years, Dad said. About me doing all right, coming a long way.

Well, I must have forgotten myself. I let my guard down. Don't count on it happening again.

I know. I learned that much. I'm not ignorant about everything.

He woke once more. Frank had moved his chair to a place closer beside the bed. The other two chairs were gone now. The air was fresh and pleasant coming in the window, the light still shining from the barn outside.

You're still here, Dad said.

Yeah. I'm here. I haven't left yet.

My old mother and old dad didn't come back.

No. They're gone now.

Those others didn't come back either.

Who?

Tanya. And Rudy and Bob.

No, they aren't with me.

Dad looked at him for a while. Frank had turned sideways so he could see out the window. The shade had been drawn up now. Son, are you doing all right? Dad said.

Me?

Yes.

I'm all right, more or less. I could use a better job. I never could get going right. I get dissatisfied and take off.

You always could do a lot of different things.

Maybe. But I don't know what. I don't have any college degree like Lorraine does.

You could of.

You think so?

We would of helped you like we helped her.

I couldn't do it back then.

Why was that?

I wasn't thinking about studying. I didn't have the time. Or the desire for it.

You wanted out of here, Dad said. Didn't you. That's what you wanted.

That was part of it.

Away from me, you mean.

Not just that. Away from this little limited postage-stamp view of things. You and this place both.

But you still could of gone to school. That would of helped.

I didn't think so then. I just wanted out on my own.

Well. You done that.

Yeah. He laughed. I've done that, all right. I've been out on my own. A lot of good it did me.

But you done all right, didn't you?

What are you talking about, Dad? I've been a waiter. A night clerk. A janitor. A hired hand. A garbage man. A taxi driver. You don't want to know what all I've done for money.

But that's just somebody getting started. You're still getting on your feet.

Dad, I'm fifty years old. What am I going to do now? How can I start now?

Dad moved in the bed and then lay still.

Hand me one of those pills there, he said.

Here?

Yeah.

You want some water?

Yeah. He took the glass and drank and handed it back and lay still again.

You can always come back here, he said. After I'm gone you can come back.

And do what, Dad?

Help run the store.

Lorraine's running the store.

You can help her.

It wouldn't work. It's not going to happen.

Then you can have some of the value of it, Dad said. You and Mom and Lorraine can divide it up. Take your third of it. Do something. Start over.

No. I don't want any money from you. I won't take your money. I swore I wouldn't.

Dad stared at him a long time. Frank looked past Dad at the wall and turned again to stare out the window. He lit another cigarette.

You never forgave me, did you, Dad said.

You never forgave yourself.

I couldn't. How could I? Now it's too late.

You're still alive, Frank said. Maybe you'll have a deathbed conversion.

Dad studied Frank's face. You're being cynical. You're just talking.

Of course.

You don't mean what you said.

No, I don't mean it. I've been too goddamn angry. I've been too filled up to my throat with bitterness. Oh Jesus. I could smash your dying face right now.

Why don't you? I wish you would. Go ahead. I want you to.

Frank stood up. I got to go. He stepped on his cigarette and put it out.

Wait. You don't have to leave yet, Dad said. You should see your mother. Are you going now?

Yeah. I better.

Well. Good-bye, then, son.

Frank moved toward the door.

Wait. Would you give me your hand? Dad said. Before you go. But he was gone on out into the doorway now. Dad still watched him. This tall middle-aged balding man. Broad in the doorway. Not too old yet. But wearing old clothes. Ragged-looking. Still, there was something there. He was still a good-looking man. There was something there yet. It hadn't come out yet.

38

THE NEXT MORNING Mary lay in the old soft double bed with Dad until the sunlight streamed into the room. She got up and went into the bathroom and returned and put on her shirt and jeans and leaned close over the bed to look at him.

Dear. Are you waking up now? He didn't move. Dad?

He lay staring up at the ceiling out of half-open eyes. Then he breathed deeply, a kind of rattle. She felt his forehead. He felt cool, clammy to the touch.

Can you hear me? she whispered.

She bent and kissed him and went quickly upstairs to Lorraine's room.

Honey, can I come in?

Lorraine had just gotten out of bed in her light summer nightgown.

What's wrong?

He's going now. I'm afraid he is.

Is something different?

He won't wake up. I can't get him to talk. He feels cold.

Lorraine put her arms around her. We knew this was coming, Mom.

Come down with me, would you. I want to turn him on his side. The nurse said he'd breathe a little better on his side if we turned him.

Lorraine put on a robe over the nightgown and followed her mother downstairs. Dad's eyes were shut now. He breathed and stopped and breathed again, rattling in his throat. They folded back the summer blanket and the sheet and turned him so he was facing the door, and placed an old flat pillow under his head, and put another between his knees. His feet looked mottled with blotches climbing up his legs and his hands were blue and on the undersides of his arms were more blue spots that were like faint bruises.

Look at his poor fingernails, Mary said.

Yes.

They covered him again with the sheet and blanket and stood together beside the bed, watching him. His mouth stayed open. He breathed and made a little involuntary noise and breathed again.

He never woke that day. He lay quietly in the bed, his mouth open and dry and his lips cracked, his face yellow and washed out. Lorraine called the nurse and she came and examined him and looked at his feet and hands, the blue places and mottling on his arms and legs, and told them he was in the final stages. They talked about what they should do. They said they would bathe and dress him themselves after he died, they preferred that, they wanted that last duty and moments of caretaking for themselves, and the nurse said, That's fine. But you still need to call me so I can certify his death and dispose of the unused medicine. When you're ready we can call the mortician. But there's no rush. You take as long as you want.

We've already talked to George Hill, Lorraine said. He'll take care of all the details for the cremation and there'll be a service at the church and a brief graveside service. Some of his ashes will be buried at the cemetery. But we'll keep most of them here.

Just please call me if you need something, the nurse said. It doesn't matter what time it is.

What about his pain now, while he's like this? Mary said. I'm afraid he'll choke if we give him a pill.

Give him liquid morphine under his tongue, with the eyedropper. That'll be all right. And just keep him dry and clean and turn him regularly. That's about all you can do.

Will it bother him for us to talk in the room here while he's sleeping like this?

No, I wouldn't think so. He might even like hearing you even if he doesn't seem to.

I think he might, Mary said. It might comfort him.

They checked on him every half hour. And then at midmorning they turned him again, toward the wall now, and he was wet and they changed his diaper and washed him. He slept on as before, breathing, stopping, starting again, the rattle still there in his throat.

In the afternoon Berta May called and she came over, and they called Rob Lyle and he came too. Lorraine met him at the door. He put his arm around her.

Thank you for coming, she said. She brought him into the living room and he hugged Mary.

I'm glad you're here, Reverend Lyle.

I'm not a preacher anymore, he said.

Aren't you still a reverend?

No.

You do still pray?

Yes, I still pray. That hasn't changed.

Will you pray for Dad?

They went in the room and sat on the bedside chairs and Mary and Lorraine and Berta May and Lyle held hands, looking at Dad. He lay facing the door now. They bowed their heads. May we be at peace together with Dad Lewis here, Lyle said softly. May there be peace and love and harmony in this room. May there be the same in all the difficult and conflicted world outside this house. May this man—he stopped and spoke directly to Dad in the bed—may you leave this physical world without any more pain or regrets or unhappiness or remorse or self-doubt or worry and may you let all your trials and troubles and cares pass away. May you simply be at peace. May each of us here in this room be at peace as well. Now we ask all of these blessings in the name of Jesus, who himself was the Prince of Peace. Amen.

Thank you, Lorraine whispered.

Afterward they talked quietly and watched Dad and looked out the window to the hot summer day, to the flatland beyond the house.

Would you be willing to tell us about your life? Lyle said. This would be a good time to talk.

Oh, nobody wants to hear that, Mary said.

Yes, we do. Of course we do.

She looked at him and then looked at her old husband lying in the bed with the sheet and blanket spread over him.

We met on the corner of Second and Main Street in the summer of 1947 right here in Holt. I was coming out of a store and Dad was crossing the street.

What store was it, Mom? Was it the Tavern?

Don't be funny, Mary said. It was the department store. I was standing in front of Schulte's on the corner trying to think about something.

What were you thinking about?

I was deciding if I had got everything I needed. I was sewing something. And Dad was walking toward me. I was thinking about my sewing and I stepped off the curb and walked right into him. I almost fell down but he reached and caught me. He helped me back up onto the curb. I was embarrassed. Oh excuse me, I said. Please. I wasn't watching. And he said, I was coming toward you anyways, miss. You didn't have to fall for me.

They looked at Dad in the bed, trying to see him as a young man. They looked at his back and the shape of his sharp hip and puny legs under the blanket.

That was his little joke. I suppose it doesn't sound very funny anymore. But I did fall for him. That's the whole truth. I did with my whole heart. And that's how and when I fell.

Then what, Mom?

Oh, you've heard all this before.

I want to hear it again. We all do.

Well, then we went to the pharmacy. Brown's Drugstore. They had some little round drugstore tables to sit down at, at the back. We drank soda drinks and got acquainted. Then he asked me out that weekend to a picture show and six months later we got married and two years after that you came along and in three more years we had your brother.

Lyle and Berta May looked at Lorraine now and looked again at Dad, breathing so slow and hard.

What were you wearing? Lorraine said.

What was I wearing when?

When you met Daddy at the corner on Main.

Well, it was in the summer. I'm sure I was wearing a dress. We only wore dresses back then, didn't we, Berta May.

Stockings too if we was leaving the house, she said.

What was Dad wearing? Lyle said.

Mary looked at Dad. I suppose he was wearing pants.

They laughed, but quietly.

I mean trousers. He wasn't wearing overalls, like a lot of men did. And he had on a light blue long-sleeved shirt with stripes in it. He was already working at the hardware store. His sleeves were rolled up on his arms. Oh, I can still see him.

Did he own the store then? Lyle said.

Oh no. He was only a skinny young single man then. He had been in the army. But the war ended while he was still in training. He never got sent overseas. He felt bad about that. I didn't. Who knows what might have happened to him.

They left Dad to himself for a while, he seemed to be making some private effort that he had to make, and they went out to the living room where Mary brought them each a cup of coffee. They sat down on the couch and Mary sat in the rocking chair, leaving Dad's chair by the window empty.

You all just please help yourselves if you want more coffee, Mary said. She sipped at her cup. She looked at Lyle. I don't think we ever asked you. I guess we just assumed. So I want to ask you now.

Yes? he said.

We'd like you to do the service for Dad, for all of us. At the church.

Lorraine and Berta May looked at her, then at him.

Yes. I'd be honored to do that, he said. But I doubt they'd allow me to perform any kind of service in the church now. I'm not sure I'd want to anyway. We're going separate ways.

But you still live in the parsonage, Mary said. They've allowed that.

They've agreed to let me stay two months. So it's not a clean break. Is that what you mean?

I don't know what I mean, she said.

Could you perform the service somewhere else? Lorraine said.

Maybe. But it depends. The other churches in Holt wouldn't want to interfere by hosting it in one of their sanctuaries.

What about the yard here at the house? Lorraine said. We could borrow chairs from somebody, or rent them from George Hill maybe, and have the memorial right here in the shade in the side yard. That might even be better.

Yes, I've done services outdoors many times.

What do you think, Mom? It's up to you.

Well, I don't know. I haven't thought about it before. I know Dad sure looked out that window for hours on end. I never understood what he was looking at, but it seemed to give him a lot of pleasure. Yes, it might be just right to have his memorial in the very place he spent so much time looking at.

Could we still do a graveside service at the cemetery afterward? Lorraine said.

Yes, Lyle said. I'm sure we could do that too. That wouldn't involve any of the churches.

It's a public cemetery, Berta May said. We pay taxes for its upkeep. Nobody would stop us.

We'll take care of all the practical details, Lorraine said. If that's what you decide to do.

Yes, Lyle said. I think so.

Thank you, Mary said. Thank you all.

In the evening Dad woke once and looked around and asked for water. Only Mary and Lorraine were sitting with him now in the bedroom. He stared at Mary for a long time while she held his hand. He stared over at Lorraine, then he pulled his hand back under the blanket and fell into his restless sleep again.

Later that evening, Mary said, I have to go to bed. I can't sit up any longer.

Do you want me to stay with Dad? You could have my room.

No. I want to be here with him.

You're not afraid?

Why no. This is my husband. I've been with this man most of my life. Over half a century. I know him better than I know anybody else in the world.

But you're not afraid to be here now.

No, honey. There's nothing here to scare me. I might be afraid about the future, but not of this man in this room here.

Mom, I'll be here to help in the future.

I know, dear. Now you should go to bed too.

After Lorraine went upstairs Mary lifted the blanket and slid in beside Dad. He was lying on his back now. She patted his hand under the blanket and rose up to kiss him.

I'm right here. I'm not going anyplace, she whispered. You do what you have to do. Did you hear us talking about you? I hope you didn't mind.

She kissed him again on his cracked mouth and lay back beside him and lay still, peering up into the dark room where the barn light was forming dim shapes and shadows and strange figures, and suddenly she began to weep.

Later in the night she woke abruptly and switched on the bedside lamp and looked at him and felt his head, he was still breathing the same slow irregular breath. She got up and went to the bathroom and went out to the kitchen, looking out into the backyard and the corral and barn and stood staring at the darkness, and then drank a glass of water and came back and checked Dad again and got in beside him and took his hand again. When she woke in the morning he was still alive.

He lived through all of that day. He'd stop breathing for a while, then begin again with a gasp, coughing, trying feebly to clear his throat. They moistened the inside of his mouth with a swab and spread balm on his lips. He lay facing the door or the wall, or lay stretched on his back, his face gray and faded, strained-looking, and his eyes under the thin eyelids were fixed now, not moving.

They sat with him beside the bed talking softly and touching him now and then, holding his icy hands, and whispered to him, telling him their feelings for him. They cried every so often, then one would stay with him while the other went out.

In the afternoon Berta May came again and helped with the straightening in the house and brought in dinner to eat, a casserole of meat and pasta and a green salad. Can I do something else? she said.

You've done too much already, Mary said. You shouldn't have done all of this.

Yes, I should of. You would for me.

Well, you know we thank you.

Now what else?

If you wouldn't mind . . . people have been calling all morning long on the phone and some of them want to come visit. I can't have that. I told Willa and Alene to come. They're the only ones. I think they would be good. But I don't want anyone else. Could you answer the door for us, and explain to people?

———

The Johnson women drove up to the house in the afternoon and Berta May let them in. They entered the front hall very quietly and she told them Dad was still alive, that Mary and Lorraine were in the bedroom with him, they'd been sitting there almost all the day. They're just about worn out, she said.

Oh, wouldn't they be? Willa said. Is there something we can do?

Everything's done. You can go in if you want. They said to tell you to come in.

Berta May led them back down the hall and eased the bedroom door open and stuck her head in. Mary gestured for them to come in, and Lorraine got up and brought two more chairs from the dining room, then the four women sat near the bed together. Dad lay on his back, his mouth open and his eyes shut, with the blanket covering him.

We can talk, Mary said. It's all right to speak, if we're quiet.

How is he? Willa whispered. Is there any change?

He's worse, I think. Her eyes filled with tears. Willa and Alene leaned toward her and took her hands.

I'm glad you've come, she said. I don't want others to be here. That would bother Dad.

No, Willa said. We don't want to bother any one of you.

I just don't want some people.

No. Of course.

Dad coughed, his eyes opened, staring, he stopped breathing. They watched him, then he breathed in, a hard gasp, and shut his eyes and went on as before.

The poor man, Willa said softly. You know my husband always thought so much of him. Dad Lewis is somebody to know, he said. Dad Lewis is a man you can set your clock by. I don't think he was talking about time.

Yes, Mary said. He was always reliable.

Yes, but my husband meant he was somebody that was straight up and down, like the hands of a clock, somebody you could depend on, somebody to trust completely.

That was nice of him to say, Mary said.

Yes. He meant it too.

Outside the bedroom it suddenly turned dark, a cloud was passing over, and it began to rain. It pounded straight down. A sudden dark fallen curtain. Then in a moment it stopped.

I hope Dad heard that, Mary said.

The air was cool and fresh now coming in the window.

Oh, doesn't it smell good, she said.

Lorraine went to the window and opened it wider and Alene joined her and they stood watching as the sun came out again and the rain dripped off the eaves.

In the evening Mary and Lorraine stayed with Dad, sitting on into the night beside the bed. Finally Lorraine went up to bed and left the door open so she could hear if there was anything to hear, and Mary got into her nightgown and crawled in beside him. I'm still with you, she said. Don't worry about anything. I'm right here. She switched the lamp off and took his hand. She went to sleep immediately.

When she woke at midnight he was still breathing. She went to the bathroom and came back and lay down and took his hand and went to sleep. At two suddenly she woke again. He wasn't breathing, then after a long while he breathed again and shuddered. She turned on the lamp and looked at his face and got out of bed. I'll be right back. She went to the bottom of the stairs.

Lorraine! Please! Can you hear me? Lorraine!

She came to the landing. Mom. What's wrong?

Come down here. Now.

She hurried back to the bedroom and when Lorraine came they sat together beside the bed and held Dad's hands and he took a short breath and after a long time breathed again. Then he made a sound down in his throat, followed by a drawn-out choking rattle, then a little weak noise again. Minutes went by. He breathed once more, a small shallow inhalation, almost nothing, and the little sigh, they waited, watching his face, waited . . . waited, but there was nothing more, that was all there would ever be, he never breathed again.

Mary began to cry, rocking herself. I'm not ready! I thought I was. But I'm not ready! Not yet!

Lorraine began crying too and she put an arm around her mother. They leaned toward the bed and Mary took Dad's hand and kissed the back of it and held it to her cheek and then stood leaning over and pressed his quiet face between her hands and kissed his forehead and kissed him a long time on his cooling open lips. Good-bye, sweetheart. Good-bye, my dear.

Lorraine bent over and kissed his cheek and touched his face. Be at peace now, Daddy. Good-bye.

They removed his clothes and bathed his body, lifting each arm, and washing his hands, his papery fingers, they closed his mouth, pressing his jaw up, pressing his lips together though his mouth still stayed slightly open, and closed his eyes. They washed his face and ears and washed his scalp and washed all of his body front and back, holding his long thin cooling body as they did. They put clean pajamas on him and folded his hands together over his chest. Finally they lit a candle and turned off the lamp. They sat down beside him.

After a long time Mary said, I think I'm ready now. Are you, dear?

I am, Mom.

They got dressed and called the nurse. It was about five then, the sky just turning light. The nurse came in right away and looked at Dad and collected the remaining medicines and filled out the papers. She left the house and at six o'clock they called George Hill, the mortician. Before he came they went back in the room one last time. Dad's face was cold now to the touch, his eyes had come open slightly.

They sat until George Hill arrived. Then they kissed Dad's face a last time and left the bedroom weeping. George and his assistant wheeled in a gurney and lifted Dad's body onto it and spread a white sheet over him. They rolled him carefully out through the doorway into the living room, mindful not to bump anything.

We'll be going now, Mrs. Lewis, George Hill said. If that's all right.

Mary nodded. She choked and couldn't speak. She and Lorraine went with the men out of the house and stopped at the gate and watched them fold up the wheels of the gurney and lift it into the back of the van. George Hill looked at them once more and nodded and got in and drove slowly away.

They walked back into the side yard and stood with their arms around each other, facing the east as the long day began.

39

PEOPLE BEGAN TO COME to the house in the middle of the morning, to offer sympathy and gifts of food, and Berta May came over again to help. Mary and Lorraine had dressed in good clothes by now and they met the people at the door and brought a few in for a brief visit.

It rained that morning again, around ten o'clock, another of the short hard summer rains that blew through, then the sky cleared again.

Later that morning Richard arrived from Denver in a new car and came up to the house. Lorraine hugged him and he was unusually quiet and Mary allowed him to take her in his arms. I'm sorry for your loss, he said. It makes me sad to hear of it. He sat out on the porch for a while and about noon he left and went over to Highway 34 and rented a motel room for the night and stopped to eat lunch at one of the highway cafés.

At one o'clock Willa and Alene Johnson came to the house and relieved Berta May. Before leaving, Berta May made sure everything was in order, and Mary said, Would you mind doing one more thing for us? Would you take these notices around to the stores? If it's not too much to ask. I know you've done so much already. It was the one thing Dad said he wanted.

So that afternoon Berta May and Alice distributed the little stiff white cards with black borders, bearing the news of Dad's death and announcing the memorial services to be held at the house and the

Holt cemetery. The notices had been printed that morning in the back room of the *Holt Mercury* newspaper.

They drove over to Main Street and Berta May stopped the car. Now you understand what to do. Take one of these into each store and hand it to the person at the counter, whoever is there.

What should I say?

You just say this is a funeral notice for our neighbor Dad Lewis. And be slow when you do this. Don't do nothing in a hurry. Remember what you're doing here. This is a solemn occasion.

Alice got out and Berta May moved the car down to the corner of Fourth and Main. Alice went into all of the stores on the east side and crossed the street and entered the ones on the west side. When she was done, Berta May drove farther down Main Street and parked in the next block and watched as her granddaughter went in and out of those shops. She was wearing a blue dress. She looked like a nice girl. At the hardware store there was a Closed sign hung at the door and in the display window was a large piece of wrapping paper with writing in black. Our friend Dad Lewis died this morning. We're closed until further notice.

In the last block of businesses Alice came back to the car before she had finished. That woman wanted to know if the preacher at the Community Church was doing the service.

What woman?

That woman in there.

What did you tell her?

I didn't tell her anything. I didn't know what to say.

That's exactly right. Anybody who asks you, you don't know. And you'll be telling the truth. It's none of their business. People like her make me real tired.

When they returned home Berta May said, Now I'm going to go back and lay down a while. You take off your dress and put your shorts and T-shirt on.

Can I ride my bike?

Yes, but don't you make no noise. I don't want you bothering them next door.

What are they doing?

Those people are grieving. They've had a hard thing today. Other people are wanting to come and visit them and talk. They don't need no noise outside. Do you understand?

Yes.

Not a sound.

Yes, Grandma.

Okay, go on and get out of that dress and hang it up. I don't mean to sound unkind, honey. I'm just tired. You did a good job downtown just now. I'm proud of you.

Next door Alene and Willa were doing what they could to help. Alene washed the coffee cups and saucers in the kitchen sink and put them to dry. There was a dishwasher that Dad had brought home a long time ago but they didn't want its disruption in the house now.

Lorraine and Mary had gone upstairs to lie down in the two bedrooms. When the phone rang Willa answered it at once and took down the caller's name. The memorial will be held here at the house, she said, day after tomorrow. Yes, that's right. Here at the house in the side yard, with a service at the cemetery afterward. Thank you, I'll tell them.

Later that afternoon Richard came back with a handful of flowers and Alene met him at the front door. I'm Richard, he said. Maybe Lorraine mentioned me.

Yes. We've heard of you.

Is she available?

She's sleeping, but you can come in and wait.

Well. I don't want to be in the way. I'm happy to wait for her. She'll probably get up pretty soon. She never sleeps very well.

Is that right? Alene said and led him into the living room.

He'd bought the flowers at the grocery store on the highway and he was carrying them in front of himself in their thin green tissue paper like a kind of ceremonial element.

This is my mother, Willa Johnson, Alene said. This is Lorraine's friend from Denver.

Lorraine's asleep, Willa said. And can't be disturbed.

I'll just sit and wait for her.

The women looked at each other and Alene took the flowers to the kitchen and returned with them in a vase and set the vase on the coffee table.

You don't have to pay me any attention, he said.

The phone rang and Willa picked it up. This is the Lewis house. Willa Johnson speaking. She explained again about the services, and hung up.

And after a while Mary came downstairs and Richard stood up to meet her. I thought I had better come back, he said.

Yes, she said.

And then Lorraine came downstairs and he stood up again. I came back to see if I can help.

Did you.

I'd like to, if I can.

There's nothing to do right now. Thank you for asking.

I brought you those flowers.

I see that. Thank you. They're beautiful.

The women went out to the kitchen and he sat again on the couch, looking around the room, looking at the flowers. He picked up a magazine.

Toward the end of the afternoon Rudy and Bob came to the house. They were greeted at the door and brought into the living room and were introduced to Richard. Rudy and Bob had on their good wintertime suits and were sweating and red faced in the heat. They sat down on the couch.

You'll have to excuse us now, Mary said. You're welcome to stay.

She and Lorraine and Alene and Willa went back to the kitchen and closed the door.

Mary said, I can't be sitting out there with them or anybody. I just can't do it.

Mom, you don't have to.

You do what you want, Alene said. You don't need to think about anyone else today.

There will be other times later, Willa said, but today now you just go ahead and do what you feel you need to.

I don't want to be rude. But I can't sit out there. I think I need some air.

Do you want company?

She shook her head and went out to the backyard. They watched her through the window. She walked slowly into the shade under the tree and they watched her bend far over and touch the ground and lower herself onto her knees, wrapping herself in her arms, and now they could see she was crying, the top of her white head on the grass.

Oh I should go out to her, Lorraine said. Look at her, the poor thing.

No, I don't think you should, Willa said. She has to do this. This is only the beginning. This is the first day.

In the living room the men sat glancing sideways at each other and looked around the room and peered out the windows.

We kept the store closed today, Rudy said. He cleared his throat. We had to do that.

It was the right thing, Bob said. Out of respect.

I don't know if it was ever closed before on a weekday. Except for Christmas.

Or New Year's, Bob said. One of the holidays.

I brought these flowers, Richard said.

They stared at him.

On the table here.

———

After a while Richard stood up and went back to the kitchen and tapped on the door. Lorraine came out and went with him to the front porch.

I think I'll go, he said. There's no point in me being here right now.

I thank you again for coming.

So I'll see you tonight, he said.

No. I won't be going anywhere. I can't leave.

I got a motel room, he said. I thought you'd come join me.

I can't leave my mother. What were you thinking?

I thought you could for a while. It'd be good for you. You need a break.

No.

Well, he said. When's the funeral? Two days from now. I might as well go on back to Denver, if you won't see me.

You have to do what you want. But I can't leave, you know that.

I didn't, he said. He leaned to kiss her and she turned her cheek. I see, he said. You won't even kiss me.

Not now. I don't feel like that.

He looked out toward his new car. There are just all kinds of things happening today and not happening today, he said. Isn't that right.

You can understand why.

I'll see you, Lorraine.

She waited on the porch watching him walk around to the far side of the car. He got in and looked at her for a moment. He didn't wave. Then he put the car in gear and sped off throwing gravel up behind just as a gray cat darted out in the street ahead of him. Oh! she cried. Don't hit it! The car swerved in time and the cat ran out with its tail straight up and ran into the neighbor's yard. She watched the car go on up to the highway and turn west toward Denver.

In the house, when she went back inside, Rudy and Bob were standing in the living room, talking to her mother. She could see Willa and Alene out in the kitchen.

I guess we better be getting on too, Rudy said. He looked at Lorraine. If there's anything we can do, you'll let us know?

Yes, of course, she said. We appreciate all you do for us.

We wanted to be here, Bob said. You know what we thought of Dad.

Yes, we know, Mary said. You've both been very kind. You're good friends.

One thing we wanted to ask you, Rudy said.

Yes? .

We wondered what you was thinking about tomorrow.

Tomorrow? Lorraine said.

Because we figured you will want to close the store for the funeral the next day.

Of course.

But the question is. Tomorrow.

What do you think, Mom?

I think Dad would want it to be open. Keep it closed today and again for the memorial, but open the doors tomorrow like always.

That's what we was thinking, Rudy said. He was looking at Lorraine again. But we thought we should ask.

That would be the appropriate thing, she said. If you will open tomorrow, please.

Well, we better get going, then. We're sure sorry about Dad. We sure are. His eyes filled with tears. That's one thing for certain. We're going to miss him every day. It's not going to be the same without him down there.

They started to shake hands with Lorraine but she stepped forward and kissed each man on his clean-shaven cheek, red and streaming with sweat and uncomfortableness, and then they both hugged Mary in their warm good suits, their eyes full of tears, and went out the door and climbed into Rudy's car and drove away.

Then at dusk Rob Lyle came once more to the house. Mary and Lorraine and the Johnson women were out in the kitchen dishing up food and they asked him to join them.

No, thank you, he said. I only came by to see if you were all right.

You can just please stay here and join us, Mary said. We ask you to. You can see all this food. People have been so kind. You'll be doing us a favor.

Lorraine handed him a plate.

All of these gifts of food are a tribute to your father, aren't they. And to you and your mother.

People thought so much of him. All over this county, Lorraine said. Help yourself and come into the dining room with us.

They made another place at the big dining table and the women and Lyle sat down and he said a prayer of grace and they began to eat. But after a short while Mary put down her fork.

Mom? What's wrong?

I can't eat.

You need to eat something.

I'm not hungry. I don't feel like it.

You'll feel more like it tomorrow, Willa said.

Maybe I will. I don't know that.

Then suddenly the front door burst open and Berta May came rushing in. Alice! she cried. Is Alice here?

They all stood up from the table and gathered around her.

I don't know where my girl is. I told her she had to be quiet. I told her you was grieving over here so she couldn't make no noise. So I let her ride her bike. But, oh I'm afraid she took me too serious. She must of went someplace. Oh, I'm just afraid she's got hurt or some-body's done something wrong to her.

Has she been out late like this before? Lyle said.

Never. She never does this. Oh, what if something happened to my little girl. Berta May began to cry. Her chin quivered and she covered her face. Mary and Lorraine put their arms close around her.

What about her friends? Lyle said.

The old woman looked at him and dabbed at her eyes with a Kleenex. I called, she said, but they don't know no more than I do. She don't really have friends here anyway. We was waiting for school to start.

What about the police? Willa said.

I don't want to call the police. This isn't a police matter.

I could search around town, Lyle said. If you'd like me to do that.

If you could, maybe you'd see her somewhere. She might be playing with somebody that I don't know about.

Is there a part of town she liked to ride in especially?

That's it—I don't know. I never paid enough attention. She always come back in the house to check in.

I'll look, Lyle said. You don't think she went out past the highway or rode over on the other side of Main Street.

I don't think so. But I don't know now. Oh where's my girl? She began to cry again.

I'll start looking, Lyle said.

I'm coming with you, Lorraine said.

The two of them hurried out to Lyle's car and he drove along the quiet twilight street past the cars parked in front of the houses and onto the highway and back in the next street, and then up and down the alley, looking in the backyards. The light was fading out of the sky and at the street corners the streetlights were coming on.

I'm starting to get sick at heart about this, Lorraine said. What if something has happened? Oh God, I hope it hasn't.

We can't think that, Lyle said.

But what if it has? It brings up all the old feelings for me. My daughter died in a car accident. Did you know that?

Your mother told me.

I've never gotten over it. I never will. You never get over a child's death. She turned away. Lyle reached across the seat and took her hand. Now it's Alice, she said, this little girl. I've let myself care too much for her. I know I shouldn't have; it's just starting things over again. That's the awful truth. That's how I feel about it. But I'd take her in, in a minute, if she didn't have her grandma. Oh, what if something's happened to her too.

She stared out the window. Lyle held on to her hand. They crossed Main Street to the streets on the east side.

The boy that was driving the car, Lorraine said, that boy is thirty-three years old now. He's become a grown man and my daughter's life ended at sixteen. Now if something like that has happened here . . .

They drove across town and went bumping and rattling over the train tracks at the crossing and on to the north side, looking between the small houses and the turquoise trailer houses and the cars rusting in the weeds and the backyards.

My son is in trouble too, Lyle said. I won't tell you all of it. I won't say what he wouldn't want me to say, but he's in serious trouble. I'm really worried about him. He's gone to Denver to live with his mother.

Will he be better there?

I doubt it. What's wrong with him isn't about geography.

Is this trouble he's having, about you and him?

Some of it is.

They came back across the tracks. More cars were out in the evening now. High school kids driving up and down Main Street, honking at one another under the bright lights. Lyle and Lorraine turned off Main and drove along the railroad tracks to the town park. At the Holt swimming pool they stopped the car and hurried into the entrance. They could hear kids screaming and splashing. At the front counter there were two high school girls selling tickets, with the wire baskets of clothes stacked in ranks behind them.

They quickly explained to the girls who they were looking for.

No, we haven't seen her, one of the girls said.

No, we've been here since four, the other girl said.

Just send her home, Lorraine said, if she shows up. You know her, don't you?

Yes.

They went back to the car. Let's go back, Lorraine said. She might have come back.

When they drove into the street at the edge of town, they saw that all the lights in Berta May's house were turned on. All the windows were filled up with light.

The four women were standing out in front of the house. Lyle and Lorraine got out and came over to them.

You never found her, Berta May said.

No, Lyle said. But we haven't given up. We'll keep looking.

Oh, where is she? I got all the lights on so she can see the house and come home.

We should call the police now, Willa said.

No. I can't do that. Not yet.

But they could look for her in ways we can't.

I don't want them. I will pretty soon if I have to. . . . I will pretty soon.

She looked around. They were watching her.

I should go back inside. I'm not doing no good out here.

Don't go, Mary said. Stay here with us.

I'm going all to pieces. You can see I am.

We all feel that way, dear.

Wait! Alene said. She was looking up the street. Someone's coming.

Somebody was out in the gravel street, coming toward them three or four blocks away. A small figure.

I can't see, Berta May said. Is it her?

Yes. It must be.

I don't see no bicycle.

Lorraine began to run, and Lyle ran after her. The women hurried after them. Lorraine was first and grabbed her up in her arms and lifted her up and swung her around and held her tight. She set her down. The girl was dirty and scared. Oh, are you all right? She looked closely into her face.

Yes.

You are, aren't you?

I got lost. I went out on a country road and it got dark and then I went the wrong way. A pickup came by and I went down in the ditch. I cut my tire on a bottle.

Did the ones in the pickup bother you?

No.

They didn't stop?

No. I crawled under the fence and ran out in the field. But I left my bike there.

Never mind, Lyle said. We'll get it tomorrow.

Oh God! I'm so glad you're all right. Here's your grandmother.

The women had all hurried up. The girl went to Berta May and the old woman wrapped her in her arms.

Oh my oh my oh my. Don't you ever—

The girl burst into tears.

Don't you ever do that again. Do you hear me?

I'm sorry, Grandma. I'm sorry. Don't be mad.

I'm not mad. You're home now.

I got lost.

I know. But you're here now. It's all right.

I saw the streetlights. That's how I knew where to go. My bike's still out there, Grandma.

Oh I don't care. I don't care about nothing else. You came home by yourself, didn't you. I turned the lights on. But you didn't see them, did you.

I saw the streetlights out in the country.

The women stayed close around and they each hugged the girl in turn and cried over her and petted her dirty sunburned face.

We better get you in the house, Berta May said. We got to get you cleaned up. Look at you. Lord, what a mess. I expect you can eat something too.

You want me to bring over a plate of food from the house? Mary said.

No, I had our supper cooked two hours ago.

They walked back in the street to the house that was still lit up in the night and Berta May and the girl went inside. The others stood out on the sidewalk and watched, the lights were turned off one by one and the old house went dark again except at the back.

We should go home too, Willa said. It's time.

Yes. Good night, Alene said.

Lyle said good night and Lorraine put her arms around him and he got in his car and drove off and the Johnson women drove off toward the sandhills.

Lorraine laced her arm through her mother's arm and they went inside and turned on the lamp at Dad's chair by the window so the light shone out into the side yard and then they went back to the kitchen and sat together at the table and drank coffee and talked a little very quietly.

That was on a night in August. Dad Lewis died early that morning and the young girl Alice from next door got lost in the evening and then found her way home in the dark by the streetlights of town and so returned to the people who loved her.

And in the fall the days turned cold and the leaves dropped off the trees and in the winter the wind blew from the mountains and out on the high plains of Holt County there were overnight storms and three-day blizzards.

Acknowledgments

The author wishes to thank Gary Fisketjon, Nancy Stauffer, Mark and Virginia Spragg, Mark and Kathy Haruf, Gabrielle Brooks, Carol Carson, Ruthie Reisner, Kathleen Fridella, Jim and Jane Elmore, Peter and Jill Brown, Will Archuletta, Lura McKinley, Leslie Stockton, Rev. Andy Dunning, Rev. George Christie, Dr. Paul Ilecki, Rev. Saundra Nottingham, Sorel Haruf, Whitney Haruf, Chaney Haruf Matsukis, Jane Templeton, Virginia Davis, Heather Austin, and especially Cathy Haruf.

A NOTE ON THE TYPE

This book was set in Adobe Garamond. Designed for the Adobe Corporation by Robert Slimbach, the fonts are based on types first cut by Claude Garamond (c. 1480–1561). Garamond was a pupil of Geoffroy Tory and is believed to have followed the Venetian models, although he introduced a number of important differences, and it is to him that we owe the letter we now know as "old style."

Composed by North Market Street Graphics
Lancaster, Pennsylvania

Printed and bound by Berryville Graphics
Berryville, Virginia

Designed by M. Kristen Bearse